"Stop!" he shoute

She froze but didn't turn around to face him.

"What in hell's name is going on, Lisa?" Ryan caught up to her, put his hand on her arm to support her, and blew out a frustrated breath when she recoiled.

"I'm sorry. I need to go."

"Not so fast. The only place you're going is inside." He urged her to turn around and he was surprised she did.

The look on her face, the resignation, should have made him feel bad. He didn't want to go down this road with her. The one where he was basically forcing her to talk. But she was in danger and he couldn't put up with this any longer.

"He'll come back." There came the fear in her eyes again.

"Not tonight, he won't."

TEXAS HUNT

USA TODAY Bestselling Author
BARB HAN

HARLEQUIN® INTRIGUE®

My deepest thanks go to Allison Lyons for the amazing talent she brings to make
each story the absolute best it can be—I am beyond grateful. I'm incredibly blessed
to work with Jill Marsal and I'm looking forward to many more years together.

There are three people who cheer me on through late nights and weekends,
who are always quick to build me up if my spirits dip, and who inspire me to reach
deeper every day so that I can be half the person I see reflected in their eyes.
Brandon, Jacob and Tori—my three beautiful gifts!—
my world is so much brighter because of you!

And to you, Babe, because the life we've built together is so much better
than I ever thought possible—and you are at the center of it all. I love you!

ISBN-13: 978-0-373-69894-3

Texas Hunt

Copyright © 2016 by Barb Han

The publisher acknowledges the copyright holder
of the additional work:

What Happens on the Ranch
Copyright © 2016 by Delores Fossen

Recycling programs
for this product may
not exist in your area.

H HARLEQUIN®

™ www.Harlequin.c

Printed in U.S.A.

CONTENTS

Barb Han lives in north Texas with her very own hero-worthy husband, three beautiful children, a spunky golden retriever/standard poodle mix and too many books in her to-read pile. In her downtime, she plays video games and spends much of her time on or around a basketball court. She loves interacting with readers and is grateful for their support. You can reach her at barbhan.com.

Books by Barb Han

Harlequin Intrigue

Mason Ridge

Texas Prey
Texas Takedown
Texas Hunt

The Campbells of Creek Bend

Witness Protection
Gut Instinct
Hard Target

Rancher Rescue

Harlequin Intrigue Noir

Atomic Beauty

TEXAS HUNT

BARB HAN

CAST OF CHARACTERS

Lisa Moore—Haunted by her past, she's kept Beckett Alcorn's secret for too many years. So when he attacks her with intent to silence her forever, she's confused. She'll do whatever it takes to keep her family safe and protect her infant nephew, even if it means relying on the one person from her past she's never been able to forget.

Ryan Hunt—He has no intention of falling for anyone. His life has been too much about taking care of others in his family to focus much attention on his own circumstances. But he's a little too quick to jump when Lisa needs him, and his unresolved feelings for her from the past make him question if he's willing to risk his heart while protecting her.

Henry Moore—His death is all-too-easily explained as an alcohol-related accident, especially since he's the town's constantly rehabilitating drunk. But is there more to it than that?

Lori Moore—She's the younger sister Lisa has always needed to protect.

Grayson Maxwell—Lisa's nephew is the center of her universe.

Charles Alcorn—He's head of a prominent family and has been pegged as the Mason Ridge Abductor. While in custody, he manages to escape and a manhunt gets under way to find him.

Beckett Alcorn—Son of Charles Alcorn and member of the most prominent family in town. Now that his father is under suspicion he'll do anything to protect the family name from further damage.

Mason Ridge Abductor—The man who has tormented the small town of Mason Ridge, Texas, for fifteen years.

Chapter One

Lisa Moore woke with a start. She tried to push up to a sitting position. Motion made a thousand nails drive through her skin and her head split four ways. Bright fluorescent lights blurred her vision. Her arms gave out and she landed hard on the firm mattress.

"Whoa, slow down there." Before she could shift her position enough to try sitting up again, Ryan Hunt was kneeling at her side. She didn't want to acknowledge just how much his presence calmed her rising pulse.

"What are you doing here?" she asked. Looking around, realizing she was in the hospital, she added, "What am I doing here?"

"I came as soon as I got the call," Ryan said, his low, deep timbre wrapping around her. An emotion flickered behind his eyes that she couldn't immediately pinpoint. At six foot two with the muscled body of an athlete, Ryan could take care of himself and anyone else around. She told herself that was the reason him being there comforted her...but comforted her from what?

Reality dawned on her as a full-body shiver rocked her. She'd been attacked by Beckett Alcorn, son of the most prominent man in town. His father had recently been named a person of interest in the fifteen-year-old kidnapping case that had rocked the small tight-knit community of Mason Ridge, Texas. News broke yesterday that Charles Alcorn had escaped before questioning and a manhunt was under way to find him.

Fear seized her, cramping her stomach. What if Beckett came back? No one would suspect him, the grieving and confused son. Too bad she couldn't tell Ryan what had actually happened, what she really knew. She'd done her part. She hadn't told a soul what Beckett Alcorn had done to her. So why was he trying to deliver on a fifteen-year-old threat now?

"Who else has been here?" She glanced at the door.

"Our friends. Your sister." The questioning look he gave her reminded her that she couldn't afford to give away her true emotions. No one could know about Beckett.

"What really happened to you?" The sight of Ryan—his gray-blue eyes and hawk-like nose set on a face of hard angles softened by rich, thick, curly dark brown hair—settled her fried nerves enough to let her think clearly.

Beckett had misjudged her this time. She'd distracted him long enough to escape. He'd be better prepared next time. Lisa and her family were in grave danger and she needed a plan.

"A guy came out of nowhere and jumped me. I'm guessing they didn't catch him." Playing dumb with Ryan was her only choice. Otherwise, Beckett would hurt her sister or nephew as he'd promised.

"Must not've." Ryan's cell buzzed, his gaze followed hers to the door. "People have been dropping by or calling every half hour to check on you."

"Where's my sister?" Panic beat rapid-fire against her ribs.

"At work. Said she'll stop by when she gets off at three." His dark eyebrow arched.

Lori would be safe as long as she was in a public place. Beckett would strike in the dark when she was alone. Lisa had to make sure that didn't happen. She tried to sit up, but her arms gave and her head pounded.

"Hold on there. Where do you think you're going?" Ryan asked. His suspicion at her reaction evidenced in his tone.

"Nowhere like this." She tried to adjust to a more comfortable position.

"Do you know who did this to you?"

"No. Of course not," she said a little too quickly. It was true that she didn't remember much after escaping. Her mind was as fuzzy as her vision. One thing was crystal clear. Ryan asking questions was a bad idea. She needed to redirect the conversation. "How'd I end up in the hospital?"

"You crawled into the street as Abigail Whitefield drove past on Highway 7. She stopped and called 911 on the spot."

"I'll have to stop by and thank her on my way home," Lisa said, wincing. Speaking shot stabbing pains through her chest.

"The deputy wants a statement. He's been waiting for you to wake up." Ryan's cell phone buzzed. He checked the screen and then responded with a text.

"Everything okay?" she asked.

"It's work. It'll hold," he said without looking at her.

She'd heard that his construction business had been booming. "How long have I been out?"

"Just a day." He chewed on a toothpick.

"What?" She tried to sit up again with similar results, pain forcing her to still.

"Whoa, take it easy there. You shouldn't try to move until the doctor checks you," Ryan said, locating and then pressing the nurse's call button before tossing the toothpick in the trash. There was compassion in his eyes and sympathy in his tone, and for some reason she didn't like either. She didn't want to be the one he pitied. She wanted to be something else to him, something more meaningful than a friend. The thought appeared as out of the blue as a spring thunderstorm in north Texas. Both could be dangerous. They'd known each other since they were kids. Besides, relationships were too risky and Lisa didn't go there with anyone.

But it was Ryan, a little voice inside her head protested—a voice she quickly silenced.

Waking in the hospital was messing with her head. Her nerves were fried and she was reaching for comfort. And those thoughts about Ryan were as productive as harvesting burned corn.

"I just need a minute to clear my head. I'll be okay." The last thing she remembered was seeing Beckett's face as she ripped off his ski mask while he was trying to strangle her. He'd panicked for a split second, which had given her the window of opportunity she needed to push him away, kick him in the groin and run. Lisa was lucky to be alive.

"We'll find the person who did this to you. He won't get away with it. You have my word." Ryan's voice was barely a whisper, but there was no mistaking the underlying threat in his tone. "In the meantime, the doctor or nurse should make sure you're okay."

"So, what's the verdict so far? Have you spoken to anyone?" She scanned her arms for bruising, remembering the viselike grip that had been clamped around them. Black and blue marks were painted up and down both. "I'm guessing I have cracked ribs based on how painful it is to breathe."

"Let me go find that nurse." He made a move to stand, but Lisa grabbed his arm, ignoring the piercing pain.

"Please stay." The words came out more desperate-sounding than she'd planned. "It's just nice to see a friendly face." She added the last part to cover, praying he believed her. In truth, she was scared to be alone in her current condition.

Ryan followed her gaze to the door again.

"I'm not going anywhere." When his gray-blue eyes intensified, they looked like steel.

She didn't want to acknowledge the relief flooding her or how much his presence sent tingles of awareness deep in her stomach. Whatever spark he might've felt had to be long gone by now, replaced with sincere friendship. He showed no signs of experiencing the same electricity humming through her when she touched his arm. Maybe if she'd handled things differently between them years ago...

A young dark-haired nurse wearing glasses and aqua scrubs entered the room, shuffling to Lisa's side.

"I'm Shelly. How are you feeling today?"

"Good, considering I've been dead to the world for the past twenty-four hours."

"You've been drifting in and out. There've been times when you responded to questions. The answers didn't always make sense." Shelly smiled and the look made her plain round face more attractive.

Had Lisa muttered something in her sleep she shouldn't have? Panic rolled through her. If she had, Ryan would be asking very different questions.

Shelly asked a few questions that were easy to answer, ensuring Lisa knew who she was and where she was from.

"Are you sure you don't want something for the pain?" Shelly asked.

"I can manage."

Ryan stood and took a step back to give the nurse room to work.

"How long before I can get out of here?" Lisa checked the door again, half-afraid Beckett would show.

Ryan's eyebrow lifted for the second time.

"The doctor will be in to see you shortly and talk to you about your injuries. Your numbers are strong, but I'm sure the doctor will want to keep you awhile longer for observation. You took a couple of big blows to the head." There was sympathy in her voice, too.

It shouldn't annoy Lisa. Maybe the bumps on her head affected her mood. She should be grateful that everyone seemed genuinely concerned about her.

Except that she knew this was far from over. Beckett must believe she'd told someone or was planning to start talking. With his father in trouble, Beckett might do anything to keep his family's name out of the papers. Either way, she wasn't out of danger.

"I'm sure you'll be up and around soon," Shelly reassured her.

"That's the best news I've heard so far. Think there's

any chance I'll be discharged later today?" Being at home in her own bed sounded amazing about now.

A thought struck her. Beckett knew where she lived. No. She couldn't go there. She'd have to find a safe place to stay until she recovered from her injuries and could do something about Beckett. A flea could take her down in her present condition, and leaving herself vulnerable would be foolish.

"The doctor can explain everything to you when she comes in, but I'd put money on you staying here another night." Shelly had stopped playing around with gadgets and stood sentinel next to the bed. She'd be all of five feet two inches in heels, or in this case thickly padded tennis shoes. "Do you have family in the area other than your husband?"

My husband?

"Why?" Lisa glanced at Ryan, who shot her a look before intently studying his cell phone screen.

"We like to have additional contacts on file in case your husband has to leave," Shelly said casually.

Hold on. Did that mean what Lisa thought? Her dad hadn't been up to see her? She might understand her sister, Lori, being preoccupied with her infant son or work, but wouldn't Dad come by to make sure she was okay? Ryan had said people had been stopping by. She made a mental note to ask him about it as soon as the nurse left the room. "I can give more names. There are others here in town."

"Great. I'll send someone up from Records to take more information."

"Perfect," Lisa said, trying to sound casual.

"The doctor should be in soon." The nurse paused at the door.

"Terrific." Lisa shot a look at Ryan. "I'm sure my husband will bring me up to date in the meantime."

His lips were thin and his arms folded. He fired off a warning look. She understood. He didn't want to be caught in a lie. He must've felt that he had no choice. Ryan was one of the most honest people she knew. He wouldn't take giving false information lightly.

"What else can I get for you while I'm here? Another blanket?" Shelly asked.

"No, thank you. I have everything I need." Lisa glanced from the nurse to Ryan. If he'd been a cartoon character, steam would've been coming out of his ears from embarrassment.

"Press the button if you change your mind," Shelly said before closing the door to give them privacy.

"Was it a big wedding?" Maybe it was the pressure mounting inside her that needed release, but Lisa couldn't stop herself from poking at him.

"Cut it out," Ryan groaned.

Even when they were twelve he didn't like hopping a fence to retrieve a ball in a neighbor's yard without asking first. More than that, he detested outright lying. His older brother hadn't had the same conviction before he'd cleaned up his act. Lisa figured most of the reason Ryan despised untruths had derived from living through the dark periods in Justin's life.

"Sorry. I couldn't resist. I know why you did it and I appreciate you for it. I'm sure they needed consent to treat," she said.

"Yes. You're welcome." The corners of his lips up-turned in a not-quite smile. Something else was bothering him. She could tell based on his tight-lipped expression. Whatever it was, he seemed intent on keeping it to himself.

"Has anyone contacted my dad?" she asked.

He shrugged.

"What a minute. How did you even know I was here?"

"Mrs. Whitefield called. She said you asked for me right before you passed out on her. She needed help getting you in the car." He cocked an eyebrow at her. "She said it seemed like there was something you wanted to tell me."

"You could've called my father," Lisa redirected.

"Guess I didn't think of it at the time." Something dark shifted behind his eyes and he looked uncomfortable.

A light tap at the door sounded and then Lori rushed in.

"I came as soon as I heard you were awake. Thank God you're all right." Her hands were tightly clasped and her gaze bounced tentatively from Lisa to Ryan.

"I thought you were at work." Had Ryan really sent a work text earlier or was he covering for connecting with Lori? Why would he do that?

Oh no. Something had to have happened. Lisa's heart raced thinking about her nephew. "Is Grayson okay?"

"Yes. He's fine. Great actually." Lori's face muscles were pulled taut. "It's Dad."

No. No. No. "What happened?"

"He had an accident." Lori shifted her weight to her right foot and bowed her head.

"Where is he?"

"He's gone." Huge tears rolled down her pink cheeks.

Wait. What? No. This couldn't be happening. She

stared at her sister waiting for the punch line. If this was some kind of joke, it was beyond twisted. Tears already streaked her cheeks. Deep down, she knew her sister wouldn't say something like that if it wasn't true.

"What happened?" Lisa forced back the flood of emotions threatening to bust through her iron wall and engulf her.

"He was on the tractor, drinking again," Lori said, raw emotion causing the words to come out strained. "He must've had too much because he flipped it and was pinned. The coroner said he died instantly."

Ryan had moved to her side, his hand was on her shoulder, comforting her. She needed to know the details, to know if Beckett had anything to do with it. Dozens of thoughts crashed down on her at once. She also had to think of an excuse to get her sister and nephew out of town and far away from any threat.

Of course everyone would assume he'd been hitting the bottle again. It wouldn't be the first time he'd relapsed. No one would believe her if she denied it. And yet Lisa knew he'd been clean. There was always a pattern. He was on an upswing. Lisa forced back the flood of tears threatening to overwhelm her. A few streamed down her face anyway.

"Do they know for sure Dad was drinking? Did they perform an autopsy?" she pressed. She'd seen on TV that the coroner could screen for alcohol level.

"Why would they do that? Isn't that for, like, people who are murdered or something?" Lori's voice rose with her panic levels. Her grip on Lisa's hand had tightened to the point of pain.

Lisa gently urged their fingers apart.

"Oh, sorry. This is just happening so fast. First, what

happened to you yesterday morning. Then Daddy later that afternoon." Lori broke down in a sob. "I'm scared, sis. He's gone and I didn't know if you'd—"

"I'm here," Lisa reassured, fighting back her own emotions. She'd always tried to be brave for her little sister. "I'm not going anywhere."

"I know. It's just all…surreal or something. Everyone keeps saying that bad news comes in threes and I keep waiting for the other shoe to drop. It's crazy. I mean, who would want to hurt you? You're like the nicest person. Everyone loves you. You're a kindergarten teacher for heaven's sake. Who would do this to you?"

"Random mugging, remember? I have just as much chance as everyone else. It's like lightning striking," Lisa said even though her heart wasn't in the words. When it came to lying, she fell on the same side of the scale as Ryan. Her father's drinking binges had always been preceded by lies. In bad times, she and her sister would be hauled off to stay with a relative. In the worst cases, they'd end up in the foster care system for a few months until their dad straightened out.

Even though she hated lying, she had no choice. She had to protect what was left of her family. "Where's Grayson?"

"I'm sorry. I didn't want to bring the baby here. I know he's still little, but I thought he might be afraid if he saw you like this," Lori said. The words gushed out. She always spoke too fast when she was a nervous wreck.

"You did the right thing, sis," Lisa said in her most calming voice.

"He's with Dylan and Samantha. Maribel's keeping an eye on him. She calls him her little brother. It's cute." Lori broke into another sob. Dylan and Samantha were longtime friends. Maribel was Dylan's three-year-old daughter. The three of them made a beautiful family. Grayson would be safe in their care. "I know he wasn't always there for us, but he was our dad. And now he's gone."

"I loved him, too." It was surreal to speak about him in the past tense. "It's okay to cry."

"No, it's not. I should be more like you."

"Calloused?" Lisa said quickly before she shattered into a tiny thousand pieces. The only thing worse than holding on to her horrible secret was seeing her baby sister in pain.

"I was going to say brave." Lori leaned into Lisa and sobbed.

With Beckett's father being hunted, this might be the right time to expose the family for the monsters they truly were. And yet she hadn't reported the crime fifteen years ago. Could she come forward now and accuse Beckett? Would anyone believe her?

Maybe Ryan knew about Beckett's family. Hadn't the Alcorns tried to take his father's land? Then again, if she asked him too many questions he might just figure out she was hiding something and force her hand. He was more persistent than a pit bull searching for a bone when it came to finding the truth. She'd also seen how dedicated he'd been to his brother when Justin had been in trouble. Would he do the same for her?

If anyone could understand or help, Ryan could.

He'd been devastated when his own mother walked out on the family. He'd acted tough on the outside, but Lisa saw past the front he'd put up. She'd seen the pain buried deep down because it was just like hers.

Lisa knew pain.

On second thought, exposing Beckett now was a bad idea. First of all, he'd take away everything she loved. Then he'd kill her. Or worse, he wouldn't.

She needed to figure out a way to keep her family safe without alarming them. The Alcorns' number was almost up and she'd be on the front row of the court trial when it happened, cheering when the sentence was delivered.

Until then, she had to figure out a way to keep her family safe.

Every fiber in her being urged her to warn her sister about what might come next, that she and Grayson could be in grave danger. But what if no one believed her?

She lay in a hospital bed with possible head trauma. She had no evidence for an accusation against Beckett. Most people believed him to be a good person and felt sorry for him after news broke about his father.

Lisa had to weigh her options carefully. If she told Lori and Ryan the truth and they questioned her, the risk would only increase. Beckett's attack on her family wouldn't be straightforward, either. He'd watch Lori. Hide. Strike when she least expected it. Considering she had a baby on her hip most of the time, she'd be an easy target.

Doing nothing was a pretty lousy option.

There had to be something she could do to keep her family safe. Lori and Grayson were all Lisa had left and she'd trade her life for either one.

LISA'S EMOTIONAL PAIN hit Ryan far deeper than her physical bruises did. He didn't like those, either, but experience had taught him the stuff on the outside healed. The marks on her heart wouldn't go away in a few weeks. He fisted his hands and then shoved them in his pockets so he wouldn't punch a hole in the wall.

The promise he'd made to Lori to keep quiet about their father had been sitting sourly in his stomach since Lisa's eyes opened. Ryan had wanted to be the one to tell her what had happened, but it wasn't his place. The news about her family needed to come from her sister, not from him. All he could do was be there to help pick up the pieces.

Seeing her lying there, helpless, had stirred more than a primal need to protect a friend.

Instead of acting on it, he'd watched her sleep as he'd held back from stroking her rosy skin as it shone even under the harsh fluorescent light. Her long brunet hair with light streaks that caught the sun seemed brighter.

Listening to the pain in her voice as she spoke to her sister was the second time he'd nearly been done in. He shouldn't allow his past feelings for Lisa to cloud his judgment. Because if they had their way he'd be in that hospital bed with her, holding her until she stopped shaking, comforting her until she felt safe again. It was obvious that the attack had left a serious mark. The way she kept looking at the door as if expecting her assailant to walk through even had Ryan jumpy.

As far as anything else between them went, Lisa was a puzzle in which he'd never quite fit the pieces together. There was no way he could risk his heart twice trying.

Get a hobby, Hunt.

Besides, he had other, more pressing things to focus on, like why she kept checking the door with that frightened look on her face. She had to know a person from a random mugging wouldn't follow her to the hospital. Ryan bet there was more going on than she let on.

"I better go. Grayson needs to nurse soon," Lori said.

"I've been lying here thinking about getting away for a few days. You should, too. Especially now. It's not good for the baby to be around all this and stress can affect your breast milk," Lisa said, looking as though she was grasping at straws. Her sister was almost militant about breast-feeding. Since Grayson's dad wasn't coming back, Ryan figured her sister compensated by throwing all her energy into being Grayson's mother. It was beyond Ryan how a father could walk out on his family. Then again, it didn't seem to have bothered his mother all that much.

Lisa made a good point but when did she have time to think about a getaway option? She'd only woken up a few minutes ago.

"I don't know. I'd rather be here for you. Plus, we need to make arrangements for Dad." Lori's voice hitched on the last couple of words.

"All we need is an internet connection to do that. It'll take a few days to settle everything anyway before the service. I can meet you somewhere. The nurse said I might be out of here later today."

Ryan had no idea why Lisa was skirting the truth, but after all she'd been through he figured he'd toss her a lifeline. "A buddy of mine has a fishing cabin a couple hours from here in Arkansas. It's right on the lake. I'm sure he wouldn't mind if you took it over."

"Are you sure that's such a good idea?" Lori glanced from Ryan to Lisa. "I have Grayson to think about."

"It's nice and big. The place sleeps eight. He bought it so his wife would want to bring the kids," Ryan said.

He intended to have a heart-to-heart with Lisa as soon as her sister left. Then again, her attack was followed by devastating news about her father. Maybe she needed to get her bearings and figured this was the best way. Plus, the Mason Ridge Abductor was still out there and even though Grayson was a baby, not a seven-year-old, which was the usual mode of operation for the kidnapper, she had to be thinking about his safety. With Lori on her own with a baby and Lisa the overprotective older sister, maybe Ryan shouldn't be surprised at how out of sync her reactions seemed to be.

He needed to reassure her that he intended to make certain she was okay.

"It might be nice to take the weekend," Lori said. "There's been so much going on that I don't even want to go to the grocery anymore for fear of running into people. They're well intentioned and all, but my phone's been ringing like crazy. I answered it a few times and it's a game of twenty questions. I can't talk about either one of you without bawling. Plus, work gave me time off to make…arrangements." She wiped away another tear.

"Then it's settled. Ryan will call his friend." Lisa turned her attention toward him. "I'll owe you big-time. You're certain this will be all right?"

"More than sure. He gave me a spare so I could check on the place for him this month while he's out of town for work." Ryan fished in his pocket and then produced a key. "I'll text the address. You should probably take off now. There's a small corner store at the turnoff to get to his place. They're used to weekenders, so they'll have everything you need to get by for a few days with a baby."

"Okay." Lori stopped chewing on her lip and took the offering.

Ryan zipped off a text with the address, waiting for her smartphone to ding.

When it did, she said to Lisa, "Good. Will I see you tonight?"

"I hope so. I'm out of here as soon as I get clearance," Lisa replied.

"Then I'll feed the baby, pack a bag and head out," Lori conceded. The idea seemed to be growing on her when she smiled at her sister.

"Be safe driving. Let me know when you get there, okay?"

They hugged and both had tears in their eyes when Lori left.

"Thank you," Lisa said as Ryan settled into the chair next to her bed.

"You're welcome." Whatever was on her mind, she had no intention to share just yet. He could tell by the set of her jaw and the look in her eye. Lucky for her, he was a patient man. "The deputy should be here shortly to take your statement. You hungry for anything? I could run out and pick up whatever sounds good."

"I doubt I could eat anything," she said. Those bluish-green eyes pushed past his walls—walls he'd worked damn hard to construct.

Lisa was attractive. Only an idiot would argue that point and Ryan didn't put himself in that particular category. He'd be lying if he didn't admit to a certain pull he felt toward her every time she was around.

But that was where it ended. Where it *had* to end.

Sure, a few of his friends had found true partnerships with other people recently. Even though Ryan had been against Brody and Rebecca's relationship early on because of their history, the two were the happiest he'd ever seen them. Dylan and Samantha seemed perfect for each other. Love seemed to suit his friends. Denying the nose on his face wouldn't change anything. Besides, Ryan was truly happy for his best buds.

But only a man with a need for punishment did the same thing over and over again expecting a different result. Lisa had shot him down before when he thought he'd picked up on a mutual attraction. Even though he felt that same sizzle between them now, only a fool would act on it. And not only because she was in a hospital bed, hurt. That just made it inappropriate.

Ryan had other reasons not to get involved with anyone. For one, he didn't need anyone to take care of him. He was perfectly fine living the bachelor's life.

Brody and Dylan might have found their other halves and taken up relationships, and Ryan didn't begrudge them. No two people deserved that kind of bliss more than his friends. He had to admit that they seemed happier than they'd ever been. And that was all pink lemonade and roses *for them*.

Ryan didn't need anyone else to "complete" him. He'd come into the world a whole human being and planned to leave the same way. Living on his own suited him. He liked waking up with the sun and going where he pleased. Was he selfish? Maybe. He was so used to taking care of family members for most of his life that he didn't have much left to give anyone else.

Had his life seemed a little lacking lately? Sure. It would cycle around again.

And if it didn't, he'd get a dog. People were so damn disappointing.

Chapter Two

A hospital was no place to sleep. Even with the lights
turned off Lisa couldn't relax, especially since Ryan had
gone home. To make matters worse, a nurse or technician padded in every hour on the dot to wrap gauges
around her arm or take more blood. After what felt like
the fiftieth time but was more like the fifth, Lisa was
beginning to lose patience.

Lack of sleep and constant ache did nothing to im-
prove her mood. Plus, the news of her father…she
couldn't even go there. Grief would engulf her if she
allowed herself time to think about it. Emotions were a
luxury she couldn't afford. Beckett was still out there.
The rest of her family was in danger. As difficult as it
was, Lisa had to maintain focus.

At least she'd convinced her sister to leave town.
Lori and Grayson were in a swank fishing cabin on a
lake in Arkansas. That was the only bit of good news
in what had been one of the worst days of Lisa's life.

Dad.

Thinking about him, about what had happened
brought a whole new wave of sadness crashing down
around her.

She tried to ease to a sitting position, searching her

memory for any sign he'd been relapsing. Pain pierced her chest, her arms and her back with movement. No use. She'd refused pain medication, needing a clear head. She was still reeling from the news of losing her father while trying to sort out why any of this was happening now. She'd kept Beckett's secret, dammit. Shouldn't that have bought her a pass?

One of the lab techs padded in. *Great.*

Trying to sort out the day's events while Prickzilla jabbed another needle contributed to a dull ache in the spot right between her eyes.

Take a deep breath. Count to ten.

It wasn't a magical cure but she felt better.

"Try to get some sleep," Dracula-in-an-aquamarine-jumpsuit whispered before she closed the door behind her and disappeared.

If only it were that easy.

Lisa tossed and turned for another half hour at least. As frustration got the best of her she resorted to counting sheep.

Still didn't work.

Just like when she was a kid, the darn things shape-shifted into snakes, their slimy bodies slithering after her. The closet had offered a perfect hiding spot when she was six. Another half dozen years later, Beckett Alcorn had been the beast that kept her awake nights. There wasn't a closet big enough now for the monster she faced.

In the category of "not making it better," she was wide-awake at—she checked the clock—three fifteen in the morning. *Great.* Even the chickens were conked out at this hour. Lisa had been drifting in and out, but every time she got close the door would creak open and a nurse or technician would pad inside. It was probably just as well. Anytime Lisa got anywhere near real sleep, she'd jolt awake from one of several nightmares ready to cue at a moment's notice.

In one scenario, hands were closing around her throat. She woke screaming, giving the nurse who was attending to her quite a scare.

In another dream, fists were coming at her from every direction and she felt blood spilling out of her cracked skull with each jab.

After the last round of fifty ways to beat up Lisa, she gave up checking the clock. There was no use realizing just how late it was and how little REM she was getting.

The worst-case nightmare involved being held under water, drowning, only to bob to the surface and find that it was Ryan holding her down. There was no doubt in her mind that he would never try to hurt her in her waking world. Absolutely no way could she even consider him doing her harm on purpose. The dream must represent something she feared. Didn't need a phycology degree to know she'd been afraid of the opposite sex ever since that summer, ever since Beckett.

What did it say about her that even a male friend scared her to death?

She thought about that as she drifted off to her first real sleep.

A hand clamped around Lisa's throat so hard she feared her windpipe would crack. She struggled against the crushing grip. It was like trying to peel off custom-fitted steel.

Her fight, flee or freeze response triggered as she railed against the force pushing her deeper into the mattress. She tried to scream, but no sound came out. In her other dreams she'd always been able to shout.

Coughing, she had the frightening realization that this wasn't a dream.

She was wide-awake.

A soft object, maybe a pillow, was being pressed against her face, suffocating her.

More coughing came as her lungs desperately clawed for air.

Could she somehow signal one of the nurses? Where were they? How had someone walked right past them in the middle of the night and gotten into her room? She felt around for the call button, but came up empty.

Oh. God. No.

Desperate and afraid, she reached for her attacker. Her hand stopped on denim material. Must've been his leg, meaning he was most likely straddled over her. Beckett?

At twelve, Lisa had blamed herself for what he'd done to her. She'd been too embarrassed and too scared to tell anyone. Beckett had threatened to kill everyone she loved if she so much as breathed a word of his actions, and he had the power to follow through with his warning. He'd threatened to do worse to Lisa's little sister. And if Lisa told, he'd said it would be her word against his, and who would believe her, anyway? He'd made a good point. She'd been a shy girl, in and out of the system, who'd mostly kept to herself. Worse yet, she was daughter of Henry Moore, the town's constantly rehabilitating alcoholic.

Lisa wasn't a little girl anymore. No way did he get to destroy her. She followed the inseam straight up to his groin, grabbed and squeezed with every ounce of strength she had.

He muttered a curse as he shifted position long enough for her to take in a swallow of precious oxygen. She clasped harder and he groaned, cursing her.

The weight on top of her lifted for a second as he wriggled his groin out of her grasp. His hold loosened on the pillow pressed against her face so she fought the pain burning through her as she drew her knees to her chest and then thrust them toward his face. They connected with his chin.

His head snapped back.

Lisa screamed for the nurse. She tried to launch another attack, pushing through the agony that came with every movement. Her arms felt like spaghetti and even a boost of adrenaline didn't give her enough strength to keep fighting.

The mattress dipped and then rose as he pushed to his feet.

"I'll be back. You'll regret this, bitch." The voice wasn't Beckett's. It was too dark to get a good look at the details of his face.

A fresh wave of panic seized her as she searched for something, anything on the side table. Her fingers reached the landline phone, so she hurled it toward the stranger's back. "You won't be able to hurt me from jail."

What was taking the nurse so long?

The dark silhouette slipped out of her room and disappeared moments before the door reopened and the night nurse rushed in.

"Someone was here. He's out there. In the hall," Lisa said through coughing fits.

Light filled the room as the concerned nurse's face came into view.

"I was just out there and didn't see anyone. My name's Alicia. I'll be your nurse this evening." She spoke slowly, calmly, as if she were talking to a three-year-old in the heat of a temper tantrum.

"I'm not making this up. I swear." Lisa sat upright, heaving.

The way the nurse stared at Lisa, the questioning look, she knew Alicia was ready to call for a psych consult.

"I promise. A man was just in here. He had a pillow over my face. Can't you see what he did to me?" Her breath came in bursts.

Alicia's forehead crease and raised eyebrow gave away the fact that she was skeptical. With a quick look communicating that Lisa should be grateful Alicia was about to indulge the fantasy, she retreated toward the door. "I'll check again, but I was just out there and I didn't see anyone."

All Lisa could think about based on Alicia's reaction was that she most likely attributed this outburst to a very realistic nightmare or head trauma.

The expression on her face when she returned convinced Lisa of the latter.

"I know how this must seem to you but someone was in here," Lisa said defensively. She glanced around on the floor. "Look. The pillow he used is there."

"It's okay," Alicia soothed. The words came out slowly, again.

Great. The woman thought Lisa was crazy. Lisa wasn't about to let the nurse get away with it.

"Look at me. I must have red marks or bruising. He

shoved that pillow in my face and held me down." She held her hands out to check herself over. A pillow on the floor wasn't exactly a smoking gun. Even Lisa rationalized she could've knocked it off the bed during a nightmare.

The only real evidence was a black-and-blue display up and down both arms.

"You've been through a lot recently. Let's see if we can get you to lie down again," Alicia said as she began her exam, evaluating Lisa's injuries.

She moved to the computer. "We'll send someone down to speak to you."

Either Alicia believed Lisa or the nurse was following hospital protocol. Neither mattered; the only person Lisa wanted to see right now was Ryan. He'd said to call if she needed him, day or night. As much as she didn't want to push the boundaries of their friendship or drive him away she needed to be with someone she trusted.

Would he even pick up at this ridiculous hour?

What choice did she have? Her father was dead. Her sister was more than four hours away, not that calling her in the middle of the night was an appealing thought anyway. Lori would have too many questions and that could be deadly.

Once again, Lisa was frightened into silence. Could she call the sheriff? Tell him everything even after she'd lied to Deputy Adams earlier and said she didn't know her attacker?

The deputy had simply shaken his head while taking down the details for his report, cursing the luck of her family to have both of these things happen within twenty-four hours of each other. He'd warned her to watch out because bad things usually came in threes.

And with her father's alcohol history, maybe the deputy had really wondered why something like this hadn't happened sooner.

Adams had confirmed that her father's death had been considered an accident. No one had argued differently. Her heart knew better.

Lisa knew for certain that her attack yesterday hadn't been random. She'd seen Beckett with her own eyes after ripping off his ski mask. But whoever had slipped into the hospital wasn't him. Maybe her brain was damaged and she'd imagined another person's voice. Who else would do something like this?

Beckett could've hired someone to do his dirty work for him. Attacking her in a hospital setting was high risk. There'd be cameras. Maybe he feared getting caught this time. It might not have been him carrying out the actual crime, but her instincts said he had to be responsible.

What good did it do her to know? If she told anyone he'd be back to kill all the family she had left—her sister and nephew.

Panic gripped her. She couldn't even think about anything happening to them.

They were safe. *For now.*

Lori and her infant son were everything to Lisa. And if she gave up the name of the man who did this to her, both of them would be dead in a heartbeat.

There had to be another way.

Calling Ryan was a risk she had to take. He'd be even more suspicious and he might think she was a little crazy. What was the alternative?

Stay there, unprotected, and she'd be dead by morning.

Try to leave by herself and she wouldn't make it out the door.

As soon as Alicia stepped into the hallway, Lisa grabbed her cell from the side table.

Calling Ryan was the only reasonable option. He'd volunteered his assistance. She'd take him up on his offer.

If he pressed her for more information, she'd have to cut him loose or risk putting him in danger. She hoped it wouldn't come to that.

Chapter Three

The sound of fear in Lisa's voice when she called had shocked Ryan out of a deep sleep.

All she'd said was "I need you."

Those three words had kicked Ryan into action faster than buckshot. Her voice had blasted a different kind of heat through his chest, sent it spiraling through him. He'd dismissed it quickly as an inappropriate reaction and focused on the terror coming through the line. He'd hopped out of bed, ignoring the aftershocks of sexual awareness, thrown on clothes and raced toward the hospital. He'd made the drive in record time, parked and still hadn't come up with a plan to get past security.

Something had happened to Lisa. He intended to find out what was going on. She'd convinced him she'd been too tired to talk earlier that day and he hadn't wanted to put undue pressure on her, given all that she'd been through. This was different. No way could he go back to sleep without answers. And no one could stop him from getting them, not even her.

"Sir, visiting hours are over," the nurse warned as he stalked toward Lisa's wing.

"I received a call from a patient of yours. She's expecting me." Like hell he wasn't going into her room.

"I can't allow it. Hospital policy." The nurse sprang from her seat and moved around the desk too late to block him from entering Lisa's hallway.

"Call your supervisor if you have to, but I'm not leaving until I know my wife is okay." Ryan used the earlier lie he'd given in order for her to receive treatment. He'd had to think quickly then. Surely they wouldn't refuse a husband access to his spouse now. He figured he had at least a few minutes before hospital security could catch up in order to toss him out of the building.

"Sir." Her voice trailed off, which meant she wasn't following him. She'd most likely doubled back so she could call the security desk.

Ryan pushed Lisa's door open and rushed to her side. Desperation was a net, casting a wild animal look over her normally soft, feminine features.

"I don't have long. The nurse will have me evicted in a few minutes. Tell me what happened," he said.

"Someone was here, Ryan." The urgency in her words nearly knocked him back a step.

"Who?"

"I'm not sure." An emotion he couldn't quite put his finger on flickered behind her eyes. It was more than fear.

"Was it the guy who attacked you?"

"Yes. No. I don't know." Her bluish-green eyes were wide and scared.

"I need you to tell me what's really going on." When he sat on the edge of the bed, he realized she was shaking. It took every bit of strength not to pull her into his chest and comfort her.

"I would if I could." She looked away.

What the hell did that mean? He'd been exposed,

firsthand, to people in trouble. Make no mistake about it, Lisa was drowning. He couldn't do anything to help her unless she gave him something to hang on to.

If he'd learned one thing from trying to save his brother, it was that people helped themselves. Sure, sometimes they needed an extra pair of hands. Ryan never hesitated to be there for a relative or friend in need to offer support. But drowning people were notorious for pulling others down with them. Ryan had learned to keep a healthy distance until they took those first few strokes on their own.

"Why can't you?" Seeing her looking so small in that damn oversize gown overrode rational thought. He fisted his hands to keep them at his sides.

Didn't work. He brushed the hair from her face, ignoring the urge building inside him to hold her until she stopped shaking.

"Believe me, Ryan, you're the only one I would tell if I could, but this is…complicated and innocent people will be hurt if I don't play this right." Her words broke at the end and sobs racked her shoulders.

Ryan didn't debate his next action. He just hauled her into his arms, where she buried her face. "I'm here. It's okay."

He half expected her to push him away and tell him she was fine. She didn't. Instead, she pressed deeper against his cotton T-shirt while he whispered reassurances in her ear he couldn't guarantee.

There was no worse feeling than watching someone he cared about in pain and not being able to help.

Against his better judgment, he told Lisa he would do whatever she needed.

She broke away and stared him directly in the eyes.

"If you really want everything to be all right, take me home with you."

Hold on a minute. She couldn't leave the hospital. The determination in her bluish-green eyes said otherwise. Maybe he could talk her off the ledge.

"Is that wise?" He glanced at the bruises on her arms.

"I'd walk out of here on my own if I could," she said, and he had no doubt she meant it.

Could he convince her otherwise?

"The doctor wants to keep an eye on your head injury." Was it safe for her to leave the hospital against medical advice?

"I can't stay here. He'll come back, or send someone. I'm in danger here. You're the only one I trust."

"Did you tell the nurse?"

"Yes, I did. She didn't believe me. She's most likely calling in a psychiatrist. I won't make it that long. He'll slip right back in and…" She bit her bottom lip as if to stop if from forming the next words.

"Tell me exactly what happened." They were running out of time. Security would burst through that door any second now. Ryan believed something had happened and he needed to know more. Whatever it was had scared the bejesus out of her. But how could it be the same guy who'd attacked her earlier? That was supposed to be a random occurrence. Ryan had been sitting in this very room when she'd given the deputy her statement.

"Maybe he works here." Her shoulders sagged and she looked to be in considerable pain every time she moved. "That's impossible, isn't it?"

"Security will be here any second. What if we explain what happened to them? Maybe we can get them involved."

"It's no good. The nurse will tell them not to believe me." She held her arms up as though she wanted him to inspect them. "She thinks I'm crazy and she's sending me for a psych evaluation. End of story. It's the middle of the night and my doctor isn't here, but what would she do, anyway?"

She gestured toward her arms again.

Ryan didn't want to say the bruises could've been from the earlier attack. She needed to hear that someone believed her. Otherwise she'd jump out of her own skin if someone sneezed. "I see what happened and I believe you. I won't let him get to you again. I promise."

He didn't say that might not be an option if he was booted out. He'd figure something out. Lisa had been afraid before, but there was a grasping-at-her-last-straw quality to her voice now that didn't sit well with him.

Touching her was a bad idea because his emotions started taking over his logical thought. Nothing good could come of that.

There was more than her reaction that bugged the hell out of him. The persistence of this guy was unsettling. It took guts to attack at a well-staffed hospital even in the middle of the night. Then again, dress in scrubs or a maintenance uniform and he might blend right in. Ryan needed to get into contact with their friend Dylan, who owned a personal security company. He might have enough contacts to get hold of the footage at the hospital.

The questions of the day were…who was doing this and why was he being so persistent?

Lisa had never been a liar, but one look at her said

she was at the very least holding back something that could get her hurt or killed. Plus, she'd practically forced her sister out of town for a few days. A storm was brewing and Ryan needed to know just how big this squall was going to get.

"Take me out of here. *Please*." The way Lisa emphasized the last word shredded Ryan's resolve. This was a bad idea. Being there was sketchy enough. Walking her out the front door in her condition was borderline insanity.

Leaving her there, alone, was out of the question.

Voices down the hall neared. Security would walk through the door at any second. Ryan had about two seconds to make a decision. All of his experiences, instincts railed against doing what he was contemplating. He'd be stepping in a boot full of sludge trying to justify this.

Not to mention the fact that his feelings for her clouded his judgment. Logic told him to bolt, to let authorities handle this. And yet she hadn't trusted them enough to tell them everything.

Only a fool or someone in serious trouble would do that.

"What if I stay here with you? I'll stay awake and keep watch." He'd be irresponsible if he didn't put that out there as an option. The fear widening her eyes said she wouldn't take the offer.

"So he can come back and kill us both?" She sank deeper into the bed like a deflated airbag. "I didn't consider this before, but I'm putting you in danger. You can't be here. I didn't think this through all the way. I'm sorry. Forget I ever called you."

Wait a minute.

Was she kicking him out?

"Fine. Where's your stuff? I'll grab a bag." He stood as she stilled, staring blankly at him in disbelief. "We need to get moving. Several people are going to come through that door and none of them are going to be happy to see me in here."

"I can't let you do this. It was a mistake to get you involved." She stared toward the window, blankly.

"You've already told me the risks. Consider me informed. I'm going to take you home with me, but we gotta go now."

The door opened so hard it smacked against the wall.

A guy close to Ryan's height wearing a blue security uniform with a squawking radio filled the frame.

"Sir, I need to ask you to leave," he said. His polite words were delivered with a clipped tone. "You can come back to visit between the hours of eight a.m. and seven p.m."

"My wife is ready to go now," Ryan said, folding his arms across his chest as he assumed a defensive stance. The name on the security officer's badge read Steven. If Steven wanted to go a few rounds, Ryan had every confidence in his own fighting abilities. That said, he preferred to save his energy for more important things. It would be up to the big guy which path they took. "I'm not walking through that door without her, Steven."

"I'm leaving." With great effort, Lisa pushed off the bed and stood. Ryan was by her side, urging her to lean on him for support before she lost her balance again. All kinds of heat fizzled through her where they made contact, but she pushed it out of her thoughts.

"You heard her. She's ready to leave."

Steven glanced at Alicia.

"That's not a good idea," Alicia said. "Let's all settle down and think this through."

"You're assuming I haven't already." Lisa winced as she took a step forward. Ryan was there to catch her as her knee gave out, his steadying arm around her the only thing keeping her from falling flat on the floor. "You aren't keeping me safe here."

"I'm afraid I can't allow you to go. Doctor's orders." Alicia's resolve was steady.

Panic overwhelmed Lisa. Ryan couldn't help her and deal with the big security guard at the same time. The air in the room was thinning. Her heart thumped wildly in her chest in part from stress and the very real feeling of contact with Ryan. What was it about him that could calm her and send her body into such a pinball machine of awareness all at the same time?

Trying to take another step toward the door, she faltered.

Ryan hauled her against his chest and made a move to kiss her.

He was giving them a show. She understood that on some level, but his hand guiding her lips toward his sent heat rocketing through her.

Ryan's moment of hesitation—a brief pause to catch and hold her gaze for a split second—sent her heart soaring and caused a hundred somersaults to flip through her stomach.

His lips, tentative, barely touched hers. Her breath caught and she could've sworn she'd heard him groan right before deepening the kiss.

She tilted her head back to give him better access as she parted her lips for him. For one dizzying moment when his tongue slid into her mouth her pain disintegrated and all she could feel was his lips moving against hers and how right it felt to be in Ryan Hunt's arms.

The thought was startling. She didn't belong there.

Breaking away first, she forced her mind to the present because for a moment she got lost—lost in the moment, in the feeling of awareness, in the feeling of life being right for just a second.

Turning toward the folks intent on keeping her in that room, Lisa put one hand on Ryan's shoulder and the other on her hip. No way could they push past Alicia and the big guy. Ryan was not small, nor was he incapable of handling himself. She was the weak link. She was the liability. Anger surged through her for being the one to hold them back. "Do you have a court order keeping me here, Alicia?"

The nurse's lips thinned as she shook her head.

"Then I suggest you step aside." The look of approval on Ryan's face, the way he smiled out of the side of his mouth shouldn't make her this happy. It did. She told herself it was because he was putting himself on the line for her. She owed him this at least.

He squeezed her waist and more of that fiery electricity shot through her, warming her in places she didn't want to think about with him standing this close. Or maybe it was just that she didn't want to go there with other people in the room.

Her thoughts couldn't be more inappropriate under the circumstances. Because that kiss made her wonder if Ryan was feeling more for her than he'd let on.

And what exactly was she supposed to do with that? Her life was a mess and he deserved so much more than she could give him.

In times like these, Lisa had to remind herself to take it one moment at a time.

"Well?" she asked point blank. Her confidence had returned.

"We can't keep you here against your will. However, I would like to ask you to stay, anyway," Alicia said flatly.

They couldn't keep her safe. They didn't believe her. They gave her no other choice.

"I'm fine." She looked up at Ryan. "Let's go. They can throw away the rest of my things for all I care. There's nothing in here that can't be replaced."

He gently leaned her against the bed and she missed his warmth as soon as he took a step away from her.

"Hospital regulation requires her to leave in a wheel-chair," the nurse said. "Will you at least sign the paper-work and let me take you out?"

Lisa nodded. "As long as it's quick."

The nurse disappeared, taking the security guard with her.

"My clothes are over there." She motioned toward the tall cabinet next to the wall-mounted TV. "That's all I have with me other than my cell, which is nearly out of battery."

Ryan retrieved her folded-up outfit of shorts and a halter top along with her underclothes.

She hoped he didn't see her cheeks warm with em-barrassment at the idea of him handing her underwear to her.

Once they got outside, she'd breathe much lighter. As it was, tension threatened to crack her already bruised and hurting shoulders.

"I can step into the hallway for a minute to give you

privacy while you dress if you'd like." Ryan placed the clothes on the bed next to where she stood.

"Here's the thing. I'm going to need your help." She smiled weakly.

His gray-blue eyes darkened to steel. An almost-pleading look crossed his features for a nanosecond. Then he half smirked. "I guess it would be weird for a husband to leave the room while his wife dressed."

"Hadn't even thought of that. It shouldn't take too long and I probably only need help getting things over my big size eights." Did she just complain about her shoe size? Was she rambling? The thought of Ryan in the room with her while she was completely naked was almost too much.

"I happen to like your feet." He helped her ease onto the bed and then he pulled the blanket over her, covering her midsection. With athletic grace he moved around to the other side of the bed, behind her, and then untied each bow on her hospital-issued gown.

Gently, he rolled the material down her arms. His breath was so close it warmed the sensitive skin along the back of her neck.

The white cloth hit the floor in front of her. She secured her sheet as Ryan moved in front of her. She was so aware of just how naked she was beneath her cover and how thin the material was that kept her cloaked. She white-knuckle gripped the seam with one hand while she reached for her clothes with the other. Thankfully, her ribs weren't broken, just a hairline fracture on one, the doctor had said, but the pain was still excruciating.

Without saying a word, he bent down and then cradled her ankle in his hand. He slipped her black lace panties over one foot, then two and she could've sworn she heard him groan.

Her body went rigid trying to fight the attraction overwhelming her senses.

His hands moved up the sides of her legs, his eyes trailed and when his skin touched hers it blazed a hot trail.

She lifted her bottom long enough for him to slide the panties around her hips. He didn't immediately move. His hands rested on either side of her.

Lisa couldn't remember the last time she felt this intimate with a man. Maybe never.

A few seconds later and with similar ease, Ryan slipped her shorts on.

At least for her bra he stood behind her and she couldn't see his intense expression—intense because they both had to know deep down that anything more than friendship between the two of them would be a bad idea.

After her bra and then halter had been secured, he moved to her side, eyes down. Was he thinking about the kiss they'd shared, too?

He lifted his head and made a move to speak.

The door opened, interrupting the moment. And that was probably for the best. The last thing Lisa needed to hear was just how much he regretted their lips touching. Or worse, an apology.

The nurse pushed a wheelchair in front of her. She helped Lisa into the seat and then handed her a stack of papers on a clipboard. The words *Against Medical Advice* had been scribbled in huge letters across the first page.

Lisa initialed all the places the nurse had highlighted as Ryan positioned himself behind the chair.

When she'd signed for what felt like the hundredth time, he wheeled her out of the room, off the floor and into the night.

The air was still hot. It was the time of year in Texas when she went to bed and it was hot, she woke and it was hot. Midday, the rubber soles on her shoes could practically melt against the sweltering pavement.

"I'm parked in the front row," he said, his voice still husky.

"That was lucky."

"Turns out there aren't that many visitors in the middle of the night," he said, and she could tell he was smiling without looking at him. She could hear it in his voice.

"Thank you for breaking me out. If Nurse Ratchet had her way, I'd be zonked out with an IV drip that would have me slobbering down my chin as she spoon-fed me mashed potatoes."

"Not a problem." He chuckled. "I'm not that big on sleep, anyway."

"Either way, I owe you a big favor for everything you've done today."

"It's nothi—

"Hold on a second. What the hell's going on?" He abruptly stopped. Based on the shift in tone, this wasn't going to be good news.

"What is it?"

"Someone slashed my tires."

"You haven't been here for long. Whoever did this must be close." Lisa glanced around and gasped. "He must still be here."

"I'll arrange another ride. We need to get you inside." He spun her chair around and wheeled her toward the hospital as she kept watch for any signs of movement in her peripheral.

Ryan parked her near the elevator, away from the automatic sliding glass doors. His cell phone was already at his ear by the time Lisa could see him again.

"Who are you calling this late?" she asked, panic written all over her features.

"Dawson lives close," Ryan said, the line already ringing.

"Please don't say anything," she begged. That damn desperation still in her tone.

Their friend picked up on the third.

"I'm at the hospital with Lisa and we need a ride." He paused, not eager to lie to his friend. "Must've picked up a nail on my way over. Left tire's flat."

Ryan said a few uh-huhs into the phone before he ended the call. "He's on his way."

She couldn't quite feel relief yet; maybe it was hope. Her danger radar was on full alert after everything she'd been through. Every noise made her jumpy.

"Is there any way you'd consider not sharing any of this with Dawson yet?" she pleaded.

"I don't even know what's really going on." Ryan kept his fisted hands at his sides as he kept watch.

A few quiet minutes later, Dawson pulled up in his SUV.

Ryan looked Lisa dead in the eye before he made a move to help her. "I won't force you to say anything in front of Dawson. We're going to my house. And when we get there, you're going to start talking."

Chapter Four

"I'm sorry about your father," Dawson said once they were safely inside the truck. Based on the look in his eyes, she knew he meant it. He had questions. Ditto for Ryan.

"Thank you," she said, unable to suppress a yawn. Exhaustion had worn her body to the bone and for the first time since this ordeal began she felt that it was safe to go to sleep. The burst of adrenaline she'd felt during the struggle in the hospital was long gone.

Dawson seemed content to leave things at that for now. She leaned against Ryan, put her head on his shoulder and closed her eyes. By the time she opened them again, they were parked in front of Ryan's house.

"No need to go out of your way for me. I'll be good on the couch," Lisa said to Ryan as he helped her up the few steps to his house.

He turned and waved at Dawson, who'd been waiting for a signal that it was okay to leave.

Lisa was grateful that Ryan hadn't forced her say anything in front of their friend. More than that, she was thrilled that she'd been able to let down her guard enough to fall sleep.

"Okay." Ryan unlocked the door and led her inside.

It was the first time she'd seen his house, a bungalow on an out-of-the-way street five miles from town. He'd already told her that the place sat on three acres and that he especially liked being on the outskirts of Mason Ridge. He was close enough to get anything he needed and just far enough to feel that he was away from it all when he went home.

He flipped on a light, walked her right past the leather sofa and moved toward the hallway instead.

"Ryan. What are you doing?" She tried to stop, but he nudged her forward.

"Giving you a place to sleep, remember?" He had the upper hand. He knew full well she couldn't walk into the other room without support.

"You said I could sleep on the couch."

"Did I?" His grin shouldn't make her want to laugh. Maybe she just needed to think about something light for a change.

She should throw more of a fit about sleeping on the couch, too, but she didn't have any fight left inside her after all she'd been through. Fatigue weighted her limbs, making it difficult to hold on to Ryan, and the new bruises she'd acquired were already tender.

"Can we close those blinds?" she asked, biting back a yawn as Ryan helped her ease under the covers.

"If that would make you feel better." He paused. "No one can hurt you out here."

He was already moving toward the window.

"I feel rotten for kicking you out of your own room. Are you sure you don't want to put me on the couch? I'd be fine."

"You're in my house. That means we play by my rules. You get the bed." He winked at her, but she could see the storm brewing. "I'll leave the door open in case you need anything. Just give me a shout."

"Where will you be?" She must look pitiful for him to hold off his questions until morning. Maybe she'd figure out what to tell him by then.

"On the couch." He walked toward the hallway. "It's not the first time."

Even so, it didn't feel right.

"No, Ry—"

His hand came up before she could finish her protest. "My rules, remember?"

She was biting back another yawn as she conceded. For tonight, she wouldn't argue. However, she hoped to stay a few days, at least, and she had no plans to force him out of his bed for that long.

"I'll be in the next room," he said, turning off the light. "Unless you need me to stay until you fall asleep."

"I'm good. Thank you, though." Lisa knew that Ryan wanted answers and normally she'd trust him with her life, but more lives than hers were on the line. She had Lori and Grayson to consider. Maybe she could get word to Beckett that she had no plans to reveal his secret. Leave her family alone and she would never bring the truth to light. Would it work?

No. Wasn't that the deal they'd had all these years?

There had to be a reason for the change. A family like his would be savvy. Maybe he figured she would come forward. No way could he allow this accusation to come to light given the depth of trouble his father was already in. The Alcorn name was worth a lot of money. Their reputation was big business. Between that and ruining their family name, their history in the town, maybe Beckett figured he needed to ensure only positive press for him and his father in the coming months. It was the only thing that made any sense.

If a plea wouldn't work, then she'd threaten him if she had to. If he didn't leave her family alone she would go to the law and then to the media and tell them everything.

His voice echoed in the back of her mind. What were the chances the sheriff would believe her? And especially after all these years? Would the media? It wasn't as if she could produce any tangible evidence, not now. She'd believed Beckett's threats as a little girl because she wasn't aware of rape kits and forensics.

A good attorney could turn her testimony upside down. And then she, Lori and Grayson would have to watch their backs for the rest of their lives. Wealthy men had long reach and she doubted she'd be safe no matter how far away she moved, which was precisely why that plan wouldn't work.

Either way, she couldn't see an out. Plus, there was this new guy to worry about. The man who'd attacked her in the hospital was not Beckett.

Trying to think made her brain cramp. Frustration ate at her. Exhaustion threatened to pull her under. She was toast. No way could she think clearly.

For now, Lori and Grayson were safe.

She let that thought carry her into a deep sleep.

LISA WOKE THREE times throughout the night, screaming from nightmares. When she opened her eyes for the fourth time, the sun was bright in the sky. She glanced over and saw Ryan, shirtless, still sleeping in a chair. He'd stayed after the first round, saying he wanted to be close if she needed him.

His presence comforted her.

Her lips tingled with the feel of the kiss they'd shared. She didn't want to be thinking about that first thing when she opened her eyes. And yet there it was all the same.

His chest was a wall of muscle and she had to force her eyes away from his sculpted abs. That body was built from hard work and she admired him for it. There were other marks on his body, too, and she didn't want to think about the scars left behind at his father's hand. She'd witnessed one of the beatings as she was skipping home from school one day. Thinking about it even now caused her heart to squeeze and anger to flair through her.

She didn't ask, didn't know what had triggered Ryan's father that day. Everyone knew how bad the man's temper had been. Ryan was quick to step in to cover for his brother, Justin, and she wondered if Ryan had done it on that day, too.

It had been two weeks until summer break, and the Texas heat had arrived early that year. Lisa couldn't have been more than ten or eleven at the time. She'd stayed after school to finish a science project and passed by Ryan's house on her way home.

His father had him around the side of the house, his hand clamped around Ryan's arm as the man beat his son with a belt, buckle still attached.

There were no screams from her classmate, no begging for mercy, and that was a fact that would haunt her for years.

Ryan's pain was endured in silence, like hers. He never spoke about that or any other beating afterward, either. She could see in his eyes when they'd been exceptionally brutal. His father was always careful to hit Ryan in places where the bruises wouldn't show in plain sight. Every time Ryan had worn long pants in ninety-eight-degree temperatures to school, she'd noticed. Every time he had eased onto a chair, she'd noticed. Every time he'd worn long sleeves in the summer, she'd noticed.

And she'd known why.

Fire burned through her veins, boiling her blood at the memories. Only a coward hurt a child. Ryan's father had been one. And so was Beckett.

"How'd you sleep?" Ryan's voice surprised her.

"Good," she said quickly, trying to slow her racing pulse. She'd slept better than good actually, even with the nightmares. She didn't want to tell him how comfortable she felt in his bed. The sheets were soft against her skin. The mattress was like sleeping on a soft cushion. And his clean, masculine scent was all over the pillow.

The pain was messing with her mind. This bed was no nicer than the one at the hospital, she tried to tell herself.

He stood and fastened his jeans, and she forced her gaze away from the small patch of hair on his chest leading down toward the band of his jeans.

Walking toward her, he yawned and stretched, and she noticed just how powerful his arms were. There was enough muscle there to hold off a bear, let alone a man who liked to hurt women. She told herself that was the only reason she noticed—to see if he could protect her—and not because of the awareness she felt every time he was in the room.

The mattress dipped under his weight as he sat on the edge of the bed.

"Are you hungry?" he asked.

"I think I can eat."

"What sounds good?"

"Don't put yourself out. Anything is fine. A piece of fruit or yogurt would do." She hated feeling so helpless.

"I can make an omelet," he offered.

"No. That's too much work, seriously."

"Would you stop worrying about being a pain already? I don't mind. I can scramble some eggs and heat sausage. But first, how does a cup of coffee sound?"

"Like heaven on earth." She waited for him to leave the room before she tried to sit up. Pain shot through her with every movement. She fought through it. No way was she asking him to help her to the bathroom.

Carefully, she inched her legs toward the side of the bed until her feet hung off.

How long did the nurse say it would take before Lisa felt better?

At this rate, it was going to take a long time to make it to the bathroom let alone go for a run again. She shook it off and forced her legs over the side of the bed.

Pushing up on her arms, she winced. A good look at the bruises there only made things worse. At least she could use her anger to fuel her determination to get up. She focused all her energy on standing.

The first few steps were like walking on stilts for the first time. A few more and she started getting the hang of how to lean in order to reduce the pain that came with movement. By the time she returned to the bed, she was energized. Being able to do something for herself so soon was a huge win.

"Hold on there. Let me help you." Ryan stood in the doorway two-fisting cups of coffee.

"No problem. I got this," she said, in too much pain to outwardly express her excitement.

"I'd ask if you're always this determined, but I already know the answer." His genuine smile was better than any painkiller, and that probably scared her more than anything else.

"I hope it's okay that I opened the toothbrush on the counter. I figure you left it out for me." She eased onto the bed and pulled the covers up.

Ryan returned to his earlier seat near her and handed over a cup of fresh brew.

"Good," he said, and his voice was husky. He cleared his throat and took a sip.

This close, she could see the horrible reminders of his painful childhood up and down his back and her heart nearly exploded.

"How's Justin?" she asked to distract herself.

"Good. He's living in Austin now with a wife and a pair of kids. The oldest is about to start school and Maria isn't thrilled." Ryan perked up.

"It's good that he got out of here," she said. She'd never met Justin's wife. Once he left, he never turned back.

"Too many memories, I think."

"What about you? You ever think about leaving Mason Ridge?" She sipped the coffee, thinking it was about the best thing she'd tasted all year.

He leaned back, positioned his elbow on the bed and said, "All the time."

"Then why do you stay?"

"Not sure. Work's here. Still have a little bit of family in the area, friends."

"You know you can stay in touch via cell phones and social media now. People don't have to live in the same area to keep a friendship going anymore." She wondered if a little piece of him waited for his mother to return. He'd been hurt the most when she left.

"I have a cell phone, which is brand-new, but I use it to as a means to call people so we can meet up somewhere. Call me old-fashioned, but I like to look my friends in the eye when I talk to them, have a beer together and not have to plug in a device or stare at a screen to do it."

"Wow. You really are sounding like a relic now," she teased, enjoying the easy conversation. The heavy discussion would come and she'd have to figure out a way around giving straight answers.

"I'LL LEAVE YOU with that as I make your breakfast, in the kitchen, using old-fashioned machines like a toaster," Ryan said.

She laughed, which shouldn't have put a smile on his face as he left the room. It did. If he had any sense at all, he'd wipe off his silly grin.

Talking to Lisa came easy. It had always been the case with the two of them. He'd misread that to mean something more in the past. Being wiser now, or maybe just older, he realized that their conversation flowed when everything was light, right up until they tried to talk about anything important.

Then there were the nightmares she kept to herself. She woke screaming, traumatized, but refused to talk about them.

He'd also noticed last night that she recoiled when he touched her. If his arm so much as grazed her skin, she involuntarily tensed. What was that about?

There was an electrical current running between them, too. The chemistry that had existed before was as strong as ever, and that just confused the hell out of him.

He might have maturity on his side, but that still didn't explain why he couldn't accurately read her intentions even after all these years. And it wasn't as if that had ever been a problem for him with other women. His relationship was Lisa was the definition of complicated.

Right now there were more pressing questions that needed answers. And he had a feeling he was about to make her uncomfortable.

Right after he fed her.

Ryan brought in a plate of toast and scrambled eggs, which she made short work of.

He'd been reviewing all the possible reasons she'd wound up lying in a hospital bed, none he liked. In fact, most made him downright angry because if this wasn't random, then his mind snapped to the very real possibility that a boyfriend or someone she cared about had done this to her. Fire raged through his veins, burning him from the inside out at the thought. He'd nearly caught on fire last night thinking about how she'd kept watching the door yesterday, afraid. She'd evaded all of his questions even when he'd made sure her back was against the wall. She would rather toss him out than give him the truth. He'd suffered enough at the hands of his father to know when someone was covering for an abuser. Ryan had been that person.

Giving a false report to the law could get her in real trouble. They needed to have a discussion about that.

"So, tell me what's going on with you, Lisa. Are you seeing someone?" She wouldn't come out and tell him she was being abused. He'd need to let her know she could trust him first.

"No." She shook her head for emphasis.

Okay, fine. Looking at her expression, he believed her. Lisa was a bad liar and it was mostly because she had no practice at it. After dealing with his family, Ryan appreciated that about her. But that didn't mean a guy from her past hadn't resurfaced. Maybe even someone who knew her sister. He thought about how protective she'd been over Lori and Grayson.

"Then what?" he asked, not wanting to own up to the relief he felt knowing she didn't have a boyfriend. It shouldn't matter. He had to be hands-off when it came to her.

"I appreciate everything you're doing for me, Ryan, I do." She paused, looking as though she was searching for the right words. "Maybe I should go."

"No, you don't." She was in too deep, and he needed to be delicate with what he needed to ask. "You're staying here. Just give me a reason why you won't tell me what's going on."

"I would if I could. Can we leave it at that?" There was that fear in her eyes again. If he said, "Boo!" she'd bolt. Anger roared through him.

"We can for now." He needed to know what he was up against, but there were other ways to get at the truth without pushing—pushing would only drive her away. Ryan knew that from personal experience, as well. Lisa looked as if she might explode from fear and he didn't want her getting the idea that she had to go home. At least while she was at his place he could keep an eye on things, make sure she was okay. They already had history and he could build on that to get her to trust him. Then, as soon as he found out that bastard's name, Ryan would make sure the guy never touched anyone else ever again.

"Promise me something?" she asked, and he could hear the fear in her voice no matter how much she tried to mask it.

He nodded.

"Don't tell anyone I'm here. Or where Lori and Grayson are staying at least until I get my head around everything that's happened and we make arrangements for my father." A few tears fell, streaking her cheeks.

He thumbed them away, ignoring the impulse to lean forward and kiss her.

"You have my word. I won't tell a soul. But if I'm going to protect you, then I need to know what I'm up against." That seemed to strike a chord.

She pursed her lips and then nodded.

Chapter Five

"The swelling is worse on my cheek, isn't it?" Lisa asked as she walked into the kitchen, where Ryan was doing dishes.

"Let me help you." He made a move toward her but was met with a hand.

"I want to do this on my own. Can't stick around here forever."

"You just got here last night." Ryan was used to people leaning on him. This was the first time he met a wall every time he tried to help. Lisa and her sister had been bounced around when they were kids and he suspected that was the reason she kept everyone at arm's length.

"It doesn't hurt as much to do this, though." She stretched her arms out and then lifted her hands above her head.

The move caused her breasts to press against the fabric of her shirt. Spending 24/7 together wasn't doing good things to his hormones. Those feelings from the past had resurfaced and that was most likely because he hadn't spent much time around her since then. You'd think he was still eighteen for how much his body reacted to her. He needed to keep himself in check.

"That's a good thing. Do you want a couple of pain

relievers? I have over-the-counter stuff, but it'll take the edge off." Ryan handed her a fresh cup of coffee. She'd been tight-lipped so far about what was going on. She kept reassuring him that she'd be fine, but those nightmares told a different story.

Ryan had a fleeting thought that her attack could be related to Charles Alcorn slipping out of police custody. His capture brought up the old trauma from their friend and her brother being abducted fifteen years ago.

Would that cause Lisa to wake up in the middle of the night screaming? Ryan's gut instinct said no. Something like that came from deep-seeded fears. He knew all about those.

"No, I'm fine. I need to check in with my sister. Have you seen my cell?"

"Spoke to her this morning. She and Grayson are doing great, enjoying the view of the lake."

"When did you do that?" She moved to the kitchen window, wearing his boxers tied off at the waist and an oversize T-shirt, drinking her coffee.

"Early. Figured she'd be up with Grayson."

"How long has your SUV been here?" The fear was back.

"Since about eight o'clock. I called in a few favors to expedite the process. Having a friend in the private security business helped. Why?"

"No reason." She shrugged off the comment, trying to make it look as if she didn't care.

This might be the opportunity he'd been looking for to get her to open up a little more. He needed to find the right words or he'd scare her into her shell faster than a sea turtle being hunted by a shark.

"What made you become a teacher?" he asked.

"It sounds corny but I like working with kids. See-ing their eyes light up when something clicks is the best feeling," she said, and her mood instantly improved. She settled down at the kitchen table with her coffee.

He'd found a less threatening subject. Good.

"I can see in your eyes that you love your job." He joined her at the table. He wondered how much her own difficult childhood played into her career choice.

"I can't imagine doing anything else," she said, her face glowing.

And that shouldn't make Ryan smile, but it did. He chalked it up to enjoying seeing his friend happy.

"Did you know that my dad never finished high school?" she asked.

"I probably should know that. You know me. I'm not one for gossip." Hadn't he always had his hands full with his own family?

"He didn't. I think it always bothered him, too. He always pushed me and Lori to graduate and go to col-lege." Tears welled in her eyes.

"I'm sure he's proud of you both," Ryan said.

She turned her face toward the window and he could see that she was struggling to control her emotions.

He gave her the space she needed, resisting the urge to move across that table and haul her into his arms.

"You know what keeps me awake at night?" she fi-nally asked, turning to face him. "My sister and Gray-son. I worry about her bringing up a child alone."

"Lori isn't alone. She has you." Don't think he didn't notice that she'd just changed the subject before he could dig deeper. Okay, fine. He didn't have it in him to press when she was barely able to tamp down her emotions. But he was determined to make progress with her at some point today. He'd go ask her coworkers if school was in session. Maybe he could dig around a little, anyway. Surely someone knew about her personal life.

"True, but Grayson needs a father and that doesn't look like it's going to happen." She took a sip of coffee. "Jessie cut off all contact with her when he found out she was pregnant."

"Better it happen now than later."

"How do you know it would have happened later? He never gave her a chance." She shot fire at him through her eyes.

He held his hands up in surrender. "That didn't come out right. I'm just saying that it would hurt less now, while Grayson's little, than if he had the chance to get to know his dad before he took off."

She hesitated for a second. "I can see why you'd think that."

"I know what you're thinking and you're exactly right," he conceded. How in hell's name did she flip this into a conversation about his family? "I learned that lesson the hard way."

"I remember when your mom left. It changed you," she said softly. He hadn't expected her to remember, or to hear so much compassion in her voice when she talked about his family.

"A mother choosing to walk out doesn't do good things to a ten-year-old boy."

"No, you're right. That never should have happened." Lisa didn't add the fact that she'd left her sons with a cruel man, and he appreciated her for it. "For what it's worth, I'm sorry."

Those last two words spoken from Lisa did more to ease the ache in his chest than almost two decades of going over and over it in his own mind, reminding himself countless times that it wasn't his fault.

"Have you spoken to her since then?" she asked, studying her coffee mug.

"No. I don't even have a good address on her." This discussion wasn't the one Ryan wanted to have. The only reason he'd keep going is that it just might help bridge the gap between them, help her to trust him to talk about deeper issues.

"It's not hard to find people these days. All you need is a name and you can search the internet," she said.

"Sure. If you want to find them."

"And you don't?" she glanced up from her mug, curious.

"I've already told you. I'm not that good with technology," he countered.

"Oh no, you don't, mister. You're not getting away with it that easily. Nice try, though."

"You got me, then." How did he put this without sounding like an SOB? "She's the one who walked out. Why on earth would I go chasing after someone who could just as easily find me if she wanted to? Just in case you haven't put it together yet, she hasn't even tried."

"How do you know?" Lisa's brow furrowed in the way it did when she studied something intently. She might have been looking at her coffee mug, but she was carefully considering his responses. And from the look of it, she was also holding back her true opinion.

"Why is any of this important to you?" He didn't mean to sound so clipped. Talking about his mother never seemed to get any easier.

She glanced up at him.

"I'm sorry. I shouldn't be so nosy." She ran her finger along the rim of the cup. "I guess I was thinking of all the good times I would've missed with my own father if I hadn't forgiven him for some of the things he did when he was drinking."

"There is one big difference between our parents."

"Which is?"

"Yours cared enough to stick around."

LISA NEEDED TO change the subject. Witnessing the hurt in Ryan's eyes when he spoke about his mother was a shot to the heart and she feared she was only making the situation worse by dredging up the past. Some topics weren't good to revisit.

Ryan did it for her when he stood and took his mug to the sink, mumbling something about making plans for the day.

And it could just be the fact that she was missing her own father that made her want to heal Ryan's relationships. Speaking of her family, she needed to talk to her sister.

"Did you say that you saw my cell?" she asked while he seemed to intently focus on whatever he had going on in the sink.

He stopped what he was doing for a second.

"Is there something going on with my phone?" she asked.

"Are you sure you want it? That thing hasn't stopped vibrating and buzzing."

"What did you do with it?"

"Nothing. Well, I turned it off. You needed to rest and I was afraid it would wake you. I brought it out here and then it kept me up, which is the other reason I slept in that chair last night."

Normally, the thought of her smartphone being stuffed inside a drawer or tucked away on a counter would create a level-five panic. In this case, she was grateful. Everyone would most likely be trying to figure out what was going on with her or sending their condolences. Even though people were well-intentioned and she would get back to them as soon as she could, she wasn't strong enough to face it yet.

"We need to stop by the funeral home later today to make the arrangements," he said.

"Did they call?"

"No. I made contact with them. I knew you and your sister weren't in the right place to be able to handle it yet. I didn't want them leaving messages, so I figured I'd reach out and keep them posted on your progress. They said they'd have someone available early evening today, after closing, so you'd be assured privacy."

Ryan had no idea how comforting those words truly were. "Can we go see Lori and Grayson after?"

"I have a few things to take care of tonight. We can leave for Arkansas first thing in the morning. We'll go at first light."

"Great." She could live with that. Besides, that would give her another night of rest to heal. As it was, she was afraid that she'd scare her nephew. She could hide the bruises with makeup.

Most of the day she spent curled up on the couch watching TV.

Lisa was determined to dress herself. Ryan had washed her clothes and it felt good to have on something clean that fit. The drive to the funeral home went by quickly.

There were only two cars in the parking lot when

they arrived. She noticed a late-model blue sedan parked near the front door. The second, a pickup truck, was positioned around the side of the building. The bed was loaded with mulch and equipment that looked like gardening supplies. The sun was bright. It wouldn't be dark in this part of Texas for three hours and yet the place still had a creepy feel to it.

Maybe it was the knowledge that there was so much death around her that made the hairs on her neck prick. Or the fact that she knew her father lay inside, breathless, gone.

Tears welled, stinging the backs of her eyes.

"Can we stop by my place on the way home?" she asked. "I need to pick up clothes and makeup."

Ryan seemed to pick up on her anxiety because he leaned forward and kissed her on the forehead before helping her out of his SUV. He held out his hand. She took it, the warmth in his touch calming her, and ignored the pain shooting through her chest with every step toward the sales office. This pain was different than what she'd felt for the past few days. She felt that, too. This hurt from the inside out, sucked the air from her lungs in one whoosh and made her want to fold onto her knees and cry without stopping.

The emotions that she couldn't afford to allow herself to feel about her father's death threatened to explode. The inside of her head felt like raging storm clouds gathering, clinging thickly in the air, making it difficult to think.

Her father's body had already been identified. At least she didn't have to do that. Oh, but Lori had and Lisa hated that her baby sister had been the one to do it. Even worse was that Lisa had been in the hospital

and Lori had had to deal with it alone. Ever since their
mother had died, it had always been the two of them together, supporting each other through their dad's antics.
Lisa had stepped up to try and fill their mother's shoes.

The door was locked, so Ryan tapped on the glass.

An older man appeared from down a hallway, wav-
ing and smiling. He opened the door and shook each
of their hands, beginning with Lisa's.

"Please come inside. I'm pleased to meet both of you.
My name is Arthur." His spoke in a soft, even tone. He
was a short man in his late fifties. He wore a simple
suit with a button-down shirt and no tie.

Inside, the walls were painted taupe, a calming color,
and the decor was simple. There was a cherrywood desk
with matching bookcase and cabinets. The leather ex-
ecutive chair was tucked into the desk. It was eerily
quiet and no one else appeared to be inside the building.

"Thank you for agreeing to meet this late," Lisa said.
"I'm Lisa and this is my friend Ryan. I believe you two
spoke on the phone."

"It's my pleasure to assist you in putting your loved
one to rest." Arthur's hands were clasped, his shoulders
slightly rounded.

He isn't at rest, Lisa thought, *he's dead*. Tension
tightened the muscles in her shoulders and back. Arthur was being polite, doing his job, so it wasn't him
causing her to tense up. Maybe it was the thought that
her father didn't have to be…gone.

She took in a deep breath and refocused.

"Please, follow me." Arthur turned and then walked
down the hallway, stopping at the second door on the
right. There was a Bible verse written on one wall that
she remembered from her childhood. On the other was

a poster that read Celebrate the Life of Your Loved One. Ask Your Representative for Details.

Two chairs sat opposite the cherrywood desk in Arthur's office. Ryan helped her to the nearest one. He bent down so only she could hear him and said, "You say the word and we're outta here."

She nodded slightly.

He took a seat next to her, and then turned so that he was facing her more than Arthur, bent forward and clasped his hands together. The older man seemed unfazed and she imagined he'd seen stranger things. She glanced backward toward the door, not liking that she didn't have a clear view.

There was a small table between her and Ryan with a few brochures promoting add-on services like all-maple caskets and the use of their on-site chapel for viewing along with a tissue box.

Arthur clasped his hands, mimicking Ryan's gesture, and placed them on top of the solid desk.

"How may I assist you today?" he asked, his voice calm and soothing.

"My father wanted to be cremated." Those six words threatened to unleash a torrent of tears.

Arthur nodded, gave another compassionate look. As genuine as he seemed, he'd probably done this thousands of times over the course of his career. He'd seen an equal number of grieving families bury someone they loved.

Lisa opened her mouth to speak but was silenced by a noise that sounded from behind. Ryan turned at the same time she did, watching the hallway.

"It's probably nothing. Fred, our groundskeeper, is

still here working," Arthur dismissed the interruption, focusing on Lisa again.

"Stay right here." Ryan was already on his feet by the time they heard a second noise.

Lisa didn't want to wait. Besides, the thought of Ryan going out there to investigate alone didn't do good things to her blood pressure. Her father was dead. She'd been in the hospital. Any number of things could happen to Ryan. And the thought of bad news happening in threes was fresh in her mind.

She pushed herself up and followed him. He must not have noticed because he said nothing to stop her. And if he'd known, he would've stopped to help her. He was locked on to something.

Only a few steps behind him, she still didn't get a good look at what had caused the noise. The front door was closing, though.

Someone had been in there.

"Fred?" Ryan called out as he bolted through the front door.

She couldn't get there fast enough to catch him. By the time she made it across the room with Arthur's help, Ryan had returned.

"You expecting anyone else?" Ryan asked the older man.

"No. We get kids running through shouting inappropriate things sometimes for laughs." This was the first time the old man broke form. Disgust was in his eyes.

"Don't they normally say or do anything?" Ryan's gaze moved from Arthur to his SUV. He must be remembering what had just happened to his tires at the hospital.

"Yes. But you never know what's going on in the

mind of a teenager." Arthur shrugged, his compassionate demeanor returned.

Ryan turned to Lisa. She tried to command her body to stop trembling.

"You want to do this by phone?" he asked.

She nodded.

"I'm sorry to have wasted your time, Arthur. This isn't a good idea for her right now," Ryan said firmly, leaving no room for doubt that they were about to walk out the door.

"I understand. Call when you're ready to talk." Arthur produced a card from his pocket.

Lisa thanked him and walked to the SUV with Ryan's help.

Once they were inside and he took the driver's seat, she said, "I've had a bad feeling the whole time we've been here."

He turned over the ignition. The engine hummed to life.

"That's because we were being watched."

Chapter Six

"I need to ask this straight out, Lisa. Did an ex-boyfriend do this to you?" Ryan knew he might make her retreat by being straightforward like that, but he needed to know.

"No."

"Are you being honest with me?" Again, he had to ask. It was the only thing that made sense to him, given everything he'd witnessed so far, and especially the way she'd watched the door at the hospital as though she was expecting someone to come in. Expecting wasn't the right word. It was more like fearing.

"I've never lied to you, Ryan." She sounded hurt.

Maybe he should've trusted his initial judgment and left it alone. This was a no-win situation. She wasn't giving him anything else to go on.

"Then tell me what's going on with you. Who hurt you? I know it's not random." He pulled the SUV onto the county road, checking the mirrors in case anyone followed them.

"I'm afraid to tell you. I don't want to make everything worse. I just need a few days to heal and figure this out."

"Figure what out?" he parroted.

"Can't we just leave it at that?"

"No. Not when you could get hurt again. Not when I can't protect you. Not when some unknown threat can pop up at any time."

"It's not a boyfriend, but it is something from my past. I can assure you that I'm the only one he wants," she said quietly.

"Tell me his name." Ryan kept his gaze focused on the road ahead, waiting for her to give him a name.

Neither spoke for the rest of the ride.

As soon as they got to his house, Lisa asked if he minded if she went to bed early.

"Eat first." He grilled a simple meal of beef kabobs with pineapple chunks and slices of green bell peppers for her while she was in the shower.

The plate he'd fixed for her was clear in a few minutes.

"That was delicious," she said with the first half smile since the ordeal at the funeral home. "At least let me help with the dishes."

"No. I got this." He waved her away. No way was he letting her help in her current condition. Besides, he liked cooking for her and taking care of her more than he wanted to admit, even if she was making it difficult by withholding information.

"I kicked you out of your bedroom. I haven't lifted a finger since I got here. The least you can let me do is earn my keep in the kitchen." Her voice rose at the end, angry.

What was that all about? She was injured and he was trying to take care of her.

Lisa started toward the bedroom. He made a move to help her.

"I can do this at least, Ryan," she said.

Ryan bit back a curse as he watched her struggle on her own.

"This is silly. Why won't you let me help you?" he asked, frustrated.

"Ask yourself the same question, Hunt."

If Ryan lived to be two hundred and fifty years old, he'd never understand a woman. All he was doing was trying to help Lisa. She was hurt and he was able. End of story. If she could do more for herself, he'd have no problem letting her pitch in to do the dishes or whatever else the heck she wanted to do around his home. Why had she turned it on him?

There was another thing that had been bugging him. She'd made a big deal about putting him out by taking his bed. He didn't mind. Hell, he'd slept in worse places than his comfortable couch. What was she getting crazy about?

Rather than spin out on questions he couldn't answer, he decided to watch a little TV before turning in.

Ryan must've dozed off because he woke to Lisa screaming. Another nightmare? He pushed off his blanket, did a quick head shake to get rid of the fog and jogged toward his bedroom.

A crashing sound. Ryan broke into a full run.

Ryan smacked at the light switch, missed as he darted to her side. The room was completely black.

Lisa was struggling…and someone was on the bed hovering over her.

Ryan dove at the male figure from behind, knocking him off balance and off Lisa.

Both he and the intruder rolled off the bed. Ryan

fired off a couple of jabs into the guy's ribs, taking a blow to the chin.

Lisa screamed in what sounded like anger and pain rolled into one.

The attacker was smaller in stature than Ryan, but he was quick.

A knee to Ryan's groin had him cursing and fighting off nausea. He had a decent grip on the jerk, and Ryan had no intention of letting go.

"Call 911," he shouted to Lisa.

Another knee to the groin, a little higher this time, and Ryan saw stars. He couldn't get a good look at the attacker in the pitch-black. The blow caused him to lose his grip just enough for the guy to push off and get to his feet.

Ryan rolled onto his shoulder and wrapped his arms around the guy's ankles. He prayed like hell that Lisa was calling the sheriff.

Still on the floor, he couldn't see what she was doing and the guy was kicking and squirming. At this rate, it wouldn't be long before he broke free from Ryan's grip. Unless Ryan made a move. It was risky. Give this guy an inch and he could break free and sprint away.

Damn, Ryan's shotgun was in the second bedroom he used as an office. Lot of good it was doing in there.

All Ryan could see was outlines and dark figures.

An object slammed against the guy's head, knocking him back. The guy tried to rebalance by shifting his feet. Ryan tightened his grip, locking the guy's stance. The attacker fell backward.

"Call 911. Now!" Ryan shouted to Lisa.

He climbed on top of the guy, pressing him into the floor with his weight advantage.

Without warning, the muscles in Ryan's body seized up. What the hell? Every muscle suddenly became rigid and he heard a ringing noise in his ears.

Pain shot through him and he couldn't move. He was paralyzed.

The charge stopped after a few seconds and his muscles relaxed, but it felt as if they were vibrating and he still couldn't coordinate movement.

His attacker wriggled free, elbowing Ryan in the process, catching him in the neck. Ryan still couldn't budge.

The guy took off down the hallway.

There were the sounds of a struggle that lasted only a few seconds. Then a door slammed. A dirt bike engine roared to life.

Ryan still couldn't move, couldn't speak. He could only lie on the floor, frustrated and helpless.

Light filled part of the room. Lisa must've flipped on the hallway light. She was next to him a few seconds later.

"What did he do to you?" Concern laced her raspy tone.

At least another full minute passed before Ryan could respond.

"Taser gun." Those two words took more effort than he imagined. Normal feeling was beginning to return to his extremities. He flexed and released his fingers, wiggled his toes.

Once the recovery process started, it moved quickly. He had full possession of his faculties within minutes.

Ryan pushed himself up to a sitting position. His nightstand had been cleared in the struggle and his alarm clock and lamp tossed onto the floor.

How had the guy gotten past Ryan to get inside in the first place?

His legs were shaky, but he moved to the window in the bedroom, realized it was open and stuck his head outside. He couldn't see anything moving and figured the guy was long gone.

"The deputy should be here any minute," he said to Lisa.

She pursed her lips.

Wait a second. She didn't call?

"We don't need to get them involved, do we?" she asked. The fear had returned.

"As a matter of fact, we do. I still have no idea who we're dealing with and this is the third incident. I don't know what kind of jerk you got yourself involved with, but I'm bringing in the law this time." Ryan didn't wait for her to respond. He located his cell and called dispatch.

He checked the front rooms, locked the door and returned to the bedroom when the house was clear.

She just sat on the floor, facing the wall.

He moved to her side and helped her onto the edge of the bed.

"It's not safe anymore," she said in a monotone, sounding as if she was in a trance.

"Whoever is doing this to you belongs behind bars. We talk to the deputy, bring in the law and they'll lock him up. It's that simple." He stared at her. The hallway light lit up one side of her face. The other was cast in a shadow. "He's bound to have left some evidence behind. They'll figure out who this is."

"You're right," she said.

Finally, he was getting through to her.

"I'll meet you in the living room in a second. I want to get dressed before the deputy gets here," she said.

"Okay." He moved into the kitchen and then brewed a fresh pot of coffee. She was starting to see logic. He was making progress. Now he might actually be able to help Lisa. All he'd done so far was provide a refuge.

But how did anyone know she was staying at his place?

His mind snapped back to the incident at the funeral parlor. Someone had been watching. Waiting to see if she showed so they could follow her and find out where she was staying.

Crazed boyfriends, if that was the story here, were known to go to all kinds of lengths to get revenge on their so-called loved ones. He'd read stories about abused women and the fear stamped on Lisa's face certainly fit the description. Her actions did, too.

The thought of anyone hurting her on purpose boiled his blood. A real man didn't raise a fist to a woman. Give Ryan a few minutes alone in a fair fight with the bastard and see what would happen.

What didn't add up was that Lisa didn't seem like the sort of person who would get mixed up with an abuser. Then again, based on the stories he'd come across, there was no type. Domestic abuse covered every race, religion and income bracket.

He'd nearly finished his cup of coffee by the time the deputy knocked on the door.

The intrusion and the fight must've shaken Lisa up pretty badly, because she hadn't emerged from the bedroom yet. If Ryan was being honest, he'd admit that his adrenaline was still pumping. He wished he'd gotten a good look at the guy. All he could give the deputy was a general description.

Ryan opened the door and invited Deputy Barnes to come inside. Barnes had been in Justin's grade and Ryan hoped the officer wouldn't hold Justin's teenage years against the whole family. Barnes was five foot nine, slim and wiry.

"Lisa Moore is also a witness. She's a friend of mine who's staying with me while she recovers from a hospital stay. I'll let her know you're here." Ryan started toward the hallway. "Coffee's fresh. There's a clean mug on the counter. Help yourself."

"Thank you," Barnes said.

Ryan nodded and then moved down the hallway. He didn't want to surprise Lisa, especially if she was in the bathroom, so he stepped heavily and called out to her.

When she didn't respond, his pulse kicked up a notch. No way the attacker could have returned, Ryan reassured himself.

He knocked on the bedroom door.

Nothing.

She could be in the bathroom, running sink water or flushing the commode. Even so, Ryan didn't have a good feeling about this.

"Lisa." He knocked once more, a little louder this time, before opening the door.

Heat hit him full force as soon as he stepped inside the room. The window had been reopened.

An ominous feeling settled over Ryan. The bathroom door was open and the room was empty.

What had she done?

He raced to the window. The porch light illuminated

a small part of the front yard, and that was about all he could see.

There was no sign of movement or Lisa.

Ryan needed to get out there and find her. He darted into the next room, where Deputy Barnes waited.

"My guest isn't here. She might be in trouble."

"What does that mean exactly?" The deputy, who was standing in the kitchen with a mug of coffee in his fist, blinked at Ryan.

For a split second he feared that the attacker had come back and snatched her from right under his nose. But, no, that couldn't be it. She would've screamed. Or fought. In which case, he would've heard something. It had been quiet. He'd been listening for any signs that she might've fallen. She could be so stubborn and insisted on taking care of herself.

Now he had no idea where she could be.

Chapter Seven

"She's injured and something's happened. Either she got spooked and ran or she's been taken." Ryan was already at the front door by the time he finished his sentence. "I need to search the grounds."

"Hold on a second. Talk to me about what we're dealing with before you trample all over my crime scene." The deputy set the coffee mug down and trailed behind Ryan, who'd stopped.

"I'm sorry. Someone broke in and attacked my guest," he said. "She's already hurt and I'm afraid she's in worse trouble."

"So this is a kidnapping?" The deputy's brow arched.

"I think she could be hiding, afraid the guy will return," Ryan hedged. He wasn't being completely honest. There was a thread of truth in his statement. She couldn't have gotten far, and hopefully she hadn't gone into the woods. That was where the attacker had gone.

"If that were true, wouldn't she come out now that I'm here?" Barnes asked.

"That's why I'm afraid she can't move. If we don't find her soon, it could be life or death."

Barnes nodded.

Within the first five minutes, he and the deputy had

cleared the shed and the yard. The deputy had insisted on going first and Ryan didn't have time to argue.

Being injured, she couldn't be moving fast. He thought for sure they'd find her somewhere on the grounds.

"There's no sign of her," Barnes said after fifteen minutes of searching. The deputy took his notepad from his front pocket and moved closer to the lights on his SUV. "Tell me what happened."

Ryan did.

"Show me where the struggle occurred," Barnes said.

Ryan followed the deputy as he examined the bedroom.

"Looks like the point of entry was the window. The latch is broken." He checked the other window and all the doors anyway, taking pictures as he worked the room. "We might be able to lift a print."

After collecting evidence there, he moved outside and examined the ground beneath the window, flashing a light around the hard dirt.

The deputy's cell phone buzzed. He took the call while Ryan turned toward the shed. He needed to think. Where would Lisa go at this hour?

"Do you have somewhere else to stay tonight?" The deputy stood and pocketed his flashlight when he was finished.

"No, sir. I'd rather stick around and protect my belongings." Ryan had every intention of finding Lisa.

"Let me know if your friend turns up," the deputy said, producing a card from his pocket. "In the meantime, call my cell if you remember anything else."

"Will do," Ryan agreed, anxious to continue his

search. He had every intention of locating her. More scenarios ran through his mind. None of them he liked.

Ryan pulled supplies from his shed to board up the window as he thought about where Lisa might go as the deputy's SUV backed out of the drive.

Thirty minutes later, he'd secured his house and put away extra nails and his hammer.

Walking back toward his small porch, he realized that they'd checked everywhere but his SUV. It was a long shot but one worth investigating.

The doors were locked. Another sign something was off. His personal belongings had always been safe on his land until tonight.

Ryan jogged into the house and retrieved keys from his jeans pocket. He heard the distinct sound of a vehicle door closing. He broke into a run.

Lisa was halfway across the yard when he returned.

"Stop," he shouted.

She froze but didn't turn to face him.

"What in hell's name is going on, Lisa?" Ryan caught up to her, put his hand on her arm to support her and blew out a frustrated breath when she recoiled.

"I'm sorry. I need to go."

"Not so fast. The only place you're going is inside. There's a fresh pot of coffee on and you're going to tell me what has you acting like a scared child." He urged her to turn around and he was surprised she did.

The look on her face, the resignation, should make him feel bad. He didn't want to go down this road with her. The one where he was basically forcing her to talk. But she was in danger and he couldn't put up with this any longer.

"He'll come back." There came the fear in her eyes again.

"Not tonight, he won't. The deputy said he'll be watching just in case. Plus, I have no plans to sleep. I won't be caught off guard again. And we're going to talk about what's scaring the hell out of you."

THERE WAS NO avoiding the discussion that Lisa didn't want to have with Ryan. Her stomach ached, not from physical pain, but the emotional kind. Everything had spiraled out of control faster than she could wrap her mind around it. In trying to keep her sister and nephew safe, she'd inadvertently put Ryan in danger.

Damn. Damn. Damn.

Once inside, Ryan helped her settle on the couch and brought her a cup of coffee. His steel eyes pierced right through her and she knew she could never lie to him. She had to tell him the truth, but she wasn't ready to share everything.

Seeing him retrieve and load his shotgun tied her stomach in knots.

He put two filled coffee mugs down on the coffee table in front of them and then took a seat next to her on the couch. He clasped his hands and rested his elbows on his knees. He was so close his left knee touched her right and she ignored what the contact was doing to her body.

"You already know about what has happened to me, the attack," she said.

He nodded, kept his gaze focused on a patch of hardwood floor to her left.

"This runs so much deeper than that." She took in a

fortifying breath and then released it. "I don't believe my father's death was an accident."

"Murder?" He sounded too stunned to say much else.

"Yes. I know it probably sounds crazy and I haven't given you any reason to believe me so far."

"Has someone been stalking you or your family?" He must've put a few things together, because his head rocked. "They have. That's why you won't talk about it."

"This person has been threatening to hurt my family if I tell anyone."

"And you think they staged your father's death to look like an accident?" he asked.

"That's part of why I was so apprehensive at the funeral home. Is it too late for an autopsy?" She took a sip of coffee, thankful for the burn in her throat.

"It never hurts to ask. I'll call first thing in the morning."

"I want to know what happened, but I'm afraid if I ask too many questions, he'll come after…"

"You?" Ryan paused. "They already have, so that can't be it." He paused again. "It's your sister, isn't it? You're trying to protect her and Grayson."

She nodded.

"No one else in your family is going to be hurt. Your sister and Grayson will be safe in Arkansas. No one knows about the cabin but me," he reassured her.

"What if she decides to come back to town and doesn't tell me?" Lisa asked.

"Lori needs to know the truth. It's the only way to keep her safe. But first, you have to tell me who's after you."

Fear made her freeze. She couldn't form the words. She shook her head instead.

"Lisa, I'm on your side, remember?" he asked with a calmness belied by his features.

She did know that on some level. And on another she knew Ryan wouldn't let up until she told him everything. Plus, he was a good guy. Why was it so hard to tell him?

Maybe it was the fact that she hadn't told anyone about the past…not her sister…not her father…not another soul.

She'd held it all inside for so many years now she'd lost count. Telling Ryan who was after her would force her to tell him why. And her unwillingness to talk about the past had so little to do with Ryan and so much to do with her.

As much as she loved her father, he hadn't exactly been someone she could trust. She'd known at twelve that she couldn't tell him what had happened. And then there was that time in high school when she'd started to talk about it with her friend Angela. Lisa figured she'd explode if someone didn't know what had happened to her.

When Lisa had brought up Beckett's name to test the waters, Angela had spent the next twenty minutes gushing about how wonderful he was. How fantastic his family was to donate so much to the town. Lisa couldn't deny it. Every year, they gave large sums of money to aid disadvantaged kids. Mr. Alcorn always graced the cover of the *Mason Ridge Courier* around the holidays for his generosity. Whether it be feeding the homeless or rounding up toys for kids, Mr. Alcorn could be counted on to give big. All carefully choreographed PR schemes, Lisa figured.

There was also no denying that Beckett was attractive. At least, before she knew what a monster he was on the inside. After that summer night when he'd abused her, she'd never looked at him in the same way again. Him or any of the Alcorns for that matter. She'd thrown out the newspapers featuring one of the family members, refusing to keep them inside the house.

Turning to look at Ryan, she noticed a cut high on his left cheekbone.

"You're hurt," she said.

"I'll live. And you just changed the subject."

"I'm sorry. You deserve to know everything. It's really hard for me to talk about it."

His hand came up to her face and he tilted her chin so she was looking directly at him.

"I'm not going anywhere. There's nothing you can tell me that will make me run away. I have every intention of seeing this, whatever *this* is, through until you're safe again."

Letting Ryan touch her was a bad idea. Her heart already pounded no longer from fear but with awareness. Being this close to him, allowing him to be her comfort, stirred up confusing emotions. And she found that she wanted more from him than loyalty, which made it that much more difficult to say what she needed to.

His expression was unreadable. All she could see in his eyes was determination and anger. His set jaw told her everything she needed to know about where his mind was at the moment.

"Now, we've been friends a long time. You can trust me. So I want you to tell me what's been going on. When did this start? And who has you this scared?" His hand touched hers and she pulled back immediately. She'd seen it plain as the nose on his face. The only thing Ryan felt for her was compassion.

Hope of anything but friendship between them shriveled as she squared her shoulders and took another sip of coffee before trying to figure out where to begin. No brilliant words came to her, so she decided to spit it out.

"Beckett Alcorn has it in for me. Has for quite a while now." There. She'd said it out loud. It was both terrifying and freeing all at once and her heart thundered in her chest.

She waited for Ryan to laugh. He didn't. His gaze intensified. He seemed to take a minute to contemplate this information. After taking a sip of his coffee, he asked, "Why you? Why now? Why your father?"

"All great questions. I'm still trying to figure out answers to those," she said.

"There must be some reason you can think of." His tone had a sharp edge to it.

What was up with that?

She shrugged.

"Have you two dated?" he asked pointedly.

"Me and Beckett?" She had to choke back vomit. The thought repulsed her, especially after what he'd forced on her. Beckett had called what he'd done to her a date. Just thinking about it again made her stomach churn. She set down her cup of coffee. "No."

"I can see that you're terrified of him. Heck, I used to think you were terrified of me with the way you flinch every time I touch you… Hold on…" Ryan stood and then began to pace. It was clear that he'd put two and two together. "That son of a bitch. I'll kill him myself."

He produced a set of keys from his pocket and started toward the door.

"Ryan, no!" Lisa stood, pushing through the pain, and blocked his path.

"Let me through that door, Lisa."

"Hear me out first. Please, listen to reason." She couldn't contain the panic in her voice.

"He hurt you, Lisa. That's all I need to know." Anger pulsed from him as he spoke through gritted teeth.

"Thank you, Ryan. You have no idea how much that means to me." She broke down in tears. Someone actually believed her about Beckett. For so many years she'd been convinced that if she'd told anyone, they'd laugh at her or say she was just trying to get at the Alcorns' money.

"What?" His right eyebrow hiked up.

"For believing me." How long had she feared that no one would? How many times had she wanted to say something to someone but stopped herself? How many times had she been on the edge of sharing but couldn't force herself to say the words?

Tears that had been stuffed deep down far too many years spilled from her eyes, down her cheeks. She couldn't stop them as she released another sob. They were sweet tears of release and her chest felt as if the boulder that had been parked on it was lifting. There was something magical about another person knowing, believing, that made Lisa's heart push out the darkness and begin to fill with light.

"Hold on there. Of course I believe you. We've known each other a long time, right?" He stood in front of her, his arm around her, comforting her.

"I didn't think anyone would." She buried her face in her hands and cried.

"It's okay. We're going to make this right." His hand came up to cradle her neck as he kissed the top of her head.

Her body tensed involuntarily. She had to force it to relax. He whispered other reassurances that her heart needed to hear.

Thankfully, he didn't ask for details and she figured none were needed. Him knowing everything that had happened wouldn't make him hate Beckett any less than he seemed to just knowing that the man had hurt her. There was something so very comforting about that. She would tell Ryan everything in good time. Eventually, he'd want to know and she desperately needed to speak the words out loud.

Sharing as much as she had so far was exhausting emotionally and physically.

"There's more that I need to tell you, Ryan. Let's sit down." She motioned toward the sofa.

He helped her to the couch.

"It's about my father. I know he wasn't drinking."

His gaze intensified.

"There are signs leading up to his binges. First off, he lies about little things. Then he gets irritable in the mornings. It's like there's a battle going on inside him every day. Also, he wouldn't let me see him drunk. Granted, I don't live at home anymore, but I always check on him on my way home. I know the signs."

Ryan seemed to seriously contemplate her words. "Why didn't you tell anyone about this before?"

"I was scared. I still am." And yet this was the most free she'd felt, too. "There's my sister to consider and Grayson. Beckett threatened me all those years ago. Said he'd do worse to my sister if I told anyone about our 'date.'"

Ryan's hands fisted. "You know, there's an easy way for me to fix this."

"Except the person who came to the hospital was not him," she said, needing to push Ryan out of his emotional state and back to a logical one.

"That doesn't mean the guy knew anything. He was probably hired by Beckett."

"That's what I thought, too. But what if he wasn't?"

"Then this would be bigger than Beckett."

"Exactly. So, if I take down Beckett, how do I know that I'm safe? That my sister won't still be a target?"

"First things first. We need to convince her to stick around the fishing cabin for a while longer. You and I need to head up there, too. I have to make sure we're not followed. I'm sure that's what led them here. They had someone watching the funeral home. I should've seen it coming," he said, frustration clipping his words.

"Beckett's a rich guy. He can afford to hire a lot of hands. Even if they put him in jail, what's to say that he won't hire someone to hurt my family from there through a friend or his lawyer? Not to mention the fact that the crime occurred more than fifteen years ago," she said, struggling to breathe while she spoke so freely for the first time. He'd had such a hold on her for so long that she'd barely whispered his name. "Let's sit down."

"Which is a good point. Why would he surface now?" Ryan followed her to the couch.

"My guess is that he's afraid I'll talk while his father is being hunted," she said.

"You think he's closing a loop?"

"If I went to the deputy and gave a statement, I doubt it would matter much. But if I went to the media while all this is going on, it could hurt his father," she said emphatically.

"He's still on the run. Turning himself in would go a long way toward helping him prove that he's innocent. Everything else is just hearsay." He paused. "You make great points, though. There are those in town who would believe that you're kicking Alcorn while he's down."

"Charles Alcorn isn't stupid. He has to be hiding somewhere, right? At least until his lawyer can straighten out this mess he's gotten himself into. Beckett might think they can't afford any bad press right now. That's the only thing that makes sense. He must believe I might come forward," she said.

"Happens all the time when bad news about a person or family surfaces," Ryan agreed.

"I'm guessing he's trying to protect the integrity of his family name and I'm certain they'll fight this charge. His father is probably out there hiding until this PR nightmare can be cleaned up." She couldn't hide her disgust.

"Why attack your father?" Ryan asked, rubbing the stubble on his chin.

"To send a direct message to me. I got away from Beckett when he tried to kill me."

"And he didn't want to get caught with his hand in the cookie jar at the hospital, so he hired someone to do it for him."

"Then it would just be two accidents in one week. Unlucky family," she confirmed. "That's what everyone thinks, anyway."

"We have to go to the sheriff."

"Except that we have no evidence, remember?" She tapped her finger on the table, still shaky from everything that had happened. "It's my word against his and my background isn't exactly solid."

"They have to believe you." Ryan captured her hand in his. "Deputy Barnes is already looking for you. I told him that I'd bring you to the station as soon as I found you."

"I'll call in my report. I can do that, right?" She ignored the shivers running through her fingers and up her arm from contact.

"I believe so," he said, and then glanced down at their fingers as he looped them together. "Is this okay?"

"Yeah, it is." Her fingers tensed, belying her words.

"Being touched bothers you, doesn't it?" he asked.

"I like it when you touch me," she said a little too quickly. "I mean, sure, it still catches me off guard if I'm not expecting it, but I actually do like it."

"Then, can I touch you here?" With his free hand, he pointed to her cheek.

She nodded.

He ran the backs of his fingers down the side of her face so tenderly they were like whispers against her skin.

"Can I move a little closer?" he asked.

She nodded.

He slid toward her until the outside of their thighs touched. Heat burned through her, but she tried to suppress it. He was trying to comfort her without scaring her and she appreciated the gesture. It would do neither of them any good for her to overanalyze the situation, or wish for more than light contact.

And yet her heart did wish for more.

It didn't help when she glanced up at him and saw something besides friendship darkening his eyes.

THE LAST THING Ryan wanted to do was scare Lisa. As he moved closer, he felt an almost overwhelming need to touch her. He shouldn't want to be her comfort. And yet she'd trusted him with a secret that she'd kept inside for more than fifteen years.

So much made sense about her past and present behavior to him now. Scars were still fresh with no way to heal them. He couldn't imagine how she could ever trust a man again. That look he'd seen in her eyes, the one that said she never would, made him realize she needed a friend more than ever now.

Yes, a very big part of him wanted to march out the door and arrive in Beckett's yard, unannounced, and then show him just how it felt to be afraid.

With her settled on his chest, his arm around her, he could feel her trembling. If that didn't make a man want justice, nothing would.

Act on it and Ryan would be the one tossed in jail while Beckett enjoyed his freedom. Lisa's family would be left unprotected. She was too frightened to confide in anyone else and if what she said about her father was true, then the Alcorns were far more dangerous than anyone realized. The town was still reeling from the fact that Charles Alcorn might have been involved in the abductions in the first place.

Ryan had personal reason to dislike the family. It was high time others saw the Alcorns in the same light he did.

What's done in darkness always comes to light.

Those bastards needed to pay.

Lisa tilted her head up and he could see an emotion behind her eyes that he couldn't quite put his finger on.

Ryan kissed her forehead and refocused.

"We'll figure this out. In the meantime, I want you by my side at all times," he said. Without evidence, her case would be a hard sell. Not to mention that he'd hate to open her up for public scrutiny. It didn't matter that she was a kindergarten teacher now. Her painful youth would be dug up, chewed on and spit out. She was strong, but no one deserved to be treated like that.

"I don't want to interfere in your life." She sat up, looking a mixture of exhausted and relieved. "You have a job."

"It's fine. Taking time off when I want is one of the benefits of owning a business."

She'd been there through the weekend, so he'd think that he'd get used to her being around. Yet every time she entered a room his body reacted. Her being at his place was right on too many levels and he told himself that it had been far too long since he'd gone on a real date with a woman who held his interest.

Or maybe it was just companionship he missed. If he was being honest, his house had had an empty quality to it before Lisa showed up. He hadn't paid much attention to it before but he was already dreading the day she would leave.

Being with Lisa 24/7 made Ryan realize how lonely he'd been up until now. When this whole ordeal was behind them, it might be time to swing by the animal shelter and pick up man's best friend, he conceded.

Until then, he needed all his attention on this case. He cursed himself for not realizing sooner the depth of what was going on with Lisa. She'd been scared to death at the hospital. She'd checked the door every few seconds. He'd brought her to his home and she immediately made him promise to lock the doors and close and lock all the windows.

"Try to get some rest. We'll leave in the morning."

Lisa leaned her head against his shoulder and he tried not to think about the citrus shampoo that smelled so good on her. Instead, he focused on the facts so far. While Lisa was healing the rest of the town was on alert to locate Charles Alcorn. The man who was wanted for questioning, believed to be the Mason Ridge Abductor, had disappeared. But where?

Given Alcorn's considerable resources, he could be anywhere. Ryan couldn't rule out the fact that Alcorn might be out of the country by now, too. If Ryan found Charles, would he be able to find Beckett? The idea was worth playing around with.

Whoever had broken into Ryan's house was neither of the two, which meant there was a third party. With Alcorn money, they could hire someone to do their dirty work. And it would be safer at this point, since they couldn't afford to be linked to Lisa.

Knowing this, Ryan figured that his place would be clean of fingerprints.

Therein lied another problem… Ryan knew the Alcorns on sight. But they could hire anyone to attack Lisa.

That meant every stranger from now on was a suspect.

Chapter Eight

Lisa's eyes widened as they approached the grand home in Arkansas early the next morning. The fishing cabin looked more like a five-star resort than a family getaway.

Ryan pulled up to the house and parked on the pad.

Lori came running from around the front of the house, Grayson bouncing on her hip.

"This place is amazing," Lori said to Ryan. "Thank you for helping us get away."

"You're welcome. I'm glad you can get some use out of it," he said in his characteristically reserved tone.

Last night, it would've been too easy to get swept away with emotion. Luckily, they'd both had better sense than to act on the chemistry firing between them.

Instead, she'd fallen asleep in his arms.

A visit with her sister and nephew was just what Lisa needed to regain her bearings. So much had gone on in the past few days that she couldn't begin to process it. Then there were all those intense emotions to deal with when it came to Ryan.

Was she falling for him? Even if she was, what on earth would she do with those emotions? She never let anyone past her walls and even though she felt a certain amount of reciprocation from him, there were lines that friends shouldn't cross. She thought about the kiss in the hospital and how much her blood heated when he'd held her in his arms.

Since then, he'd mostly kissed her on the forehead or top of the head, which screamed *big brother* more than anything else. And yet his lips touching anywhere on her sent a fiery reaction coursing through her, electrifying her.

"Are you okay?" Lori's mouth was twisted with concern as she came closer.

"Yes, of course." Lisa reached over and hugged her sister, fighting against the pain that movement still caused. Grayson leaned toward her with his arms extended, but she wasn't strong enough to hold him yet. She kissed his forehead instead.

"I'll run out and pick up lunch. There's a great barbecue place up the road. They cook all the meat outdoors. Give you two a chance to catch up," Ryan said.

Lisa thanked him and followed her sister into the house as he pulled away.

"Mind if we lock the doors?" she asked.

"Since when have you been so paranoid?" Lori asked. "And there's no one around here for miles."

"It's just—"

Lori held up her hand and made a face. "I'm sorry. That was really crappy. Of course you're still on edge."

Grayson threw his hands out toward Lisa, frowning when she didn't take him from her sister. He looked as though he was working up to crying.

"Here, let's sit on the floor," Lisa said, easing down onto the rug in front of the sofa.

The place was as spectacular inside as it was out. A

floor-to-ceiling tumbled stone fireplace was the focal point of the space. The plan was open concept, so she could see clearly into all the main rooms. The decor was rustic chic and the kitchen was fitted with all the modern appliances for a gourmet cook, including a five burner stove.

A gorgeous crystal chandelier hung over the center of the living room, with a metal installation circling it.

"I made pancakes this morning," Lori said proudly. "You?"

"That kitchen inspires me to cook."

"Maybe we should see about installing one in your apartment," Lisa teased.

Lori's smile faded. "How are you *really*?"

Lisa hugged Grayson and handed him one of the big blocks from the basket next to them. He immediately stuffed the corner of the block in his mouth, just as he did everything else. Two of his bottom front teeth had already peeked through and the others were most likely coming soon.

"Better. I guess. I keep thinking about Dad and…"

"I know. I cry myself to sleep every night after putting Grayson down. I can't help it. It's so hard to believe that he's gone." She wiped a loose tear away, then grabbed a tissue off the coffee table. "Did you know that he was drinking again?"

"No." How much should Lisa tell her little sister? *Enough to keep both her and Grayson safe*, a little voice said. "In fact, I don't think he was."

"I'm so glad you said that because I don't, either." Lori blew her nose. "Sorry, I get emotional just thinking about it. I'm trying to be strong for Grayson. I don't want to confuse him. It's just all so sudden."

"You're a great mom, Lori. I hope you know that. If Mom were here, she'd say the same thing."

"Now you're really going to get me all blubbery," Lori said.

"It's true."

"So, what's going on between you and Ryan?" Lori changed the subject.

"That question seems out of the blue."

"Does it?" Lori asked. "I see the way he looks at you. Don't tell me you haven't noticed."

"Yeah, as a friend. That's how he looks at me. I'm pretty sure he thinks I'm a pain in the butt."

"I doubt that," Lori said. "Give him a chance. I can't remember the last person you let take care of you."

"How'd we get on the subject of my personal life?" And when did her little sister get so observant?

"You say that as if you have one." Lori cracked a smile. "Maybe it's this cabin or looking at pictures of this gorgeous family, but I've been thinking. No one should be alone and that's what we are. Neither one of us is in a relationship. When was your last? Mine?"

"I hate to break it to you, but you already have a man in your life." Lisa nodded toward Grayson.

"And I love him with all my heart. Believe me, I wouldn't change a thing about having him."

"I know that."

"Except the part where he grows up without a father. I thought maybe Dad could fill the void, but he's gone now, too." Lori wiped away another tear. Raw emotion bubbled under the surface.

Lisa didn't want her sister to break down in front of the baby. She needed to change the subject, but nothing immediately came to mind. "Dad wasn't perfect but there was a lot of good about him. If he was drinking again, and I don't believe he was, then I missed the signs."

"So did I."

"You knew them?" Maybe Lori was stronger than Lisa had given her credit for.

"It always started with the little lies. I can't stand liars to this day because of it." Lori's chin quivered as she held back emotion.

"I always covered for him so you wouldn't know." Or at least she thought she had. Maybe her baby sister was more perceptive than Lisa realized.

Lori rolled her eyes. "You really think I couldn't see things for myself?"

"I guess not. Why didn't you say anything to me before?"

"You were always working so hard to protect me after Mom died. I didn't want to take that away from you," Lori said.

Wow. Lisa had completely underestimated her sister.

"It would've been nice if you'd spoken up before. You would've saved me a lot of angst at trying to hide things from you, kid," Lisa teased.

"And spoil the fun for me? Are you kidding? Playing dumb had its benefits. I mean, who else got served chocolate ice cream in bed when they were sick? Not one of my friends is who."

Lisa laughed out loud, ignoring how much it hurt.

The back door opened and she let out a scream before she could suppress it.

"Are you okay?" Lori asked, eyeing her sister suspiciously.

"Fine." Lisa tried to slow her racing heart with a few deep breaths.

"No, you're not." She glanced down at Grayson, who'd jumped at the loud shriek and was winding up to cry. She immediately picked him up and patted his back to soothe him. "We're not done discussing this. I need to feed him and then he goes down for his nap."

"I can help," Lisa offered.

Ryan came over and took the baby from Lori's arms. Both women's jaws fell slack at how easily Grayson took to Ryan.

"This is how it's done, ladies," Ryan teased.

"Didn't realize we had an expert in our midst," Lisa shot back. "The least I can do is set out the barbecue. It smells wonderful."

Lori moved to the cabinets and pulled out three plates.

By the time Lisa set the food out on the table, Ryan had Grayson in his high chair and was feeding him mouthfuls of a green puree.

"Since when did you get so great with babies?" Lisa asked as she piled ribs and brisket on Ryan's plate.

"Since Maribel. I figure if Dylan can take care of a three-year-old on his own, the least I can do is pitch in once in a while."

Lisa stared at him.

"Okay, I've watched him feed her a few times. Figured it couldn't be that hard if Dylan can do it by himself," Ryan admitted.

"Well, then I really feel bad, because I'm exhausted," Lori said. "And I never get him to eat peas. What did you do?"

"Mixed them in applesauce." Ryan supplied a wry

grin as he brought another spoonful to the baby's mouth. "I didn't like the smell of them before, either, big guy."

Lori laughed almost as hard as Lisa. Her sister was doing an amazing job with Grayson. And there was something about seeing Ryan with her nephew that made Lisa's heart ache.

Her past experiences with men had taught her that feelings could lead her right down the rabbit hole where everyone deceived her.

Chapter Nine

"The funeral is tonight," Lisa said to Ryan as she walked into the kitchen on the third morning since arriving at the cabin. Not only was he already awake, but he looked as though he'd gone out for a run.

"Are you sure you're up for it?" he asked, holding out a mug of fresh coffee.

"I need to be." She took the offering and thanked him, thinking how easy it would be to get used to this every morning. And then chided herself for having the thought in the first place.

"Just so you know, you don't have to do this," he said, his dark eyes trailing down her face, lingering on her lips.

"I can't say that I especially want to leave this place." She took a sip of coffee. "It's gorgeous here. And with the lake view out the front window...just wow."

She moved to the living room to take full advantage of the view, and to mask the flush heating her cheeks at being near Ryan. She'd thought about the kiss they'd shared too many times since the impulsive moment at the hospital. The worst part was that he'd done a little too good of an acting job. He almost had her believing he felt more than friendship.

She sat on the oversize white sofa and pulled a throw pillow in her lap.

"How are you feeling today?" Ryan sat down next to her.

"Much better." The swelling was starting to go down and her body was far less tender. He'd convinced her to take a couple of over-the-counter pain pills before bed, too.

"You slept the whole night," he added.

"It was amazing." She stretched out her legs in front of her. "No pain when I do this, either."

"You're healing fast."

"Because you've taken such good care of me." A piece of her didn't want to leave this cabin to return to real life ever.

"How long is your summer break?" he asked.

"Teachers go back two weeks before students. It's generally the first week of August. I haven't even looked at a calendar in days. This is not exactly the summer vacation I had planned," she said.

"Can I ask you a question?" Ryan asked.

"Sure."

"Why on earth would you want to become a teacher? I mean, it's one of those noble professions, so don't get me wrong, and I admire teachers for putting up with kids like me—"

"You weren't so bad." She knocked her shoulder into his.

"Then you're looking back with rose-colored glasses on," he shot back.

"We got into our fair share of trouble, but we weren't inherently bad kids."

"That's probably true of the girls in the group. Me,

Brody, Dawson and especially Dylan wouldn't exactly be called angels back then."

"What did you ever do?" she asked.

"Plenty."

"You don't even like to lie. I saw your face in the hospital after fibbing to the nurse. In fact, what did we used to call you back then?"

"No reason to dip that far into the past." He made a move to get up, but she put her hand on his arm.

"Not so fast, mister. You're not getting away that easily. Let me think… Oh, I remember now, reliable Ryan."

"Great. Thanks for that. Bringing up all my painful scars from childhood now. I've gotten into plenty of trouble in the past," he countered.

"Of course you did. You'd never lie about something like that," she retorted, playfully tapping him on the arm.

"And what about you? You were a little holier-than-thou back then if I remember correctly."

"No, I wasn't."

"True story." He put his hand over his heart. "Remember, I can't tell a lie."

"You're making this up."

"Scout's honor." He held two fingers up like rabbit ears.

"You were never a Scout and that's not the hand sign."

"Doesn't matter. I can use the oath, anyway," he said with a grin.

It was good to see Ryan smile. He'd been a serious kid who'd grown to be a serious adult. There hadn't been a lot of laughter in his childhood home. She liked being the one to put a smile on his face.

"Fine. Give me an example, then." She took a sip of coffee and waited for his response.

He seemed to take a minute to think. "Weren't you the one who went around correcting all our grammar in fourth grade?"

"Hello, what do you not understand about me becoming a teacher?" She laughed despite the pain. "I had to try to inspire the next generation of Mason Ridge youth to actually learn something while in school."

"Can't argue your point there." He took a sip of coffee. "We were pretty thickheaded even back then."

"We all had a lot going on." She thought about those beatings he'd endured and she wanted to reach out to him, to somehow make it better. "Do you see your brother's family very often?"

"I get out there as much as I can. He doesn't like to come back to Mason Ridge."

"Is it because of the way your father treated you two?"

"I imagine so. That, and other bad memories about the way he acted. Justin's changed. He's a family man now and I think he wanted to get away somewhere he could wipe the slate clean. Can't say I blame him. Some folks will never forgive him for the past. Small towns have long memories."

"He got into trouble, but he wasn't a criminal, for crying out loud," she said with a little too much emotion. She stopped short of saying that everything he'd done was rebelling against their father, feeling lost and unloved.

Ryan didn't immediately speak. He seemed to be contemplating her response and she was afraid he picked up on her heightened emotion.

"What about you? Why'd you come back to Mason Ridge after college?" he finally asked.

"I don't know." She shrugged. "My sister left for college. Dad was here alone. I was afraid he'd start drinking again. Figured I could teach anywhere and be happy, so I came back to keep an eye on him. He's getting older and I didn't want to get settled somewhere else and be uprooted if his health started failing, which it already had."

"That must've been tough. Did you want to go somewhere else?"

"I didn't want to come back to Mason Ridge," she said without thinking.

"Too many bad memories?" He looked at her curiously, as if he was trying to see something deeper.

"Yes."

"With your father or what we talked about earlier?" Those intelligent, penetrating eyes threatened to see right through her.

And that scared her to death.

"No, nothing like that." She shrugged it off, hugging the pillow tighter to her chest.

"I don't know if I said this before, but I'm sorry about everything that's happened." He nudged her with his shoulder.

Surprisingly, her muscles didn't go rigid this time. There was only a slight hesitation with contact and that was mostly because of the trill of awareness his touch shot through her. Her body warmed and her thighs heated.

"You've done so much for me. I'm not sure how I would've gotten through all this without you." Against her better judgment, she reached over and hugged him.

She must've known that he would come through for her all along and that's why she asked for him when Mrs. Whitefield found her.

Ryan leaned into the hug until his lips were so close to her ear that she could feel his breath on her neck. A thousand tiny volts of electricity coursed through her.

"You would've done the same thing for me if I was in trouble."

"Friends, right? Like you said before, we go back a long way." Lisa reminded herself that this wasn't the time to notice just how much reliable Ryan had filled out since high school.

With one easy movement, he pulled her onto his lap. His muscled arms wrapped around her waist, sending all kinds of sparks through her body. She could feel his thigh muscles through the denim of his jeans against her bare skin.

She repositioned on his lap to face him, stopping when she felt his body go rigid.

"Am I hurting you?" she asked.

"Not exactly but that would be a fun twist," he shot back with a sardonic grin.

"What does that mean?" She scooted her bottom again, worried she'd sat funny on his leg. She was stilled by two powerful hands on either side of her hips.

"You don't want to keep doing that." There was a low, husky quality to his voice.

"Oh." She paused, temporarily robbed of her voice. "And here I was worried you weren't attracted to me all this time."

"That's what you thought?" His face was stamped with shock. "Finding you desirable has never been the problem."

RYAN SHOULDN'T ALLOW himself to get caught up in the moment. But it was Lisa. His better judgment knew not to let this happen but that had gone out the window, taking his self-control along for the ride.

Spending time with her at his friend's cabin made matters worse. He'd figured spending a few days with her would be enough to quash the attraction he felt every time he thought about her or she was in the room.

The plan that had worked with so many women who had come and gone through his life had failed miserably with Lisa. In fact, the only thing he'd succeeded in doing was wanting her even more than before.

All it generally took was a few days of alone time with a woman to see what she was truly about. He'd done well for himself, so some wanted his money. Others wanted his body—them he didn't mind so much. He hadn't met one who had truly stimulated his mind or that he could joke around with so easily. He'd figured the others out in a flash and gotten bored.

Lisa was different. She was intelligent, beautiful and funny. They had history, so he didn't feel the need to put on airs for her. She disarmed him, causing his defenses to drop. Ryan didn't think a woman could get past his carefully constructed walls. But then, no one knew him like Lisa.

Was he falling for her? Again?

Not smart, Hunt.

Or maybe a better question was…had he ever really stopped having feelings for her?

When she looked up at him with those bluish-green eyes, he dipped his head and kissed her.

Her lips parted as she nibbled his bottom lip and he thrust his tongue in her mouth, wanting to taste her sweetness. Heat roared through his veins and need engulfed him like a raging wildfire.

"He turned himself in," Lori said, walking into the kitchen, breaking into the moment and staring down at something in her hand.

"Who?" Lisa scampered off his lap and pushed to her feet, ignoring the pain quick movement had to have caused.

Ryan needed a minute, or both ladies would know the effect Lisa had on him.

"Charles Alcorn." She looked up from her phone and her gaze bounced between Ryan and Lisa. Didn't seem that Lori had seen them kissing, and he sensed Lisa's relief over that fact.

"We were just enjoying the view this morning," Lisa said a little too quickly. Her voice was shaky, too. As far as liars went, she was a bad one. "That's great news."

Ryan cracked a smile. Turned out he wasn't the only honest one in the bunch.

"Yeah, maybe now the town will get some answers and that jerk will finally live out the rest of his life in jail," Lori said.

"He deserves whatever they do to him," Lisa said, her hopeful gaze on Ryan.

"I wouldn't count on it. That family has money and they can afford the best defense attorney in the country. He might just get away with it and he wouldn't turn himself in unless he had a plan. We'll have to keep watch over the next few days on what happens with him." Ryan didn't want to be the one to put a damper on their excitement.

"Well, he shouldn't be above the law." Fire raged across Lisa's face.

"Agreed."

At least he'd gotten her to open up a little bit more about her past. He suspected that he'd only scratched the surface, but she'd trusted him and that went a long way in his book.

They'd made progress, although she still froze up on him in certain situations.

The only reason he'd touched her a few minutes ago was that she'd made contact with him first, and he couldn't stop himself once she gave the green light.

She'd tensed just a bit when he had, so little that he almost hadn't noticed, but his body was in tune with hers. That wasn't something he could shut off, and he didn't want to, but would he ever hold Lisa and feel her trusting surrender?

Chapter Ten

Ryan didn't like the thought of going back to Mason Ridge, where Lisa would be exposed. He understood that she needed to bury her father, to put that piece of her life to rest, but being anywhere near Beckett Alcorn wasn't exactly high on Ryan's list.

He walked outside and called his friend Brody.

"How's Lisa doing?" Brody asked after exchanging greetings.

"It's been a rough couple of days," Ryan said, and then updated Brody on the funeral service.

"You know we'll be there," Brody said solemnly.

"Good. Because we'll need extra security."

"What's that all about?" Brody's serious tone dropped to outright concern.

"It turns out that random mugging wasn't so indiscriminate after all."

"With all the craziness going on, I thought about that. But she seemed so adamant in the hospital," Brody said.

"This is personal between her and Beckett Alcorn."

"Beckett?" Brody repeated, surprise in his voice. "What's up with that?"

"They have a history but she won't tell me exactly what it is. Suffice it to say that she's scared to death of the guy." Ryan didn't think it was his place to go into details.

"Does this have something to do with his father?" Disgust laced Brody's tone.

"No. I don't believe so." It seemed that family liked to prey on people weaker than them. "This is personal and it goes back a long way."

"I can ask Rebecca if she knows anything," Brody offered.

"Good idea. Keep me posted on what you find out." Trusting Brody to keep this quiet was a given. Ryan had always been able to rely on their friendship and maybe that was because both came from families with seriously messed-up mothers. Brody's had ripped off half the town before pulling her disappearing act. Ryan's had left her sons with an abusive father.

"Will do," Brody said.

"We'll talk more when I see you."

"Be safe driving in today," Brody warned. "Any chance you got another vehicle stashed out where you are?"

"As a matter of fact, I do." Ryan didn't think his buddy would mind if he borrowed the Jeep he kept at the fishing cabin. The spare key should be in the junk drawer in the kitchen. "Good idea."

"See you in a few hours."

"Will do." Ryan ended the call and turned toward the lake. The conversation with Brody had Ryan thinking about his own mother, a subject he deemed best left alone.

If Ryan was being honest, he'd admit that he felt no real pain at losing the man he'd grown up with when he buried his father two years ago.

Thinking back now, he'd been sure his mother would show at the funeral. He'd heard the same rumors for years that she'd only gone because of his father's cruelty and hadn't been allowed to take her children with her.

If that had been true, wouldn't she have returned? The old man was gone. He couldn't hurt her anymore. The coast was clear.

If she'd loved Ryan and Justin to begin with, wouldn't she be the first one in town when she'd heard the news?

Her answer had come in the form of complete silence. Distance.

Even then, Justin had tried to justify her actions as being afraid to come back. Ryan knew better. If she'd cared she would have found a way to contact her children or get a message to them that she loved them at some point over the years. Wouldn't she?

How many birthdays had gone by without so much as a phone call or a card? How many nights as a child had Ryan wished on a star that his mother would return? How many times had he denied missing her when Justin brought her up?

Too many.

Lisa opened the back door, breaking into his heavy thoughts.

"Breakfast is ready," she said.

"I'll be right there."

Lori sat next to Grayson, feeding him breakfast, her eyes red-rimmed and swollen. Lisa was busy at the massive island in the kitchen. The scene felt like family and Ryan was shocked it didn't make him want to turn and run right back out the door. It was friendship, he reasoned. "I hope you like biscuits and gravy. Breakfast is one of the few things I know how to cook," Lisa said, holding out a plate. Her smile was weak at best, but at least she was making the effort.

"You didn't have to do all this," he said, surprised at how thinking about his mother still affected him.

"Yes, I did. I can't let you do all the work. Besides, it feels good to be productive, especially today."

"Let me help you put out the food, then," he offered, needing something to take his mind off his heavy thoughts and noticing how difficult it was for Lisa to let anyone do anything for her.

"I already said no." She was being stubborn and he figured half the reason was that she looked as though she'd stayed up half the night crying with her sister. Ryan didn't want to upset her, so he moved to the table and took a seat next to Lori. Between him and their old group of friends, Ryan felt a lot better about their odds of keeping her safe later. He'd live off that win for now.

After breakfast, they piled into the Jeep and made the silent trek back to Mason Ridge.

Everything about Lisa's body language said she was scared as they walked into the funeral home. At least she had Lori and Grayson to keep her busy this time.

Lori unhooked Grayson from his car seat and pulled him into her arms. Lisa stood close by, watching everything around them.

They weren't the first to arrive, just as planned. Dawson and Brody hopped out of Dawson's black SUV. Texas was a conceal-and-carry state, so Ryan knew those two would be ready for any trouble that arrived. His shotgun was stashed under the seat in his SUV.

"Thanks for coming," Ryan said to Brody and Dawson as they walked over. His friends were similar in height and build. Brody still had a tight cut, no doubt left over from his time in the military, blond hair and blue eyes. By contrast, Dawson had pitch-black hair and dark brown eyes. Both carried themselves like warriors.

"Dylan should show up in a few minutes. He wanted us here first. He already checked the place out. Called it recon and I left it at that," Brody said, leaning in for a bear hug.

Dylan was most likely pulling from his own military experience.

Ryan was grateful for his friends' support. This entire summer had been hard on their friendships. First, when Brody's fiancée, Rebecca, was attacked in a grocery store parking lot and it was believed that the Mason Ridge Abductor had returned after fifteen years. That ordeal was followed by Samantha, Dylan's fiancée, being targeted by the same person—and that person turned out to be one of the most powerful men in Mason Ridge, Charles Alcorn. Now Beckett Alcorn was targeting Lisa.

When Ryan really thought about it, everyone had been on edge since the whole ordeal began earlier this summer and all his friendships had been challenged. It had become difficult to know who to trust anymore, save for a few solid friendships.

"I'll go inside with Lisa and Lori," Dawson said. "Why don't you two walk the perimeter until Dylan gets here?"

"Now you're starting to sound like him," Brody said, rolling his eyes in an obvious attempt to lighten the tense mood.

Everyone knew he was only pretending to be disgusted. Of course, they would all do everything it took to keep Lisa and her family safe and Dylan would know how to get that job done.

Lisa gave a tentative look toward Ryan, who nodded it was okay to separate. Her anxiety was written all over the worry lines in her face. Tension practically radiated off her small frame.

As soon as she disappeared inside, Brody turned to Ryan and asked, "How's she really doing?"

"She's strong, as you already know. I think she's holding a lot inside. I know that something's going on in the back of her mind, but she's not sharing."

"Give her time," Brody said as they scanned the area. "Rebecca seems to think that something traumatic happened to her when we were kids."

That was an understatement.

They kept pace with each other, rounding the corner to check out the back of the funeral home.

"Did she say what happened?" Ryan asked.

"She wishes she knew. All she remembers for sure is that Lisa started pulling away from the group weeks before the kidnappings." Brody was referring to when Rebecca and her younger brother were abducted. The event had turned the little town of Mason Ridge upside down.

"Does she remember anything else?" Ryan asked as they walked.

"The rest of her memory is hazy. Rebecca blocked out most events surrounding that summer."

"I understand why that would happen." Ryan knew that Rebecca had gotten away from their captor, planning to bring back the sheriff to save her little brother. She got lost and wandered in the woods for days before finally being picked up. Shane and his kidnapper were long gone by the time they found the shed he'd kept them in.

The entire town had searched for months. A decade later, Shane had been declared dead. Rebecca never gave up on finding him. Several weeks ago, Rebecca learned of a man named Thomas Kramer. She discovered that he'd been involved in her brother's kidnapping, and then she and her friends uncovered a trail that led them straight to Charles Alcorn. He'd escaped the deputy as he was being brought in for questioning. Given that he was the town's wealthiest resident, Ryan had no doubt that justice would suffer.

"I'm sure you already heard about Alcorn," Ryan said.

"About time they caught the SOB," Brody said, disgusted. "You and Lisa have been spending a lot of time together lately."

"Because I'm helping her."

Brody shot him a look that said he wasn't buying the simple explanation. "You had a thing for her once, right?"

"Don't say it." Ryan already knew what this would be about.

"Why not?" Brody asked plainly.

"Because me and Lisa aren't the same as you and Rebecca." Ryan held up his hand to stop his buddy from saying anything else. "Hey, I'm thrilled for you and Rebecca. You know that, right?"

"It goes without saying."

"And I don't think two people could be happier if they'd been matched by the big guy upstairs." Ryan motioned toward the blue sky.

"And?"

"So don't take this the wrong way when I tell you that not everyone's ready to find their forever mate."

"That's a cop-out," Brody said, shaking his head.

"What makes you say that?"

"I have eyes. I'm not stupid. There's something going on between the two of you."

"Lisa and I have been friends for a long time. She finally opened up to me a little bit recently. And I'm talking a tiny speck. That's all you're seeing." If Brody had come at Ryan with the physical-attraction thing, he wouldn't have had much to deny. Ryan could admit to himself that he felt a draw toward her. She was beautiful, intelligent and funny when she let herself be. But no relationship flourished when kept at a safe emotional distance. *Relationship?*

He was referring to his friendship as a relationship now? *Damn, Hunt.* It really was time to get a dog.

Instead of firing back a witty retort, Brody just gave Ryan that knowing look—the look that made Ryan want to haul off and punch the guy. If they weren't friends, he just might.

"Why do I have the feeling if I hang around you for much longer I'll be surfing the internet for his-and-hers bath towels?" Ryan teased. He was only half joking. It was time to change the subject to something more productive than his relationship status. "What do you think about Alcorn? Have you been following the story?"

"Rebecca hasn't turned the TV off or stopped checking her phone since the news broke." Brody shook his head. "I don't know what to think. One minute we're chasing Thomas Kramer. The next he's dead and we've shifted our attention to Alcorn. She remembers that he helped out with the search. *Shocked* isn't the word for her expression when she found out he was allegedly involved in the first place."

"You think there's a chance he's innocent?"

"Half the town is ready to march up to the jail and hang him. The other half is disgusted with those who are demanding justice before the facts have been heard."

"What do you think?" Ryan asked.

"I don't know. After talking to Dylan and Samantha, I think there's more to the whole story than just Alcorn."

"More people involved in the kidnappings? Like a ring?" Ryan asked.

"I don't doubt Alcorn's involved somehow even though Rebecca was thrown off guard when we found out it was him." Brody paused, scanning the lot and surrounding mesquite trees. "After Maribel was kidnapped, Dylan said he was taken to a warehouse on the outskirts of town and beaten by Alcorn's security team. If the guys work for Alcorn, I'm guessing he has to be involved in some way. Is he the leader? Are there more involved?" Brody shrugged. "That I don't know."

"You're thinking he's part of some kind of organized operation?"

"It's possible. Dylan's been searching the county for this warehouse. Think about it. They could house a lot of people in an abandoned warehouse on the outskirts of town."

Ryan wasn't sure he wanted to. "Whatever happened to Kramer?"

"He burned in a car accident."

"Didn't they find a boy in Kramer's house?" Ryan asked.

"They did. And it was all kinds of messed up. Turns out that years ago Kramer had lost a son around the same age as the boy, something to do with his wife neglecting the kid. Kramer believed his child was unfairly taken from him and that's how he justified taking a little boy. I think he was trying to replace his child, since he was fixated on taking seven-year-olds."

"So he kidnapped two boys years apart?"

"Yes. The first was Shane fifteen years ago and then the new boy last year. Kramer, among others, was most likely scouting kids for Alcorn or whoever is in charge. They like them younger, though, so it could be an illegal adoption ring. Taking Shane might've been this guy being greedy, taking for himself when he was supposed to keep his eyes on the prize. And that wouldn't have sat well with Alcorn."

"And then this guy ends up fried and they find a kid in his house. Sounds pretty damn sewn up to me."

"Until Samantha's father decides to come forward with what he knows and then Alcorn goes after her," Brody said.

"Plus, I can imagine that Alcorn wouldn't put up with anyone taking kids in his own backyard," Ryan agreed. "I'm guessing Shane reminded this guy of his kid and that's why he couldn't resist?"

"Me, too. And he could've been keeping an eye on Shane for a couple of years. I mean, we all went to that festival every year. Kramer was part of the cleanup crew. So he'd been watching Shane and then, and this is where Rebecca blames herself, he follows us out that night while we were playing a game," Brody said.

"That, I remember. She yelled at him and he took off. I thought she had him when she went after him or I would've helped."

"We all would've," Brody said, shaking his head. The

guilt still fresh in both of their minds based on Brody's change in demeanor. "She'll never forgive herself for what happened to him next."

Ryan knew that Brody was referring to her and Shane's kidnapping. She'd escaped, gotten lost in the woods near Mason Ridge Lake, and Shane had disappeared for fifteen years. They'd only just reunited. Since Shane had been shipped overseas on active military duty, the family still didn't have all the answers about what had happened to him. No one knew what had happened to him after the kidnapping, only that he was safe. Everyone was just relieved to have finally found him.

"There was no way a twelve-year-old could've known what was going to happen next," Ryan said.

"You and I know that to be true. I'm not so sure Rebecca will ever see it that way. Being the older sister, she always felt responsible for him."

Ryan could relate to that emotion. Even though he was the younger of the Hunt brothers, he'd always looked after his older brother, Justin. Especially when Justin had taken a wrong turn as a teenager and had gone down a path of drinking and experimenting with drugs.

"Speaking of family, how's Rebecca's mother holding up?" Ryan asked.

"She's been doing better ever since they found Shane. Rebecca said she thought half of her mother's sickness over the years was related to having a broken heart after Shane disappeared."

"I bet. After seeing what they went through, after what Dylan went through when Maribel was taken, I can only imagine the heartache losing a child would bring. Maybe that family can finally heal." The Mason

Ridge Abductor had taken so much from the town, the people.

"Rebecca never gave up and that's the only reason they found him."

"It's a shame one man can take away so much from so many." Ryan shook his head.

Brody's cell rang. He fished it out and glanced at the screen. "I better take this. It's Rebecca."

Ryan watched as Dylan pulled up and parked, leaving Brody to his call.

"Good to see you, man," Ryan said to Dylan as the two embraced in a bear hug.

"Maribel was just asking about you."

"How's baby Bel doing?" He'd bought the biggest stuffed bear he could find when she'd been returned from the kidnappers who had taken her a few weeks ago.

"This is the first time she's allowed me to leave the house since the whole ordeal." Anger flashed in his eyes as Dylan shook his head. "Her pediatrician said she'll get better over time."

Ryan's hands fisted despite the good news. "You find out what all happened to her?"

"Lucky for those bastards, they didn't touch a hair on her head," Dylan said through clenched teeth. Maribel coming into Dylan's life a year ago had turned the man's life completely upside down. Ryan shouldn't be shocked at the changes in his friend, except that Dylan had walked the line closest to ending up in juvenile detention save for Justin.

The military had helped Dylan clean up his act. He'd served his country, gone to war and come back stronger. And he was a devoted father. His relationship with

Samantha seemed to be getting serious quickly. If anyone deserved happiness, it was Dylan.

"Having a daughter changed you in a good way," Ryan said.

"It'd be impossible not to keep things in perspective every time I look into those green eyes. Seeing the world the way she does has taught me that the earth is an amazing place even though there is still evil in it."

"Evil that needs to be eradicated." Ryan nodded toward the funeral home.

"She really doesn't believe her father had an accident?" Dylan asked.

"Nope. There's no proof, but she says she knew her father wasn't drinking."

"Her word is all I need. She knew him better than anyone else. With his background, it'll be harder to convince the rest of the town," Dylan said matter-of-factly.

"She doesn't think anyone else will believe her," Ryan said. "It's her word against everyone's preconceived notion about her father."

"I can see where that would be a problem. People get an idea of who you are and it's hard to change that perception."

Ryan nodded his agreement. Both of them had lived it.

"You look good…happy," Ryan said. He'd never get over the changes in Dylan. Good changes. Changes that had Ryan thinking that if his friend could do it, then why not him? Maybe when this ordeal was over he'd recommit himself to dating. If he was being honest he'd admit to slacking off in the meeting-new-people department. The women he'd met so far could too easily be shoved into one of two categories, too boring or too greedy.

Then again, maybe he wasn't trying hard enough. Weren't those the words of the last woman he'd been interested in? When was that? Six months ago? Seven?

Sticking that thought on the shelf, Ryan motioned for Brody to join them.

"What did Rebecca say?" Ryan asked Brody as he rejoined the conversation.

"Said that Judge Matheson set bail for Alcorn," Brody said with disgusted grunt.

"Which he'll easily make," Ryan agreed. "That jerk will be right back out on the streets."

"What jerk?" Lisa asked.

"CHARLES ALCORN." Ryan's voice had an apologetic quality.

Anger burned through her at the thought that her father was dead and yet Alcorn was about to be free again. That entire family could burn if anyone asked her opinion. She'd gladly supply the match.

"The service will start in fifteen minutes," Lisa said, deciding that her family was the only thing she wanted to focus on at the moment.

"Did you want to wait for the others?" Ryan asked, scanning the almost-empty lot.

"This is probably it," she replied, masking the hurt in her voice. Of all the years her father lived in Mason Ridge, he hadn't made many real friends.

"Rebecca and Samantha are almost here," Brody supplied.

As if on cue, a sedan came down the highway, turned onto the lane and then into the parking lot.

Lori popped out the funeral home door. "Lisa, we need you."

"Okay," she shouted back, and then turned to Ryan, "See you in a few minutes?"

He nodded.

She was surprised when a second car turned into the parking lot and then a third. The fourth came as she walked inside the building.

"Who's out there?" Lori asked.

"Some of the old gang I used to hang around with when we were kids." That accounted for a few of the people. She had no idea who else was showing up. Maybe her father hadn't lived such a small life after all.

"Everything okay in here?" Lisa asked. Being inside the funeral home again sent a chill down her spine. She tried to ignore it as another emotion overwhelmed her. How was she supposed to say goodbye to her father?

"I'll be back. I need fresh air," she said. It was hard to breathe.

"Sure," Lori said, distracted with Grayson.

Lisa knew she was most likely being overly optimistic thinking that her father had friends. He worked and spent time on his small farm, trying to beat the dry soil and unpredictable Texas weather by growing a few vegetables in his garden. He'd always prided himself on his herbs. The vegetables had been finicky. Even so, every summer he'd bring in bell and banana peppers, the easiest things to grow in Texas, and cut them up to cook with eggs. Scallions had been reliable for him, too. The rest was hit or miss. He'd had some luck with cucumbers but none at all with squash.

Those were the happy memories she'd take with her and cherish.

The others, the ones involving him drinking and doing stupid things, she'd find a way to let go of and find peace. All in all, her father had tried to be a decent man. Did he fall short? Yeah. But then didn't everyone at some point in their life?

Saying goodbye to her father was going to be just as miserable as she'd expected it to be.

Pushing the door open to outside, sunlight hit her in the face. She put her hand up to protect her eyes from the bright light. She needed to go somewhere quiet to get a handle on her emotions before facing everyone again. She needed a minute to herself.

Walking out back, she noticed the small white chapel.

Inside, there was a small alter with a tray of candles, three rows of hand-carved wooden pews and a stained-glass window to allow in some light. The place could hold a maximum of a dozen people.

She kneeled in front of the alter as tears streamed down her face.

The door to the small chapel opened. A burst of light followed. She looked up expecting to see Ryan and got a shock instead.

Beckett Alcorn stepped inside.

Chapter Eleven

"What are you doing here?" Lisa shot to her feet and took a step back until she was against the altar, hating how shaky her voice was as the door closed behind Beckett. No. This was her father's funeral and Beckett Alcorn didn't get to take that away from her. Not this time. She took a few steps toward him, and then poked her finger in his chest. "Get out!"

His hands came up in surrender. "I just came to—"

Another burst of light and Ryan, Dylan and Brody filed in. The trio flanked Beckett.

Ryan put his hand out, signaling the others to stop as though he sensed Lisa needed to be the one to stand up to Beckett.

Lisa had been standing on shaky ground as it was, but seeing her friends, seeing Ryan, gave her full confidence. Her father was dead and she knew in her heart that Beckett had to be involved, even if she couldn't prove it yet.

"Your father is a scumbag who deserves to be behind bars for the rest of his life," she said to Beckett, shooting daggers at him with her eyes.

Beckett sneered, seemingly aware that he was outmatched.

"And he will be."

"My father is innocent. His lawyer will prove it and the jury will see it," Beckett countered.

"By the time I'm done with you, you'll be in the cell next to him," she bit out, poking him again until he took a step backward.

The move caused him to run into Ryan, who stood his ground.

For a split second, fear shot across Beckett's black eyes.

"What do you think you're going to do?" he sneered. "Lay a hand on me and I'll have all of you arrested."

If Lisa heard correctly, Ryan just growled at Beckett. That couldn't be a good sign.

"Like I said already, get out."

Defeated, Beckett turned, but Ryan didn't budge from his athletic stance. Instead, he and Brody held ground, blocking the door. His fists clenched, he looked ready to go if anyone said the word.

The last thing she needed was Ryan, or any of the guys, for that matter, in jail. Any one of them acted on the threat bouncing off them in waves and Beckett would temporarily gain the upper hand. His father's lawyer had already filed a motion to have his case moved to Dallas County, saying he'd never get a fair trial in Mason Ridge, not with all the news coverage surrounding the case. Lisa had heard criminals liked having their cases tried in Dallas because it was harder to get a conviction there.

Beckett must also have realized their hands were tied, because his demeanor changed. He stood tall when he pushed past Ryan, who didn't budge. Brody had to allow Beckett passage.

Lori burst in as Beckett sauntered out. "I've been looking all over for you, Lisa. We're ready to start."

Walking from the chapel to the funeral home's viewing room, Lisa watched Beckett climb into his expensive SUV.

He spit gravel from his tires as he pulled out of the parking lot.

She smiled her satisfaction on the inside. It felt good to stand up to that jerk. He wasn't so big after all. In fact, when she really thought about it, she was a hell of a lot tougher than him. She'd survived being molested by him at a young age.

Despite looking over her shoulder for years, she'd managed to put herself through college and become a teacher, a job she loved. She'd thwarted his attack and his plans to silence her.

When she really thought about it, what had he done? He'd intimidated someone weaker than himself. He'd forced himself on a little girl. No, sir, he wasn't such a big, scary man after all.

Sure, she still had the emotional scars to prove the damage from the past. However, Lisa's fear of Beckett Alcorn ended today. All she had to do was come up with a way to keep her sister and Grayson safe.

Lisa shelved that thought as she walked into the service.

A few townspeople were there. Their postman of twenty years stopped by to pay his respects, as did the town's butcher. A few others came. They were all workingmen, like her father, who lived quiet lives.

Her heart swelled as she thought that there were a few other kindred spirits in town.

The room was small but had adequate space for

them. A large picture of her father sat in front of his urn. His wishes were for him to be cremated and spread over his land, the land he loved so much. A simple man who'd lived a simple life. A good man when he wasn't drinking, which caused him to do things he later regretted. A man who'd let her sit on his lap every evening while he read the newspaper.

He'd come from a large family of nine in the Houston area. There were two girls and seven boys. He'd been the oldest, so he'd gone to work instead of high school to help put food on the table for the family. He'd been great with his hands. The handyman jobs he was able to pick up when he was sober kept the bills paid. She and her sister had had to live with their relatives a few times when times were lean or when he fell off the wagon.

As a child, Lisa had been heartbroken to have to leave Mason Ridge when her father was having one of his "episodes" as Aunt Jane liked to call them. Too many times in the middle of the night, a relative would pluck her and her sister out of bed and take them to live with them until her dad got straightened out again. He always did. Said it was for his girls.

Her dad was a mess, but she loved him. And she'd never doubted his love for her. Maybe that was why she had been able to forgive him.

When the room emptied save for Lisa, her sister and their friends, she knew it was time to say goodbye. But how would she do that? How would she say a final good-night to the man who'd tucked her into bed more nights than she could count? A man easy to love despite his many weaknesses. The one who'd put her to bed with a kiss on the forehead before tucking in her sheets.

A sob tore from her throat before she could suppress

it. She dropped to her knees in front of the table holding his urn.

Good night, Daddy.

"Everyone out!" came a frantic voice. She recognized it as the attendant's. "Now! Go!"

"What's going on?" Lisa asked as she was being pulled to her feet. She glanced up in time to see Ryan's face, the determination in his features to get her the heck out of there. His hands were underneath her arms and he was practically carrying her as he raced toward the nearest exit.

"We gotta get outside," he said, his tone stern and focused.

"My sist—"

"Is fine," he said.

She glanced over in time to see Lori and Grayson being helped out by Dylan and Brody.

"What's going on?" Dylan asked.

All Lisa heard clearly next was the word *bomb*.

The few people still inside were scattering toward exits. Doors slammed against walls as a wave of panic rippled through the room.

Her pulse kicked up to her throat, thumping wildly.

"I can run," she said to Ryan as he half carried her out of the building. "It'll be faster."

He nodded, let her legs down a little more until she could gain traction. Then he gripped her hand.

She kept pace, pushing until her chest and legs burned. Her lungs clawed for air as she and Ryan ran through the thicket.

Everyone had taken off in different directions and Lisa had lost visual contact with her sister.

Was that why Beckett had shown up? Had he meant

to distract them so one of his thugs could plant a bomb in the building, taking out Lisa and what was left of her family?

"Cover your ears." Ryan slowed down when they could no longer see the building through the thick trees.

Lisa folded over onto the ground just in time for the blast. The earth shook underneath her.

Ryan took a step for balance and grabbed on to a tree trunk.

"We're far enough away. We're okay," he said.

"Where are Lori and Grayson?" Panic filled Lisa's chest. She hopped to her feet, her fight, freeze or flight instinct having been triggered as her brain tried to process what had just happened.

Ryan's cell was already to his ear by the time she regained her bearings and looked at him.

"Come on, Brody. Answer the phone," he said. "It's gone into voice mail."

"Lori," Lisa shouted.

"Don't do that. Don't yell. Beckett or his people might be in the woods, waiting to finish the job."

She started back in the direction they'd just come from. He caught her by the arm.

"We can't go back," he said. "In fact, we need to get the hell out of here. We'll have to wait for Brody or Dylan to make contact."

For the first time, Lisa saw panic in Ryan's expression. "I can't leave without them, Ryan. What if they're hurt? What if my sister needs me?" Shock and horror filled her, making it hard to breathe.

"You're scared and I get that. Believe me when I say that I'm freaked out, too. I saw Lori with Brody and

Grayson with Dylan. We have to trust that they'll take them to a safe spot."

"Wouldn't Brody answer the phone if everything was okay?" Just thinking about the possibility of her family and friends lying hurt somewhere in a field was enough to kick off another wave of anxiety.

"Dylan has survived much worse. If he's not picking up, then I have to believe he's been separated from his phone and that's not necessarily bad. He'll take good care of Grayson. If I was out here alone with one other person, I'd want it to be him. You know his background."

Ryan was making excellent points. And that should ease her mounting panic. It didn't. Until she put eyes on her sister and nephew, Lisa's blood pressure would stay through the roof.

"Since we don't know where Beckett is, we need to stay on the move," Ryan said.

"Are you sure we can't go back and check the funeral home? The dust has to have cleared by now."

"That's the last place I want you to be," he said emphatically.

Beckett Alcorn wanted Lisa silenced. If he had his way, it would be permanent. She got that. She wouldn't argue with Ryan.

"Where should we go?" she asked, resigned to the reality that she'd have to wait for word on her sister and nephew.

"Let's keep moving until I get my bearings. I'm not sure where we ended up. Do you need help walking?" He held his free hand out.

"No. I'm okay." That wasn't entirely true. Although

she was grateful to be alive and prayed like everything no one else was hurt.

"I can use the GPS on my phone to help figure out where we are. Then we'll get a read on what's close by," Ryan said, heading the opposite direction from where they started.

If Beckett wanted to take them down, it would be easier for him to do now. He'd managed to separate Lisa from her sister. She had no idea how many men he had surrounding the area, waiting.

Ryan stopped, staring at the screen on his device.

"Looks like we need to head east to get to the main road." He paused. "But then Beckett's people could be waiting there."

"What about the sheriff? They have to believe something happened now," Lisa said.

"You're ready to file a complaint against Beckett? To tell them he's the one who attacked you last week?"

"I think I have to, don't you? I mean, I didn't want to say anything before because I was trying to protect my sister and Grayson. Now I realize we'll never be safe until he's behind bars. Maybe not even then, with his family's money. It isn't like a conviction will stick." Frustration ate through her. "I feel like I'm right back at square one. Damned if I do. Damned if I don't."

"It's not the same thing now."

"What makes you say that?"

"You didn't have all of us before," he said, taking her hand in his, spreading warmth through her. "I promise that I'm not going to let that jerk hurt you or your family. We'll have to be more careful now that we know what he's capable of. I know the others will pitch in to help. We won't let up until you can walk around without looking over your shoulder."

Lisa had to admit she had never felt this strong, not since Beckett had stolen her power when she was twelve. Well, guess what? She was no longer a scared kid. She realized she'd been acting like one by caving to his threats, but taking action made her feel strong again.

And her horrible secret had a shelf life. By keeping silent all these years, she'd fed the monster.

Tonight, when they were safe and alone, she would tell Ryan everything.

RYAN'S RINGTONE SOUNDED with his phone still in his hand. He immediately checked caller ID. "It's Dylan."

"I'm here with Lisa," he said. Lisa moved closer so she could hear.

"Thank goodness you're all right," Dylan said. "Grayson's fine. I didn't realize you'd called a few minutes ago until I got him settled down. Are the others with you?"

"No." He looked at Lisa, whose eyes closed. "It's just me and Lisa."

"We all scattered pretty good. I'm sure everyone will meet up." Dylan sounded confident and Ryan hoped that provided some measure of comfort for Lisa.

"Where's a good place for that?" Ryan asked.

"My place isn't too far from here. Plus, I have baby supplies. Where are you guys? Maybe we can make the walk together."

Ryan supplied their coordinates from the GPS on his phone.

"That's not far at all. I'll swing by and get you, and then we'll head to my place."

Sirens sounded in the distance. No doubt, the cavalry was about to arrive.

"We'll have to call the sheriff and let him know where we're headed," Ryan said.

"Good idea. Normally, I wouldn't leave a crime scene but in this case we should be okay. I'll give the sheriff a call and let him know our plans." With Dylan's security business, it was good for him to keep the lines of communication open with local law enforcement. His connections should prove a benefit.

"I'll try to reach Brody again," Ryan said.

"Try Rebecca and Samantha's phones, too," Dylan said.

"Will do."

"I've been trying to get a hold of you, Ryan," Rebecca said as soon as she answered. He'd had no such luck with Brody.

"Dylan and Grayson are safe. Lisa's with me. Who do you have?" Ryan asked.

"Samantha and the funeral director, but we're scared to go back," Rebecca admitted.

"Have you heard from Brody?"

"No. I was about to ask you the same thing." Concern laced her tone.

He already knew that Brody was with Lori. He'd seen him helping her out of the building.

"So he hasn't called you, either?" Rebecca asked, sounding deflated.

"Not yet. I'm sure he will. He might've dropped his phone while he was running."

"I haven't seen him since he made sure I was out of the building. He sent Lori running while he hung back to make sure everyone made it out okay."

Damn. Ryan was afraid of that.

"Lori's phone would be in her purse or diaper bag. I doubt she had the presence of mind to grab either," Lisa said. "There's no way to reach her now to find out if she's okay or tell her about the meet-up point."

Ryan squeezed her hand as tears rolled down her cheeks.

He finished the call with Rebecca, telling her where they were headed at the same time he heard branches crunching to his left.

Ryan spun around in time to see Dylan, carrying a baby against his chest, coming toward them.

Lisa ran to them and embraced them both. She took her nephew and Ryan could see that she was struggling to hold the baby. He also realized that she'd have to be dead for anyone to pry that child from her arms.

No matter how much pain she was in, she wasn't giving her nephew to anyone else.

Having Dylan with them increased their odds of making it out of any situation alive.

Ryan didn't doubt his own skills, but Lisa had to take it slow. Their odds of making it out of the thicket alive just doubled.

"Is there any chance we can stick around and look for my sister?" Lisa asked, the expression on her face said that she already knew the answer.

"I spoke to the sheriff. The law is nearby, so if she's anywhere near here, she'll be safe. Beckett and his men would have retreated as soon as they heard sirens. It'll do us no good to stick around. The bomb team will most likely be called in to secure the area and investigate. They might find evidence linking this crime to Beckett. That happens and they'll lock him up. I'm calling that the best-case scenario," Dylan said.

Ryan didn't voice his worst-case concern that Beckett had somehow gotten to Lori and would use her as a pawn against Lisa.

For the moment, she was preoccupied with soothing her nephew.

"What else did the sheriff say?" Ryan asked.

"That he's fine with sending a deputy over to my place to take statements. Said it was a good idea for us to steer clear of the crime scene and that he was committed to getting to the bottom of this."

It sounded as though the sheriff had given Dylan the typical party line.

The walk to Dylan's was long and hot.

By the time they arrived, the deputy was there.

Samantha and Rebecca must've been standing at the window watching for them, because the pair popped onto the porch as soon as the trio cleared the trees.

"Maribel is napping. She's completely unaware of everything that's going on," Samantha said, not stopping until Dylan embraced her.

Rebecca and Lisa exchanged worried looks.

"Do you think he's hungry?" Rebecca asked Lisa.

"He must be by now," Lisa said.

"Does he take formula or milk?"

"Formula."

"Let's go inside and fix him up with a bottle," Rebecca said.

"I'll go help." Samantha reached up on her tiptoes and kissed Dylan. He patted her bottom before she walked away.

Ryan would be lying if he didn't admit seeing them

so happy made his own bachelor life seem a little bit empty. He shoved the thought aside.

With every ticking second that went by with no word from Brody, Ryan's muscles tensed a little bit tighter.

The deputy came outside and took down Ryan's and Dylan's statements. Lisa joined them with Grayson on her hip. Babies could be intuitive during stressful times, and his clinging to her probably meant that he was picking up on the heightened stress levels. That, and the fact that he most likely missed his mom.

"Rest assured our office is committed to finding out who did this and why," Deputy Adams said before getting into his SUV and disappearing down the drive.

"Am I the only one who feels like I was handed a party line?" Lisa asked.

"I'm not thrilled with the response, either," Dylan said, and then excused himself to check on Maribel. "But then, they have a lot on their plates concerning the Alcorns and they'll have to be extra careful. If a deputy makes a mistake, the Alcorns' lawyer will chew him up and spit him out."

Ryan had the same sense. "At least we got Beckett on the deputy's radar."

"I just keep thinking about Brody and my sister out there. I'm afraid they're hurt or worse," Lisa said.

"Don't do that to yourself. We don't know what happened to them yet. They might've stuck around and been detained by law enforcement on the scene. If Brody dropped his phone along the way they'd have no means of reaching us or getting word to us that they're okay."

"That's true," she conceded but the stress lines didn't let up on her face. She kissed Grayson's forehead. He leaned his angelic cheek on her shoulder and closed his eyes. "He's tired, but I don't want to put him down yet. I don't want him waking up in a strange place without his mother."

"He has you. And she'll be back."

Lisa started pacing in the yard. "And what if she doesn't...come back? It's my fault we were there in the first place."

"There's no use beating yourself up over this, Lisa. All you'll do is make yourself sick. You had no idea any of this was going to happen. We took every precaution possible to ensure your safety. No one saw this coming." Against his better judgment, he pulled her into an embrace.

She stiffened for a slight second before relaxing.

"Does it bother you when I touch you?" he asked. The last thing he wanted was to fry her nerves even more or bring back bad memories.

"No. I'm just not used to it. And it's only for a second until I wrap my mind around the fact that you're not going to hurt me," she said.

Ryan didn't like the fact that she had to think through his touch. He reminded himself not to catch her off guard again. Or maybe it would be best for both of them if he kept a safe distance.

"I hate what he's done to me," she said, hugging the baby to her chest.

Ryan kept his facial expression neutral. He knew two things for certain. First of all, Beckett Alcorn had done something so horrible to Lisa that fifteen years later she still had to remind herself being touched was okay. Second, if Ryan saw the guy again he couldn't be certain what he'd do to him. As it was, he imagined his fingers closing around Beckett's throat.

There was a special breed of people who preyed on innocents. Any person capable of hurting a child didn't deserve to live.

Biting back the rage growing inside him, Ryan kissed Lisa on the forehead and put his arm around her and Grayson.

"Is that okay?" he asked to be sure.

"I like it when you touch me, Ryan. Even though it takes a minute for my brain to tell my body that it's okay. But I do like it."

What was he supposed to do with that? Tell her that he wanted to do more than touch her? Most of the time she acted like a spooked cat and he finally understood why. The Alcorns needed to pay for everything they'd taken from the town, the people, his friends.

Before he could ask the question he wanted answered the most, he heard a shuffling noise coming from the trees on the side yard.

"Take the baby in the house and tell Dylan that we have company."

Chapter Twelve

Lisa nodded, tucked her chin to her chest and wasted no time rushing to the house. *Good.* Ryan jogged to the edge of the yard, wishing he'd brought his shotgun with him.

A few seconds later, the back door smacked against the wall. Ryan glanced back in time to see that Dylan was coming and he'd brought reinforcement in the name of Smith & Wesson.

Thirty feet in front of him, through the trees, Ryan could see two figures huddled together. One looked to be struggling to walk. If one of them was going to shoot, he or she would've done so by now, so he forged ahead into the trees.

The sight of Brody was a welcomed relief. His arm was around Lori, who was hobbling toward Ryan.

"It's them," Ryan shouted back to Dylan. "They're okay."

He hurried to Lori's other side to take some of her weight from Brody, who was wincing in pain.

"My sister and Grayson?" Lori asked immediately.

"Both fine," Ryan replied.

"Everyone's good?" she asked.

"You guys were the only two missing," Ryan reported.

A wave of relief washed over Brody's face, and Ryan knew immediately that it was because he was worried about Rebecca.

"She's fine. We all got out okay," Ryan said to confirm. "What happened to you guys?"

"Guess we were a little too close to the initial blast. It knocked us both off our feet and into the trees," Brody said. "I must've taken a blow to the head." He felt around for the knot. "I was unconscious for a good ten minutes. Took me another five to find and wake Lori."

"Everyone's been worried sick. I've been trying to call you on your cell," Ryan said as Dylan rushed to them.

He helped Brody, who'd been masking what turned out to be a pretty bad limp.

"Have no idea what happened there," Brody said.

"I'm just glad you guys are okay. Everyone else is already here," Ryan said. "The deputy just left. I'm sure the sheriff's office will want your statements, as well."

"All I want is to see my fiancée," Brody said. "Then I'll tell the law everything they want to know."

As they approached the house, everyone else spilled out the back door.

Rebecca ran into Brody's embrace and Ryan noticed the look of adoration that passed between them.

He'd seen them together before. So why was he suddenly noticing it like it was the first time?

DYLAN HAD ORDERED pizza for pickup and then insisted everyone stay at his house for the night. After cleaning up dishes and putting the babies to bed, people dispersed. A few went out the back door to take a walk around the property before it got too late and Lisa figured Dylan followed in order to check the perimeter. Samantha's father had insisted on sleeping on an air mattress in Maribel's room and giving the others the bed in Dylan's guest room.

The day had gotten so crazy that Lisa didn't feel that she'd had a chance to remember her father. She stepped outside to get a breath of fresh air and to take a moment to think about him.

As she looked up at one of those endless starlit skies that she'd grown up taking for granted in Texas, she thought about how much her father would've loved a night like this. There were no clouds, just piercing blue landscape covered with a sea of white dots, lighting up the otherwise pitch-black night.

The back door opened and then Ryan stepped onto the small porch.

"Everything all right?" he asked.

"Yeah." She turned toward the trees, trying to hide the fact that she was crying.

"Do you mind company?"

"Sure." She wiped away the tears.

He moved closer, examining her expression. "You know, you always were a bad liar."

"I miss him."

"Of course you do." Ryan didn't make a move to hold her and she figured half the reason he was holding back was because he wasn't sure when it was okay to touch her.

"Worse than that, it just feels useless. I mean, I finally get the courage to stand up to Beckett and look what happens," she said.

"He's trying to take back control. You've rattled him and that's a good thing. He'll make a mistake and the sheriff will arrest him."

"And then what? Do you really think he's going to let me get away with sending him to jail?" Of course he wouldn't. Beckett Alcorn was going to have the last laugh no matter what it cost him. Lisa knew that the price would be even higher for her. The situation couldn't feel more hopeless. "He's most likely already planning his next attack."

"The law can't deny that someone is after you and your family now. We didn't have that protection before," Ryan said earnestly.

There was no arguing that point.

"What good will it do? A man like him has unlimited resources. He won't stop until he gets what he wants." She shivered thinking about just how Beckett Alcorn liked to take what he wanted.

Ryan's voice lowered when he asked, "Can I ask a question?"

She nodded.

"Why didn't you tell anyone about your past with him?"

"There are a thousand reasons. First of all, I was embarrassed. I was convinced I'd done something to deserve it," she said, fighting the sense of shame that accompanied the admission.

"He's a bully. There's no indignity in being picked on or threatened by someone stronger than you. I just think it was a shame that you had to suffer alone."

"Who would've believed me, anyway? I'm the daughter of the town's most notorious drunk, remember?" She'd fired the accusation, but she knew that she wasn't being completely fair. Her friends had never treated her as less than because of her father.

"I would have, for one. There's a houseful of people in there who would have backed you, as well," Ryan said, hurt lacing his tone.

"I'm sorry. You're right. I'm just off today with the funeral service and then all that happened." Lisa hadn't told a soul what really had happened fifteen years ago. She wanted to tell Ryan, to get out what had been festering inside far too many years. How did she even begin to discuss the nightmare that had paralyzed her in her sleep and made her afraid to open her eyes in the morning for fear he'd be standing over her bed? "Ryan, do you really want to know why I don't talk about what Beckett did to me?"

"I do." There was comfort in his gray eyes, compassion his expression.

And yet it was still so hard to discuss. Lisa had read countless stories over the years trying to make sense of the incident, of her own behavior afterward. Even though a shocking number of young girls and women were raped by someone they knew, very few ever reported the crime. Both of those points were certainly true in her case. The words were all there to tell Ryan, but her brain refused to form sentences with them.

"It's okay. You can tell me anything. I'm not going to think any different of you," Ryan reassured her.

Would he, though? She'd certainly put herself through the wringer, asking herself a string of questions. Why had Beckett chosen her? Had she done something to bring the abuse on? Should she tell her father?

Guilt and shame washed over her, causing her shoulders to slump forward. She suddenly felt like that same twelve-year-old girl scrubbing her skin with soap in the shower, hating the feeling of Beckett touching her.

A sick feeling of frustration had been building. The powerlessness and stigma about what had happened to her and so many others had finally reached critical mass. The need to speak out finally overwhelmed her fear.

Keep quiet and he wins, a voice inside her head said.

"I was molested." There. She'd said it. Out loud.

Something dark moved behind Ryan's eyes. Hatred? Sympathy? Both?

"What did that bastard do to you?" he asked, not bothering to mask the anger in his tone.

"He touched me. He made me do things to him. I didn't even consider it rape before because he couldn't… penetrate. He threatened it, though. Said he'd wait for me. That he'd come back when I was ready. And if I told anyone then he'd come after my sister instead." Tears streamed down her face as she said the words. Getting them out, letting them go was the most frightening and yet freeing thing she'd ever done. She didn't overthink it this time. She just said it. "Looking back, I feel like I should've said something to someone but I didn't."

"You were just a kid. And you didn't report him because of his threat."

"I tried to forget about what happened. It didn't help that I started seeing stories on the news of women being torn apart on the witness stand and treated like they were the ones who'd committed a crime. I figured no one would believe a kid and especially not over Beckett."

"The way the legal system treats victims is repulsive," he agreed.

"So I withdrew from everyone and I've been keeping this terrible secret too long." Talking about it made her feel she was taking back some of her power. "It didn't help that my sister and I were being bounced around from home to home because of Dad's drinking. I guess I thought if I told anyone that they'd take us away from him permanently and we might be separated. I know our life was hard with Dad when he drank, but it was much harder to be divided between relatives."

"Thank you for trusting me with this, Lisa."

He didn't push her away or look at her as if she were tainted. She'd felt that way about herself for so many years.

"I was so afraid you'd look at me differently. That others would look at me strangely if I told anyone."

He lifted her chin. "I'm looking at you right now and all I see is a strong, beautiful woman. If anything, I respect you even more than I did before."

Slowly, Ryan pulled her closer to him and she felt as if she'd been bathed in the sun from his warmth. He kissed the top of her head.

"I felt so helpless for so many years. Anxiety and fury had built to a level that was almost intolerable. By storing the incident inside, it was gnawing away at me like it had to get out one way or another. It feels surprisingly freeing to talk about it with you. My only regret is that Beckett is winning again. He wrecked my father's funeral. That bastard has taken away so much from me. It infuriates me that he'll get away with it."

"We won't let him this time. I promise." Ryan didn't

try to mask the threat in his tone. He bent forward and looked her in the eye. "Can I have permission to kiss you?"

"Yes." She had never felt closer to another human being. There was nothing she wanted more than Ryan's lips on hers. She reached up on her tiptoes to meet him halfway.

His kiss, tender and soft, brushed against her mouth so gently. She could feel his warm breath on her skin. He tasted like the fresh coffee he'd sipped while helping with dishes a few minutes earlier.

"You're a survivor, Lisa. And you amaze me." His mouth moved against hers as he spoke.

She brought her hand up around the base of his neck and tugged him closer. His arms encircled her waist. His strong hands on her back caused her body to tremble.

He pulled back. His eyes had darkened to steel. "Is this okay?"

"It's more than okay," she said, pressing her body flush against his. She let out a sensual moan as Ryan pulled her closer, deepening the kiss.

In that moment, she got so very lost. Nothing else mattered except the two of them under a starlit sky. The crescent moon hung low and heavy and her body trembled under his fingertips.

She could stay like this all night, except a tiny part of her brain questioned whether or not *this* was a good idea. It was Ryan, and the two of them had a long history of friendship. They'd just crossed a line. And in doing so might be putting everything on it.

As if Ryan had a similar realization, he pulled back a little.

"It's late," she said when they broke contact, reconsidering. Then she was the one to pull back a little more. Her body fizzed with awareness with him this close and one look in his eyes said he felt the same. What was really going on between them? Chemistry? Sexual awareness? A leftover childhood crush?

No matter what box she fit "it" in, the result was the same. She had no idea what to do next or even if this was a good idea in the first place. Whatever was happening between them was so powerful that the air charged around them every time they were close, and especially now. It had been such a long time since a man looked at her like that—hungry and as though she was all woman and he was all man. And she couldn't ever remember wanting one to in the way she did with Ryan.

She wasn't a virgin. And yet nothing had felt so powerful, so new, as whatever was happening between them.

"Ryan."

"Yeah."

"I don't regret kissing you and I hope you don't, either."

"Kissing you is the best thing I've done in a long time," he said, and she almost laughed again at how frustrated that admission made him sound. "It's been a long day and we should try to get some sleep."

Ryan took another step back, looking as confused as she felt and as if he wasn't sure what to do with his hands. Based on his tense expression, he'd clearly felt whatever it was buzzing between them as strongly as she did. And it almost made her laugh that he didn't seem to know what to do with it any more than she did.

"We'll regroup in the morning after everyone's had a chance to get some sleep and figure out our next move."

Sleep? There'd be no sleeping tonight for her. Not with all those confusing feelings rolling around inside her head.

Chapter Thirteen

Ryan had tossed and turned all night thinking about what Lisa told him the night before about Beckett.

Rage had kept Ryan from being able to let go of his emotions and give in to sleep. And everything inside him wanted to crush Beckett Alcorn. Lisa felt alone, but someone like him didn't stop after one victim. Ryan was realistic enough to know that it would be next to impossible to find out who else Beckett had preyed on.

Trying to figure out a solution had kept Ryan in tangled sheets.

If it wasn't for that, he would've been awake thinking about the couple of kisses he and Lisa had shared. Ryan honestly didn't know what to make of what was happening between them. There'd never been so many sparks in a room with two people or so much fire in a kiss before Lisa. All he knew for certain was that this was different than anything else he'd experienced. He chalked it up to the string of bad dates he'd had in the past year.

What dates, Hunt?

There hadn't been a real date, someone he was truly interested in, in a very long time.

For one person to be everything he needed seemed

a tall order, especially since Ryan didn't particularly *need* anyone. Had he truly been looking for a partner? Or had he given up after Maria, Chelsea and Sandy consecutively had made no qualms about caring more about what he did for a living or what SUV he drove than anything else?

Was Ryan being too hard on women? Expecting too much?

Freud would have a field day with that.

Heck if he had answers. The only thing he knew for certain was that he wasn't checking the time every five minutes or thinking about how many NBA games he was missing when he spent time with Lisa. In fact, he liked talking to Lisa more than almost every other activity he could think of. Well, except for one, and sex with Lisa was totally out of the question.

Most likely their history and a natural curiosity gave that extra pull toward her. How many times in high school had he tried to work up the nerve to ask her out but couldn't? She'd shot him down cold when he finally mustered the courage.

Looking back, he might've done the same thing if the shoe were on the other foot and she'd come up with the same lame line he had. What was his brilliant phrase? *You wanna go grab a mocha with me and do some homework?*

In all fairness, she should've laughed in his face. He remembered how uncomfortable she'd become when he moved closer to her. He'd thought it was because she couldn't get away from him fast enough. Now he knew the real reason.

Ryan untangled himself from the sheets, threw on a pair of jeans and shuffled down the hallway. No good could come out of too much thinking before a man had his coffee. He stabbed his fingers into his hair, trying to tame his curls so that he looked respectable before shuffling into the kitchen in case there was mixed company.

Lisa stood at the sink, looking out the boxed window. "Morning."

"I'm not sure yet," he teased, needing to get things back on a lighter note with her after the way they'd left it last night. They needed to focus on figuring out how to connect Beckett with his crimes and especially while his father was under scrutiny.

"This might help." She handed over what he was looking for.

"Thanks." He took the mug filled with manna from heaven and breathed in the smell of fresh coffee.

"Can we talk now?" she asked after he'd finished his first cup, refilled his mug, and then took a seat at the breakfast bar.

"Now would be a good time," he said, smiling. "Your turn to sit down while I fix breakfast."

"No way," she said, emphatically. "I've got this."

"All right. What else do you know how to cook?" he asked, noticing how uncomfortable she seemed with him doing anything for her. Even though they'd made up ground last night, there was still a huge gap between them. He could be patient and wait for her to be ready to allow someone in. Until she did, there could never be anything more than friendship between them no matter how much he was starting to think he was ready for more.

"Mostly just the eggs. I hope you're okay with that," she said, rolling her eyes and clucking her tongue at him.

"Like when you decided to cook for the group when

we were working on that project in eighth grade?" he teased.

"No. Not like that." She shot him a look. "I managed to get through college without burning down any buildings, didn't I?"

"You only set a small fire. I'm still trying to figure out how you managed to get through college fed. Meal plan?" He couldn't stop himself from laughing any more than he could keep the armor around his heart from cracking a little more. Ryan didn't want to feel this way for anyone. It was only a matter of time before they'd let him down. Life had taught him that lesson early and the hard way.

She stalked over and jabbed him in the arm.

"Ouch," he said, pretending it hurt.

"See what happens, funny man?" she shot back.

In one impulsive motion, he wrapped his arm around her waist and pulled her onto his lap. Her laugh was the sweetest music, but when she turned to look at him, her eyes glittery with desire, he couldn't stop himself. "I'm going to kiss you. If that's not okay, then you need to tell me right now."

Her answer came in the form of wiggling around to give him better access. Her movement gave him a new problem to deal with…one he didn't care for the entire house to see, especially since kids could bounce into the room at any moment. Not to mention the fact that his jeans were uncomfortably tight. Need took over and he claimed her mouth. Everything about Lisa felt like coming home. Shouldn't that freak him out?

He deepened the kiss and she tasted like peppermint toothpaste and coffee. Good thing he liked both.

"Are we the only two awake? I didn't hear anyone

else when I came down the hall." He pulled back enough to brush her lips with his when he spoke.

"Dylan took Maribel out to the playground to run out some of her energy. He's been up since before the sun, I think," she said, smiling. "And you need to eat."

He kissed her one more time before helping her up and he tried not to watch her sweet bottom as she walked to the fridge and pulled supplies.

"Having a kid keeps him on his toes," Ryan said.

"The crazy part, and I noticed this with my sister, too, is that they don't seem to mind getting out of bed at ridiculous hours and staying up too late just to get basic stuff done. In fact, I've never seen either of them happier," Lisa said. "By the time I get kids at school they can already walk, talk and go to the bathroom themselves. Spending time with Grayson has changed my perspective on how hard it is to care for kids."

"Meaning what?"

"I used to look at my college friends who had babies and all I could think of was how much work they were and how tired my friends sounded. Now I get it. You don't mind being awake for three nights in a row with a sick baby when it's your child or a child you're close to. All you can think about is making them better," she said, mixing ingredients into a bowl.

"Does that mean you want one?" he asked nonchalantly, wanting to know the answer more than he cared to admit.

"A baby?" she asked in pure shock.

"No, a puppy. Of course, a baby," he retorted.

"A puppy I can handle. I'm not quite ready for a baby. I haven't even dated anyone seriously for longer than I care to admit."

Why did that statement put a smile on Ryan's face? He clamped it down before she caught him. "I was just thinking about picking up a rescue from the shelter myself." He had no plans to share the real motivation. That anticipating the loneliness he'd feel after she left was the reason he needed to fill that void.

"I'd be happy to go with you, if you'd like. When this is all over," she said, the smile fading from her lips as her mind seemed to come back to the reality facing them.

Ryan couldn't help but think the cabin was the safest place for her. "Be careful," she said, a pleading look in her eyes.

"I will." Knowing an Alcorn had put it there made Ryan tense that much more. His family had a long history with that family, dating back to a dispute about land with Ryan's father. It was time the town knew who the Alcorns really were.

"I just keep thinking about my dad and the fact that he should still be alive. I can't let the Alcorns take away everything I care about."

Ryan had no intention of allowing that to happen.

THERE WAS A sad quality to Ryan's voice every time they talked about family, which had Lisa wondering about his mother again as she put the last of the dishes in the dishwasher.

Maybe it was the fact that she'd lost her father, but if Ryan was ever going to have a chance to heal, then he needed to face his mother and deal with his emotions.

But how would she reach Mrs. Hunt? Did she even go by that name anymore?

Lisa didn't have the first idea how to contact his

mother, but didn't he have the right to know where she was and what she was doing? How sad would it be if she stayed away because she was worried that she'd be intruding on his life?

It probably wasn't Lisa's business and a voice in the back of her mind warned her not to interfere. Losing her father made her realize how short time was and how quickly people could be taken away, and she suspected Ryan's sadness wouldn't go away until he had answers.

Lisa cleaned out her mug and tucked it away in the cabinet.

The kids were down for a nap. Lori was resting with Grayson. Brody and Rebecca had disappeared to check on their horses. Samantha was taking a nap.

Lisa sought out Dylan, finding him in his office. He was in the process of converting the detached garage in order to make more room for Samantha's father to move in with them.

She knocked and then waited for an answer.

"Come in," Dylan's voice boomed.

She opened the door to find him already on his feet, palming his gun.

"It's just me," she said, her heart jumping into her throat at the sight of his weapon. Growing up in Texas, she'd gotten used to being around guns, but this seemed different. It was a stark reminder of how dangerous their circumstances were and how ready they needed to be at a moment's notice. "Can I come in?"

"Sure." He set his weapon on the desk, motioned toward a chair opposite him and took his seat.

"This place looks great." The office was nicely set up. There was a solid wood desk in the middle of the room. The place had a comfortable Western feel to it. A large rustic barn star hung on the wall behind the desk. On a long side table sat a substantial bronze of a bucking bronco. She recognized it as work from a local artist.

She figured the potted plants had to be Samantha's contribution to the decor. The green was a nice touch to the masculine room. There were a few unpacked boxes shoved against the wall.

"If I wanted to find someone, where would be the first place to look?" she asked, wishing she could come right out and ask for his help.

His expression tensed. "I can help with that."

"It's not about this case. I'm looking into something that's not connected to the Alcorns," she said, realizing he thought she was planning to poke around somewhere that might get her deeper into this mess.

"Okay. I'm guessing this isn't something you want to share with me." He leaned back in his chair. "So, if it were me looking for someone, I'd start with the most obvious place, the internet. I'm presuming you know this person's legal name."

"I do. Well, actually, I used to know her name. She may have remarried or gone back to her maiden name."

That got his attention. "Do you know her date of birth?"

"No, but I think I can find that out easily enough." Could she outright ask Ryan for the information? He'd be the only one who would know for sure, right? She could sidestep him and go directly to Justin. Oh, but the two of them were close. Justin would most likely tell his brother and then she'd have to face him. Could she come right out and tell Ryan what she was doing? Would he try to stop her? Going behind his back didn't feel right. Except what if she got him on board with the idea of finding his mother and something bad had happened to her? Or, worse, what if she didn't want to see Ryan?

It might be safer to explore on her own first and then bring him in when she knew it was safe. The last thing he needed to feel was rejected by his mother again. His pain was palpable at her abandonment, even after all these years. She understood why he would feel that way. Lisa had been let down by her father many times over the years, but Ryan was right that his saving grace was how much her father loved her. He kept fighting his way back to his girls. It was difficult to fault him for his weaknesses when he'd tried so hard to overcome them.

The bouts when he was drinking were some of the worst times of her life. But he'd figured out a way back to his family every time. Even though he fell down, he'd claw his way back up. She knew, despite everything, that he loved her and Lori above all. And that was the reason she was able to forgive him when the cops had shown up searching for him after he'd "freed" a pack of cigarettes from the gas station. She'd found him, drunk, hiding in the shed behind the house. He'd fallen asleep with a lit cigarette in his mouth. Child Protective Services hadn't liked that move.

She and her sister had been passed around to various relatives and when no one could take them in, they'd done a stint in the foster care system where Lisa had had to defend them both from a predator in one of the houses they'd been assigned.

Lisa took a sharp breath. "If I brought you in, how much is your fee?"

"No charge."

"What about confidentiality?"

"Absolute," he said without hesitation. "But I have to

admit that it worries me you would ask. What are you getting yourself into?"

She wasn't sure how Dylan would react to her trying to find Ryan's mother, especially without his permission. She wouldn't be doing it at all if she didn't think he needed to know. In her heart, she knew that in order for Ryan to heal, to be able to move on with his life and really trust people, he needed this. Ryan deserved that.

There were those in town who'd felt sorry for Mr. Hunt, saying that a wife should never abandon her family. But when Lisa's dad had been hitting the bottle a little too hard once, he let it slip that she'd had no choice but to leave.

Others whispered about it for years and Lisa had always thought there'd been more to the story. Plus, she'd had no idea what her father meant and it was obvious that he knew something. Others must know something, too.

A new scandal had broken and people had shifted their attention to the financial crisis Brody's mother had put families in when she'd taken their investment money and disappeared.

Dylan ended the call and clasped his hands. "You know I'll do anything to help you. Professionally, I have a policy against accepting a job blindly. You're going to have to tell me who this case is about if you want my help."

"That's fair. However, if you decide not to take it then I need your word you won't tell anyone I asked." Turnabout was fair play.

"Agreed."

"I'm looking for Ryan's mother." There. She'd said it. She'd dropped the bomb.

"Are you sure this is a good idea?" he asked, concern in his voice.

And that concern had her thinking twice.

"I've considered every angle. If I tell him and he wants to find her but something's happened, then he'll be devastated," she hedged.

"I can see that," Dylan agreed.

"Then there's the very real possibility that she doesn't want to be found. How can I get him all jazzed up about locating her only to let him suffer rejection again?"

"Which makes me think that he should be the one heading this search. If he doesn't want to find her, case closed."

"Only it's not that simple," she countered.

"I can see where you're coming from and it's a good place. In your heart, you want to give him this gift. But my experience has been that people who don't want to be found really don't want to be found," Dylan explained.

"And I get that. It's a risk. I'm willing to gamble if I'm the only one who'll know. Then I can help guide him in the right direction if he brings it up again."

"I can see that you care about him and you're coming from a good place—"

"We all do," she quickly added. She didn't want her cheeks to flush with embarrassment, but they did.

"Right. So I think we have to support his decision not to look for her. He's a grown man and you might end up doing more damage than you think by acting on his behalf," Dylan warned.

She slumped in her chair, feeling that this was hopeless. "Then you're not going to help me."

"I didn't say that."

"I've gone over this a thousand times in my head, believe me. But I know Ryan. It would do him so much good to put this behind him. But he's too stubborn to make the first move."

"That's the truth," Dylan agreed with a smile.

"Maybe we won't find her and he'll go to his grave never knowing the truth. I think there's more to the story of her leaving, and if we can find her maybe she can finally tell her side."

"I see the hope in your eyes when you talk about this, but believe me, not all stories have a happy ending. Look at mine," he said.

"And that's why I thought you'd understand. Do you want to see your parents? Wouldn't you like to hear from them one way or the other as to why they never came back?"

"I can tell you why—they were selfish."

"Maybe so. Have you considered other possibilities?"

"Like?" He opened his hands and put his palms flat on the desk.

"They were young and scared, and had no idea what to do with a baby."

"I've thought of that. I'm not a baby anymore. They should make the effort at this point," Dylan said, hurt still in his voice.

And that was exactly why Ryan needed to know. That hurt would never go away until he knew the truth.

"Are you the least bit curious? I mean, we know how strict your grandmother was. Is it possible that she told them to go? Asked them not to come back?" Lisa asked.

Dylan leaned back in his chair, considering her questions.

"They didn't come to her funeral. Didn't try to make sure I was okay," he said, rubbing the scruff on his chin.

"I agree that was wrong. I'm not convinced they didn't love you, though."

He laughed. "I really have become soft since having Maribel. This conversation would've had me all kinds of riled up and ready to fight in the past. Now I'm actually considering what you're saying."

"That's a good thing, right?" she asked, not wanting to push her luck but also needing to help others see how short life really was and how little of it should be wasted on a hurt feelings or a grudge.

"It is," he said. "Now you have me thinking about finding my folks. You've brought up good points. Let's think this through for a minute. Say I locate them. Then what? I'm not ready to forgive them yet."

"You don't have to be. Do you?" she asked.

He laughed again. "I guess not."

"All you really have to be is prepared to face whatever truth comes out of it. If they don't want to see you, then you have your answer. But what if they do? What if they're the ones who are scared you'll reject them after all these years? If you can handle knowing the truth, shouldn't you try to find it?" she asked.

"You're probably right." He paused thoughtfully. "You didn't come here to talk about my situation, though."

"No, I didn't. And I'm sorry if it makes you uncomfortable. Losing my father has made me realize tomorrow is never promised to anyone. I guess I want everyone to get closure with their relationships."

"That's true," he agreed.

She waited for him to give her an answer about Ryan.

"I want it on record that I still don't agree with going behind Ryan's back," Dylan said. "Any heat comes from this and it's going to be on you."

"Does that mean you're agreeing to help?" She couldn't keep the excitement out of her tone.

"It does. Mostly because I know you're going to look anyway and I'd rather be involved so I can make sure no one leads you down the wrong path."

"Thank you, Dylan," she said, feeling extreme relief and a new sense of purpose.

"I just hope this doesn't come back on either one of us," Dylan said.

Chapter Fourteen

Ryan finished the last few bites of his dinner, looking around at the friends he'd known since he was a kid. As much as this felt like family, he'd be lying if he didn't admit that a piece of his life had always felt as if something was missing.

He dismissed the thought as being melancholy.

His brother, his friends and the people he could count on were all he needed. It was surprising just how quickly Lisa had made an impact on his thinking. She'd gotten under his armor and had him considering ideas he never would've in the past. Too bad they would part ways soon.

"We'll need to move out at first light tomorrow morning," he said.

"What's the plan?" Dylan asked.

"The cabin is safe. I'll make sure no one follows us there," he said.

"I want you to take my truck. Samantha and I will take your Jeep. We can go with you to the county line. It'd be too risky to keep going after that. The more vehicles we have, the higher the risk of being noticed," Dylan said.

"Just like the president," Ryan said, noticing that

the mood had instantly changed from light to intense when he brought up leaving. But the topic couldn't be avoided. They needed a plan.

Taking back roads was a good way to slip out of town unnoticed, but he also thought about how exposed they'd be with no one around for miles. There'd be long stretches of road in front of them and behind them with plenty of chances for ambush.

Brody leaned forward. "There's the issue of getting you there safely. Small highways have their own problems." He glanced up at Ryan, clear they'd been thinking along the same lines. "Once you get there, I don't like you being at the cabin defenseless. There's no backup around."

"Good point," Dylan agreed.

"You can't leave your horses, Brody," Ryan said, referring to his friend's horse ranch. "And, Dylan, you have Maribel. No way will she let you out of her sight. You need to be around for her."

Dylan and Brody nodded.

"We can check to see if Dawson is available. Plus, I haven't spoken to James. He might want to be involved," Brody said.

"I don't mind getting others involved if need be. I still believe we'll be fine if we make it out of Mason Ridge without being followed," Ryan said. "Nobody knows about this place, and bringing along others could make it easier to track us."

"You'll get out of town without a tail. I can see to that," Dylan offered.

"We'll all pitch in," Brody said.

Ryan raised his chin. "My shotgun's too big to handle while I drive. I'll need to borrow a weapon."

"You got it," Dylan said. "I have a few spares. Take what you need from my office."

A look passed between Dylan and Lisa. What was that all about?

Ryan knew that Lisa would be fine with guns. Heck, most everyone in Texas had grown up with one in the house along with the proper come-to-Jesus meeting about keeping them inside, unloaded, in a locked case. He'd ask her about it later.

Right now he needed to come up with a plan to keep her, her sister and Grayson away from Beckett Alcorn.

"I stopped by the sheriff's office while I was out," Ryan said. "Couldn't get a whole lot out of him about yesterday's incident."

"I've been investigating this on my own," Dylan said. "We located the warehouse outside town."

"Have you turned that information over to the sheriff?" Ryan asked.

"Not yet. I wanted to put eyes on it for a while. See what's really going on first. If I gave the information to law enforcement I was afraid they'd blast in there and scare off anyone who might be using the place. If the Alcorns know we're onto them, they'll close up shop there. And something's been bugging me. I remember a weird smell that I couldn't put my finger on. At the time, I wrote it off as nothing. Now I'm wondering if they might've been using the facility to mix chemicals," Dylan said.

"Like for a bomb?" Ryan asked. "I want to see this place."

Dylan nodded. "We can check it out later if you want. We'll have to go in the middle of the night and be very careful, though. I get caught and my relationship with the sheriff will go up in flames."

DARKNESS SURROUNDED DYLAN'S HOUSE. The blinds were closed. Lisa slipped out of the foldout bed she shared with Lori and Grayson in the living room and moved down the hallway.

Brody and Rebecca had gone home for the night. Dylan and Samantha and Maribel were in their respective rooms. Samantha's father was staying at his house in town to give them all some room.

Lisa's eyes had adjusted to the dark and she was careful not to bump into anything on her way to Ryan's room. She cracked the door.

"Ryan?" she whispered.

"Come in." He sounded wide-awake.

"What time do you plan to leave?" Lisa asked Ryan, who opened the covers to allow her to slip into his makeshift bed on the floor.

"Not for a couple of hours," he said.

"You can't sleep?" She closed the door behind her and took him up on his offer.

"No. You tired at all?" he asked, his voice husky.

"Not even a little bit. There's so much rolling around in my head. I have so many questions about this whole ordeal. I can't shut it off." The case was one thing that was keeping her up. She also wondered if she was doing the right thing by going behind his back to find his mother. All the logical reasons jumped to her defense and yet she couldn't help feeling that she was betraying him.

"You know we'll figure this out, right?" Based on his tone of voice, it wasn't a question. He pulled her closer to him and kissed her on her forehead. The move was no doubt meant to be reassuring and yet it felt incredibly intimate with the two of them lying in bed together. Only a few strips of material kept them from skin-to-skin contact.

With his strong arms around her, she settled into the crook of his neck, doing her best to ignore the pulses of electricity ricocheting between them. With every breath, the room heated. With every move, her body warmed with sensual heat.

The kisses they'd shared had occupied more and more mental space and there'd been something building between them for the past few weeks. Whatever was going on between them had pushed them well beyond friendship into a new scary world—scary because she'd never wanted to be with someone as much she did Ryan. Did that freak her out? Sure. In the past something like that would've paralyzed her. Not this time. Not with him.

The first time she'd lost her virginity jumped into her thoughts. She'd been in such a hurry to lose it in college. It had been this big fear building inside her that she'd never be able to be intimate with anyone, that Beckett had taken that from her. She hadn't been dating Timothy for long when she decided it was time.

Timothy wasn't the right guy. He was barely the "right now" guy. And yet she'd gone through with it anyway. And she had no regrets. Except that she did realize that making the decision to have sex needed to be about more than ticking a box on a to-do list.

Once she'd gotten it out of her system then she'd decided to wait until she had real feelings for a guy before sleeping with him. It seemed that her late start put her behind the dating curve and she'd ended up going out with guys who were in no way right for her or good for her, either. When Darren had forced the issue of sex after too many beers at a frat party, Lisa fought back. Even though she got away from him and he didn't get his way, she had that same feeling of shame as if she'd been molested.

Being touched and not instinctively reacting with shock was an uphill battle after that.

And yet she wanted Ryan's hands on her.

"Ryan…"

"Yes."

"I want you to touch me."

"You do know what you're asking, right?" he asked, his voice husky.

"Uh-huh." She no longer cared what this would do to their friendship. She needed him to touch her, to brand her as his, to make her unafraid again. And she wanted this to happen more than she wanted air.

Breathing wasn't proving to be a problem.

The palm of his hand flattened on her stomach, causing her to quiver. She'd lost her virginity years ago and yet this felt like the very first time all over again.

"I need to know you can handle this," he said in a low, deep timbre. He trailed his finger down her stomach and then along the lacy rim of her panties. "I want you."

Turning to face him, she could feel his thick erection pulsing against her stomach, causing need to roar through her.

She struggled to gain footing as thunder boomed in her ears. Was this really happening?

"I want this, Ryan."

"It's a damn good thing you do." He cupped her face in his hands.

His lips pressed hers with an intensity that robbed her breath.

Desire started building, reaching, climbing toward that place that needed release as he lowered his hand and ran his finger along the sensitized skin of her hip. He needed to hurry this up because her body couldn't take much more.

Rather than wait for him to decide when to raise the stakes, Lisa took matters into her own hands, literally. She wrapped her hand around his stiff length and was rewarded with a guttural groan in response. Being in control felt good with Ryan and she figured that, with some practice, she'd easily let go and let him take the lead. It dawned on her why he was taking it so slowly, and the reason made her heart melt a little more. He didn't want to spook her or do anything she couldn't handle.

"You can't hurt me, Ryan. I want this more than you do."

"I doubt that's possible, sweetheart."

She smiled against his lips before he captured hers again in a bone-melting kiss. With her free hand, she stroked him a few times.

"Hold that thought," he said, untangling their legs and pushing himself off the makeshift bed. He grabbed his jeans and returned with a condom.

There was enough light in the room to illuminate the hard angles on his face and hawk-like nose. Lisa had the startling realization that she'd never felt like this toward any other man. She'd never needed to touch anyone as much as she needed to touch Ryan right now. So she did just that. She reached toward him and outlined the ridges in his stomach, ripples of muscle.

His T-shirt and boxers were on the floor seconds before he rolled the condom down his length. She stopped long enough to admire him in all his masculine glory. He was serious hotness and she desperately wanted him.

It took her a few seconds to realize his pause was meant to give her time to undress. Her own oversize sleeping shirt and underwear joined his on the floor as soon as it dawned on her. This time, they'd make love on her schedule.

"I want you to touch me," she said, knowing he needed to hear the words. "I love the way your hands feel on my body."

She moved onto her back so that he could reposition himself inside the V of her legs. His body trembled with the need for release as he brushed his tip along her wet heat.

Palming his length, she guided him.

He dipped slowly at first, but she was already ready for him. She matched his next gentle thrust and he slid deep inside her.

Matching him stride for stride, she climbed with him toward the peak of release they could only give each other. Their bodies, now slick with sweat, moved at a frantic pace as they reached that ultimate climax together.

Tension corded her body as her inner muscles clenched and released around his length.

"Ryan," she breathed as she felt his body tighten while he climbed that same mountain, stood on that same edge and free-fell to that same sweet release.

They lay perfectly still, bodies entangled, until their pulses returned to a normal beat.

Lisa couldn't be sure she'd heard him correctly, but as Ryan rolled to his side she could've sworn she'd heard him say that he loved her.

THE AIR WAS STILL. There was a cloudless sky. The stars shone brilliantly against a black canopy.

This was a perfect night for reconnaissance.

As long as Ryan could keep his thoughts on the mission he needed to accomplish and not on the silky feel of Lisa's skin. Or just how much like home it felt to have her legs wrapped around him as she called out his name.

Ryan stood out front, waiting for Brody, as Dylan pulled together a few supplies. He strolled outside, shouldering a backpack at the same time Brody's truck rolled up the gravel drive, lights out.

"This should help you out if you find yourself in trouble," Dylan said, handing Ryan a weapon.

By the weight and feel, Ryan recognized it as a Glock.

The trio left as quietly as they could, staying dark until they'd slipped down the farm road leading to Dylan's house. There were no other vehicles on the road, but Ryan knew that someone could be watching the house.

"Even with the sheriff's office keeping watch on your place, I'm not sure I like leaving them alone," he said.

"I have electronic eyes on the perimeter," Dylan replied. "And someone stationed outside. Anything goes south and there's backup. I'm not leaving anything to chance with the people we love."

"I didn't see anyone outside, so I'm guessing that was

for a reason." Ryan didn't correct Dylan. The truth was that he did love Lisa and the past few hours had been a game changer for him. The tricky part was figuring out his next move. The answer to that was probably going to be nothing. He liked the idea that she didn't bristle when he'd touched her. And he'd allow her to take the lead.

"Exactly," Dylan agreed.

"I heard you got a colt in a few weeks ago from Lone Star," Ryan said to Brody, needing to distract himself from thinking about everything that could go wrong with their mission.

"He's a good horse," Brody said. "Or at least he will be when I finish doctoring him up and training him."

"What's his story?"

"The usual. His owner saw potential and kicked up his training routine at eighteen months old," Brody said.

"Which isn't uncommon," Dylan added.

"Nope. Didn't work out so well for this guy, though. His knees are a mess and he won't ever race," Brody said.

"How'd he end up at your place?" Ryan asked.

"Owner felt horrible for the colt. Wants him to have a chance to go to a ranch or be someone's personal horse, so he asked around and was referred to my rehab ranch."

A second chance sounded pretty good to Ryan about now. His first thought was Lisa. His second was his mother. Why did she pop into his thoughts? Must've been the recent conversation he'd had with Lisa. But it didn't matter. He had no idea how to reach his mother, and if he was being honest, he wasn't real sure he ever wanted to see the woman again.

The drive to the warehouse didn't take much more

than half an hour. The closer they'd gotten, the bumpier the roads. Dylan's jaw clenched tighter, too.

"Did you see anything when you were there before?" Ryan asked.

"No. I had a canvas bag on my head the entire time we were outside the building. I remember it being dark, but that was mainly because it was the middle of the night. There wasn't any other light source around, which was one of the signs I was somewhere on the outskirts of town. I remember waking up bound to some kind of wooden table and then looking up to see a single bulb hanging from a socket." He paused as he clenched his back teeth. "There were these plastic-looking panels on the ceiling and I remember thinking that if it was light outside, sun would stream through the half wall of windows."

Ryan nodded as he thanked his friend again for everything he was doing for Lisa and her family. Facing the warehouse couldn't be easy.

Dylan stared out the front window onto the winding road lit up by the beams in front of them. "All I could think at the time was that the place would be good for torturing people. And how much I needed to walk out of there alive if I ever wanted to see Maribel again. Later, I thought that it might be easy to hide people there, too."

"They could be doing any number of illegal activities in such a remote location," Ryan agreed. Not the least of which was storing chemicals required to make a bomb.

"Looking back, I remember a distinct smell. At the time, I wrote it off as being an old building." Dylan maintained focus on the road ahead. He instructed Brody on making a few turns before saying, "We'll need to cut the lights and walk soon."

"Say the word and it's done," Brody said.

The road became bumpier as they traveled along the clay path. A mile or so later, Dylan gave the signal to stop.

Brody pulled off the road and parked.

"I brought one of these for each of us," Brody said, and then located three backpacks from the backseat. "Let's see what's in here." Dylan held his up.

"A knife for starters. We could spend hours debating which one is best, but I like a six- to eight-inch blade with a serrated edge on the back side for sawing," Brody said. "There's also a signal mirror and gloves. There again, I like something light that gives a good grip while protecting my skin."

"With the added benefit of us not leaving behind any fingerprints," Ryan added.

"To that end, there are hair nets, too," Brody said.

"Great, we'll be rockin' the lunch-lady look," Dylan teased.

"Afraid so." Brody laughed. "I didn't say we'd be pretty, but we won't leave anything behind, either. Dylan's the only one we want identified with the scene."

"Good point," Ryan agreed. That way, Dylan could direct the sheriff to the site where he'd been held captive and there'd be evidence to prove his story.

"I brought headgear with reflective strips on the back," Brody continued, securing his on his head. "We all have cells, which we're going to want to silence, but I also brought a light source and a map of the area in case we get separated. Let's grab those and circle the spot where the truck is."

Ryan did. He pulled up their location on his phone's

GPS, and then circled the corresponding spot on the printed map.

"I didn't figure we'd be out here long enough to need insect repellant," Brody said, folding his own map and securing it in his pack.

"I have to admit it. When you told me you'd pack for us, I was hesitant. We all have different ideas of what we think we might need on a mission," Dylan said with a chuckle. "But you did a good job."

Brody and Dylan had served in different branches of the military, and that meant each one thought the other wasn't doing it right in pretty much every situation, Ryan thought with a laugh. He was basically Switzerland. Working the land had taught him how to survive if he was ever stranded. Hunting had taught him what he needed to know about using a gun. He'd fine-tuned his ability to point, shoot and hit a target.

Ryan tucked the gun in the waistband of his jeans and then he secured his hair net.

"We think this is the facility I was taken to." Dylan pointed to a spot on the map that would be half an hour's hike at best. "I encountered three men who worked for Alcorn."

"With his resources he could afford an army of men watching the place. You have any intel about others?" Ryan asked.

"My technology guy hasn't been able to watch for long. I just found the place. Under normal circumstances, I'd watch and wait," Dylan said.

"There's too much at stake now and it's only a matter of time before they figure out a way to get to us," Ryan agreed.

"Bombing the funeral home was a bold move," Dylan said.

"Beckett's got it in for her. We all know he's the one behind this, especially after his visit. But he's smart enough not to get caught," Ryan hissed.

"Did the deputy ever say whether or not they had any suspects?" Dylan asked.

"None yet. Said they couldn't imagine who would do such a thing and especially at such an inappropriate time," Ryan said. "Can't say that I have a lot of confidence in them given the fact that Alcorn's been under their nose for how many years now and look what he's managed to get away with." He shouldered his pack. "We helped them find him before and they lost him after that."

"You think the sheriff's in on this?" Dylan asked.

Brody nodded. "Rebecca seems to think so. At the very least she believes he's looked the other way a few times."

"And you?" Ryan asked Brody.

"I got questions." Brody paused. "Like how do you let someone involved in kidnapping kids live right under your nose and not have the first clue?"

"Either he's being bribed to look the other way and has no idea or he's in on it," Ryan said.

"Maybe he's looking at his pension thinking he needs more when he retires, so he looks the other way for some of Alcorn's business dealings," Brody said.

"What I can't figure out is why now? If I'm Beckett, do I really want more attention on me and my family right now?" Ryan asked.

"Other than the fact that she could come forward and damage their name even more." Brody scratched his chin. "Public opinion has been split as to whether or not people believe Charles Alcorn capable of such an act. Lisa comes forward and brings charges against Beckett and people start thinking where there's smoke, there's fire."

"That was my first thought, too. And that's most likely the reason," Ryan said.

Dylan, who had been quietly contemplating the discussion so far, leaned forward. "She's a loose end."

That thought scared Ryan the most. "Meaning they won't stop until they've tied it off."

"Did you think there was any chance they'd stop?" Dylan asked calmly, his low voice carrying anger.

"Not really. I'd hoped we could end this without putting someone in a body bag. With their money, I doubt that's possible. They can reach her even from jail. It won't be enough."

"She could go into a program, take her sister and Grayson with her and disappear," Dylan said. "I had to consider all of Samantha's options when she was a target."

Ryan mumbled something that sounded like agreement, but the truth was that he couldn't think about never seeing Lisa again. It did all kinds of messed-up things to his emotions. Instead, he looked to Brody and then to Dylan. "Ready to do this?"

Chapter Fifteen

Dylan nodded at the same time as Brody, giving a thumbs up. Dylan took the lead once outside the truck while Brody and Ryan fell in step next to each other.

The walk through the thinly wooded area became easier as Ryan's eyes adjusted to the darkness. He'd first focused almost solely on the reflector on the back of Dylan's headband but now could see fairly well as he mentally prepared for a few scenarios that they might be walking into.

First, someone could be there guarding the place, making it impossible to get what they needed. It would be a whole lot easier if no one was there. They'd be able to walk right in and check it out without raising an eyebrow or alerting anyone to the fact that they knew the location of the warehouse.

After taking Dylan there, they might've cleared it of anything that could be incriminating. So this mission could be a colossal waste of time.

Feeling that he was leaving Lisa vulnerable didn't sit well with Ryan, either. He had to remind himself that she was fine and safe and that she'd be at Dylan's house sleeping, just as he'd left her, when he got back.

Dylan stopped. His fisted hand came up, so Brody

and Ryan followed suit. Then he crouched low. Ryan was beside him in a second.

Being back to this place must bring up bad feelings for him. Dylan and Brody had personal reasons for wanting the Mason Ridge Abductor put behind bars. Both of their lives and future wives had been affected by that jerk. Both had a stake in ensuring the right person was caught and put behind bars.

A man like Alcorn would be able to twist the legal system in his favor. And his son had grown up with the same entitlement. Ryan would see to it that Beckett paid for his crimes against Lisa. One way or the other, the score would be settled.

Where they crouched, the building was about fifty yards away. There were no lights on inside or around the building, casting an eerie dark glow to the windows. The place looked abandoned and like something out of a bad horror movie, and everything about being there had Ryan's danger radar on high alert.

The strategy for now would be to wait in order to make sure no one was visiting this place on rounds. There were no vehicles in the parking lot, but that didn't mean there wouldn't be any coming or that no one was inside. Ryan couldn't imagine anyone would be, but no one in his party, including him, was willing to take that chance.

A noise came from behind them and Ryan whirled around, ready to fight in a split second.

All three stilled, waited, listened.

An agonizing full minute later, a deer sprinted through the brush. And that really was the best of possible situations. This area was known for cougars and other dangerous animals, and the last thing they needed was a battle with Mother Nature to draw attention to their location.

Even though there were no vehicles parked, that didn't mean there was no one in the building. Someone could be inside right then, watching, waiting.

There were a number of things this building could be used for. None of them Ryan liked.

Crouched in the brush, he didn't want to think about all the manner of other dangerous wildlife he could be sitting next to at the moment. Aside from the usual varieties of venomous snakes and spiders, north Texas was host to other bigger creatures that could sneak up on them, like coyotes.

Ryan didn't even want to think about all those creepy crawlies slinking around on the ground under the canopy of leaves. He'd rather face something closer to his own size. His body involuntarily shuddered thinking about how much he hated spiders.

Lisa couldn't sleep and she didn't want to wake Lori and the baby, so she literally lay staring at the ceiling until she thought her brain might explode.

Nervous energy kept her heart pounding inside her chest. There was no way to contact Ryan or the guys to know if everything was okay. Her mind kept racing through worst-case scenarios.

Lisa canceled the negative thoughts, reminding herself worrying wouldn't do any good. She'd deal with whatever happened, even though not knowing was killing her.

She couldn't even begin to seriously consider the possibility that something could happen to any of them, and especially not Ryan, without pain stabbing her in the chest. She took in a deep breath and regrouped.

Thinking about everything that could go wrong wouldn't do any good. It wouldn't bring the guys back any sooner. And it would only cause Lisa to shred her stomach lining with worry.

"Are you thinking about him?" Lori whispered over Grayson, who lay sleeping soundly between them.

"Yes." Lisa would be lying if she said otherwise and she didn't want to lie to her sister.

"I miss him, too."

It was then that Lisa realized Lori was talking about their father and not Ryan. Of course their father would be on Lori's mind. Lisa hadn't forgotten him, either. He was always close to her thoughts and near her heart, and she had a moment of guilt for thinking about anything else.

Then again, she could only allow herself a few moments to think about her father before she had to focus on something else. Missing him was a cavern in her chest.

"You want me to make coffee?" Lisa asked.

"That would be nice." Lori eased away from Grayson and then positioned pillows on either side of him so he couldn't roll off the bed when she and Lisa moved.

Watching Lori with Grayson filled Lisa's heart with an emotion she couldn't quite put her finger on. It was a mix of love and fulfillment and something else. Longing?

Lisa hadn't given much thought to having children of her own. Her life was full between Lori, Grayson and the kids in her classes who felt like family. There was something magical about watching her kindergarteners successfully complete center activities or experience the joy of reading a book for the first time. The rewards of seeing those little eyes light up when children grasped a concept were as tangible today as they'd been when she first started teaching five years ago.

Lisa believed herself to be a good teacher, but was she mother material?

She let that thought rattle around while she made a fresh pot of coffee.

"You like him, don't you?" Lori padded into the kitchen.

"Yes." There was no use denying her feelings.

"Maybe when this is all over you two can spend some time together," Lori offered.

"It's complicated," Lisa said, handing her sister a mug.

"Yeah? Life's complicated, isn't it?"

"When did you get so philosophical?" Lisa teased.

"Having a baby changes your priorities, I guess." Lori shrugged and then took a sip.

Lisa motioned toward the kitchen table. She didn't turn on the light and neither did Lori.

"Remember when Dad would take us camping out by Lake Mason?" Lori asked.

"I do. He always said that you had to be made of tough stuff to camp in the summer in Texas," Lisa said.

"It would be so hot and we had those little plastic fans that squirted water to cool us off," Lori said with a smile.

"We'd stay up half the night pretending to be explorers in the African jungle," Lisa remembered.

"Discovering new lands. Watching out for lions," Lori added. "Looking back, don't you think it's kind of weird that neither one of us dreamed about being mothers?"

"I guess losing ours so early had an impact."

"Do you think about her?" Lori asked, her tone serious.

"Not as much as I should." Lisa paused. "Keeping an eye on you and Dad became a full-time job after she died."

"Thank you for that, by the way," Lori said.

"For what? We both did our fair share of watching over Dad."

"I wasn't talking about that. I was thinking about the way you've always taken care of me," Lori said.

"You would've done the same."

"Maybe. Who knows? You were a great big sis."

"If that was true, I would've been able to keep us together all the time," Lisa said. "How many times were we split up to live with relatives?"

"I didn't mind."

"Really?"

"I always knew you'd find me. I never worried about that because I had you," Lori said.

"Mom would be so proud of you with Grayson." Lisa needed to change the subject before the flood of tears released.

"If I'm a good mother to Grayson, it's because you showed me how to be," Lori said emphatically. "I don't mean any disrespect to our mother. I'm sure she was amazing. But you're the one who taught me how care for someone, how to put other people first."

Tears fell no matter how much Lisa tried to suppress them.

"But I wonder who takes care of you."

"Having you and Grayson is enough," Lisa said.

"You need more than just the two of us. I know you love your job, the kids, and I have no doubt about how much you love me and Grayson. But you need more than that. I love Grayson with all my heart, but I hope to go on a date someday, maybe meet someone who'll be a father to my son as well as a good husband to me. Someone who isn't freaked out at the thought of fatherhood and steps up for me and Grayson."

"I want that for the both of you, too," Lisa said.

"And what about for yourself?" Lori asked. "Do you ever think about sharing your life with someone else?"

"Honestly?"

Lori nodded.

"I've been too busy to think about it," Lisa said.

"Or maybe you just won't give yourself the time to," Lori countered.

Was that true? Maybe her sister had a point. For so many years Lisa had worried about making sure her baby sister was okay. And yet she was uncomfortable allowing anyone to care for her, even when she was hurt and couldn't care for herself. Frustration was written all over Ryan's face every time she forced him to sit instead of help her with something.

"I guess our upbringing taught me that if I wanted something done right I had to do it myself. I stopped relying on others," Lisa said, sipping her coffee.

"It's not a bad thing to be independent," Lori said sympathetically.

"It's hard for me to depend on anyone else, to give up that power."

"It's just that I think so many people have let you

down that you've forgotten that you *can* count on people."

Lisa thought about what her sister was saying, the truth in her words.

"When did you get to be so wise?" she asked.

"Believe me, you stay awake all night with a baby enough and you'll start contemplating the meaning of life, too." Lori laughed. She took another sip of coffee and then set her mug down. "It's different with Ryan."

"Is it?" Lisa asked, wondering if she'd ever be able to let her guard down enough to allow herself to truly rely on anyone else. Life lessons like the ones she'd learned didn't wipe away so easily on the blackboard of her psyche.

"He's a good guy."

"That much I know," Lisa responded. "I'm sure you thought Jessie was decent or you never would've gone out with him in the first place."

"Yeah, and I knew him for all of three months before I got pregnant. How much can you really know anyone in that short a time?" Lori said, twisting her mouth into a funny half smile. "Don't say I should've waited to get to know him better. I think I've already figured that one out the hard way. He was just so handsome and mysterious when he rolled through town to visit his cousin. I think I wanted something different than what I'd known my whole life, someone different than the guys in town. Boy, did I learn that something different isn't always something better!"

"So true." Lisa was still trying to sort out her feelings for Ryan, especially since they'd made love earlier, but she knew exactly what kind of person he was. It seemed that that should make her feelings for him easier to understand. When this was all over, maybe she could take some time to think about what he really meant to her. She didn't have to be back to school for a couple of weeks.

A dark thought hit her. Beckett would make sure she never returned to school or a normal life again.

For the first time, Lisa considered moving out of state. She could teach anywhere. Maybe even change her name?

No. That wouldn't work.

Not with Lori and Grayson here in Mason Ridge.

And a little piece of her heart didn't want to think about leaving Ryan, either.

"Everything is happening so fast. It's hard to know what to think anymore," Lori said.

"I was just thinking the same thing," Lisa replied. They were talking about different things, but the essential truth was the same. Life would never be the same.

Chapter Sixteen

"Let's go," Dylan said after they'd sat for forty-five minutes watching the warehouse.

The longer Ryan was away from Lisa, the more clenched his gut became. He didn't want to acknowledge all the reasons. Rather than climb on that hamster wheel again, he followed Dylan inside the building.

The air was still and it was dead quiet. He immediately smelled cleaning agents, which were common materials used in making bombs.

Inside was a long, open room. Metal bars kept the ceiling from caving in. On one end of the building was a door. All three men seemed to lock in on it at the same time. If anyone was there, they'd be inside that room.

Dylan and Brody flanked Ryan as he stalked toward it, careful not to make a sound.

There were containers shoved up against the walls and gallon jugs of rat poison. He glanced at a bucket filled with old cell phones and his immediate thought was that they could be used as remote devices used to activate detonators.

None of this was damning evidence unless he could tie the Alcorns to the building in some way. Charles

Alcorn would be smart enough to erase any paper trail leading back to him.

Ryan immediately noticed the rust on the door handle as he approached. There were two logical explanations. The first was the building's age. The second could be from chemicals used to make a bomb. They'd rust any metal nearby.

There were cords half-unraveled on the cement floor, too.

Definite signs of bomb activity.

Ryan tried the door and it was locked. He pulled out the knife Brody had packed in his rucksack. Since the doorknob was a simple push-button affair, all he had to do was jab a tiny blade into the hole and push on the locking mechanism.

He popped the lock easily and opened the door much to the wide-eyed stares of his buddies. Ryan didn't dare defend himself before he found out what was on the other side. Besides, he might be reliable Ryan but he'd had his share of reasons to pick a lock to get to his brother.

Palming his gun, he used it to lead the way inside.

The room was empty save for a wooden table that had been pushed to one side.

"The place is clear," Ryan said.

"I've been here before." Dylan focused on the table with a look of disgust. "I also saw wires out there and they tied off my head covering with something like that."

"I'm sure both of you noticed the supplies in the other room," Ryan said, leading the way back. "And the smell."

Brody stopped, his gaze locked on to something in the corner. He walked over, picked it up and held it up.

It was a toy race car.

"I don't like the look of that," Ryan said.

"Neither do I," Brody replied, setting it down gingerly in the same place. "There's so much they can do with forensics nowadays. Maybe they can lift something off it and identify the owner. Damn, that makes me think I should've left it alone."

"That's a good point. We shouldn't touch anything else we see," Ryan said. "Even though we're wearing gloves, we might smudge a print."

Dylan agreed.

They returned to the bigger room and pulled light sources out of their packs. The inside of the building was surprisingly free of graffiti, so it had been maintained or at the very least watched over by someone.

Bored teenagers generally knew every vacant building in the county because they were always looking for places to gather, drink and goof around. Another sign this place was under someone's protection.

"What's that smell?" Ryan asked.

"Could be this," Dylan held up an opened bottle of vinegar. "They have so many freakin' ways to make bombs in here. I think these are acetone and aluminum powder. Then there are these bags of sugar, nitric acid, potassium chlorate and nitrate. They've even got car batteries stacked over here."

"A good source of sulfuric acid," Ryan said. "These thermometers are a source of mercury. And this hydrogen peroxide is available at pretty much every store. One thing here and there and we have no case against the owner of this building. Put even a few together and this is worth law enforcement's time."

"How do we want to do this?" Brody said.

"We can call it in anonymously," Ryan said. "Use the tip line."

"I've got someone looking into this, as well," Dylan said. "Doesn't hurt to squeeze out whoever's involved by calling in the law."

"In the meantime, let's take pics of everything we see," Ryan said. There was dirt and sawdust on the floor. "We'll need to erase our footprints."

"You two shoot, I'll take care of our footprints," Brody said.

When they were done, they shut down their light sources and turned toward the door in time to see headlights, which almost immediately shut off.

"Spread out," Brody said.

Ryan moved near the door, behind a column so that no one could see him when they breached the entry.

He crouched low, ready to spring into action.

There were voices on the other side of the door. What was it? A police radio.

If the deputy or whoever was out there walked ten steps inside the door, he'd be face-to-face with Ryan.

He ran toward the back room. Dylan and Brody had the same idea because they both tore in the same direction.

They closed the door within seconds of the other being opened.

Dylan checked the window. "I hear two voices."

"We need to get the hell out of here. They catch us in here and we'll never be able to explain our way out of it," Brody said.

Following Dylan's lead, Ryan stealthily climbed onto the table that had been pushed against a wall. He could hear footsteps echoing louder on the concrete in the other room moving toward them.

Once the window was open, Ryan slipped out first, followed by the others.

They crouched down and belly-crawled toward the brush.

Once they found their original path, they broke into a full run and didn't stop until they were at Brody's truck again.

"What the hell was that?" Ryan asked.

"Someone must've beaten us to reporting that place to the deputy," Dylan said.

"But why? It makes no sense," Ryan said. "Unless… they wanted us to get caught. What better way to accuse us of being involved than to have us caught red-handed with bomb material?"

"You're right," Brody said. "The question is how did they know we were there in the first place?"

"It must be wired." Ryan took his seat on the passenger side after Dylan and closed the door.

"My tech guy didn't detect anything," Dylan said. "Then again, there are lots of new toys out there that can fly under the radar and we didn't have time to properly screen the location."

With Alcorn's money, Ryan figured only the best would do. And he also realized they'd walked right into a trap.

If someone in Alcorn's camp knew about them visiting this site, then Lisa might be in danger. Dammit.

"We need to get back," he said to Brody.

"I thought of that, too," Brody said. "I'm on it."

As long as Beckett Alcorn was free, none of their friends were truly safe.

Pulling into the gravel drive more than half an hour later, Ryan felt his heart sink to his toes when he saw a cruiser parked out front.

As soon as the truck stopped, he bolted for the front door.

Lisa was already coming outside, followed by Deputy Adams.

"What's going on?" Ryan asked.

She got close enough for him to see the absolute panic in her eyes.

"Ryan Hunt, I'd like you to accompany me to the station for questioning," Adams said.

"What are you talking about?" Ryan asked. What on earth could Adams want to ask him at the station that he couldn't ask right there?

Lisa's expression was complete panic by this point. "I tried to text you, but he asked me not to. He won't say what's going on."

"Don't I have a right to know why you want me to go with you?" Ryan asked, not wanting to leave Lisa alone for even a few hours.

"Like I said, I have questions." Adams was looking at Ryan as if he'd finally gotten one of the Hunt boys on a criminal charge. Ryan didn't like it one bit, and this was coming out of left field. "If you're refusing to cooperate, I can make the next visit more official."

Was that a threat?

"I'll keep an eye on things here, Ryan," Dylan offered.

Brody said he wasn't leaving until Ryan returned, as well.

At least he could count on them to take care of Lisa, her sister and Grayson until he could figure out what the hell was going on with Adams.

"Fine," he said to the deputy. "I'll go with you."

Sheer panic crossed Lisa's features. "Can I come, too?"

"That's not a good idea," Adams said.

So whatever he wanted to say to Ryan couldn't be said in front of her?

Ryan didn't like any of this a bit. It was one thing for the sheriff to look the other way and allow Alcorn free rein on the town. It was entirely something else if he knew and was pocketing money. But this screamed that Ryan's rights were about to be violated, and no Texan was about to put up with that, least of all Ryan.

He followed the deputy to the SUV and started toward the passenger side.

Adams opened the back door instead.

FROM THE SECOND the cruiser had pulled up, Lisa's panic alert had been firing on high. Never in her wildest imagination would she have figured what would come next. When Deputy Adams asked about Ryan's whereabouts, she'd been confused. Now that he was being taken in for questioning, she was flabbergasted.

"I don't like any of this," Dylan said as he ushered her inside.

Brody followed suit, sending a text to Rebecca to let her know that everything was okay in case she woke up looking for him.

Dylan pulled mugs from the cabinet and filled them with fresh coffee.

"The kids will be awake soon," he said. "I'll call in Mrs. Anderson today to help out with Maribel."

"Is it too early to call Justin?" Lisa asked.

"You sure you want him in the middle of this?" Dylan asked as a look passed between him and Brody.

"He deserves to know what's going on with his brother," she said.

"You're right. It's just that there isn't much he can do, and coming back might make matters worse for Ryan," Dylan said.

"I didn't realize that," she said.

"We all know how much the sheriff disliked Justin and I don't want to prejudice anyone else around town."

"He's not that person anymore. And it wasn't his fault when he was," she countered. "It was their father."

Dylan gave her a look and she knew exactly what he was thinking, but she couldn't let a sleeping dog lie. "He might be able to help."

Lori shuffled into the kitchen with Grayson on her hip. "He's hungry."

Lisa held Grayson while Lori mashed a banana. "You want me to feed him?"

"No, thanks. Taking care of him keeps my mind off things," Lori said.

Lisa knew exactly what her sister meant. She didn't know what to do with her hands when Lori took Grayson back.

"What else can we do?" Lisa asked.

"I need to make a few calls to find a good lawyer," Dylan said. "Until then, there isn't much."

That was about the most frustrating thing Lisa had heard tonight.

Dylan excused himself to the office out back as Samantha entered the kitchen.

"Any news?" Samantha asked.

"Nothing, I'm afraid. I just keep wondering what on earth they could think they're going to accomplish," Lisa said.

Brody finished his mug of coffee and set it on the table. "Alcorn has been after the Hunt family for years. He might be targeting Ryan, trying to make it seem like he's doing something illegal. We know the truth about him. That's what matters right now. Until we know what accusations we're dealing with, we can't mount a defense."

"So, what until then?" she asked as Samantha put her arm around Lisa's shoulders.

"We wait," Brody said.

Three excruciating hours later, Dylan walked into the house.

Lisa had been folding clothes with Samantha when she heard the back door open. She raced to the kitchen.

"What have you found out?" she asked.

"He's still being questioned. They're not finished with him yet according to Stern, his new attorney," Dylan said.

"Questioned for what?" she asked.

"Apparently, his family owns the land we visited last night," Dylan said, his tone ominous.

"What does that mean?"

"We found a warehouse full of supplies that could be used to make a few kinds of bombs," Dylan said. "Sheriff's office is saying the supplies match the material used in the one at the funeral home."

"How could he have planted a bomb there? He was with us, for heaven's sake."

"I know it. You know it. About time the sheriff's office figured it out, too," he said.

"Is that the same warehouse you were taken to?" Samantha asked, entering the room behind Lisa.

He nodded.

"That's not possible," Lisa said. "No way could he own that land. I should think he'd know about something like that."

"Not necessarily. His brother might know. They inherited it after their father died," Dylan said.

"Then we have to speak to Justin," Lisa said. "Don't stop me this time. I'm calling him right now."

She retrieved her phone. When she returned to the kitchen, Dylan was holding out a slip of paper.

"What is that?" she asked.

"Justin's phone number."

Oh. Dylan wanted her to call. Good.

"He's the executor of their father's estate. He'd know about the land. I want you to talk to him. It'll be better coming from someone like you, less suspicious," Dylan said.

She called the number.

Justin picked up on the first ring. After reminding him who she was, she asked about the land.

"It belongs to us," he said. "Why?"

"Does Ryan know?" she asked.

"I guess not."

She shook her head to let Dylan know, too.

"How come?" she asked.

"Because he didn't want anything to do with whatever Dad left behind. Said nothing good could ever come of anything connected to that man," Justin said.

Ryan had that right.

"So he never knew about the land?" she asked again.

"I never told him. After our dad died, Ryan refused to come to the reading of the will. I tried to talk to him about it a few times, but he wouldn't have anything to do with the conversation. Refused to open any mail, either."

"And what about your mother? Does she know about the land?" she hedged, following a hunch.

"I called to get her opinion," Justin said. "Do me a favor, don't tell Ryan."

"Why not?"

"He said he washed his hands of the whole situation after she walked out."

"Did she? Walk out?" she asked, unable to stop herself. "I'd heard there was more to it than that."

"I'd say. The day she left he'd beaten her within an inch of her life. She had a relative pick her up when he left to go to work and she disappeared to save her life."

"But she never tried to get in touch with you two," she pushed.

"No. For years she believed he'd find out."

"Sounds like she was scared."

"You have to understand. He broke her ribs, bashed in her face. She almost didn't make it," he said defensively as though he'd been preparing her defense for years.

Maybe he had.

"I understand. I always believed it was something more than her just turning her back on her kids."

"Much more. She wanted to come back for us, but

she was scared to death he'd track us down and kill all three of us. The only way she could ensure our safety was to leave and not try to contact us," he said. "What did you say was going on with my brother?"

"He's been taken in for questioning," she said.

"For what?" Justin sounded as shocked as she still felt.

"Turns out someone's been making bombs on your land."

"Does this have anything to do with the incident at the funeral parlor the other day?" he asked, and then it seemed to really dawn on him who she was. "That was your father."

"Yes."

"I'm really sorry to hear about that. He was a nice man."

"Thank you." Lisa was shocked to hear anyone talk about her father fondly. Most of the town seemed to want to forget he existed. "Do you mind if I ask when you first contacted your mother?"

"I hired a PI a few years ago, five to be exact. I needed to know what had happened to her and I wanted her to be able to meet her grandchild if she was interested," he said.

"And you didn't tell Ryan?"

"No. He'd been through so much and he wasn't ready to forgive her for the past. I've thought about telling him a thousand times. Every time I mention anything about her, he shuts down the conversation. I wish he would talk to her." The anguish in his voice was palpable.

"Me, too."

"It would be good for him, right?"

"I think so," Lisa said.

"Maybe you can talk to him, then," Justin said. "He sure doesn't want to hear it from me."

"Anything else about that land?" she asked.

"Charles Alcorn contacted me to buy it a few years ago."

"And?"

"I told him no dice. First of all, I can't sell it without Ryan's signature. Second, my father refused to sell that man anything."

"Is this the piece of property Alcorn had tried to buy from your father years ago?" she asked.

"It has to be. It's the only land my father ever owned. He inherited it from our grandfather, so he wanted to keep it in the family." Justin paused. "With a family now, I could sure use the money if it sold. It's not doing anything but sitting there. Apparently being used for illegal activity. Speaking of which, no way has my brother done anything wrong. He's the most stand-up guy I know."

"He is. I'm sure all this will be cleared up soon."

"I can come today if you think it'll help," Justin offered.

"No. Stay with your wife. I hear she's expecting any day now," Lisa said.

"She is. And that's important. Believe me, I want to be here for her, but I wouldn't have anything if it weren't for my brother. I can be on the next plane—"

"How about this? I promise to keep you informed. If anything else develops I'll call you and you can still grab the next flight out," she said.

A heavy sigh came across the line and she could tell how conflicted he was.

"Okay. Fine. If you promise to keep me up to date, I'll monitor the situation from here."

Lisa thanked Justin for the information and promised she'd mention the land to Ryan as soon as the dust settled. In the meantime, she said that she'd keep Justin in the loop every step of the way.

"Everybody knows that my brother is a good guy," Justin said again. "I can't believe anyone would suspect him of doing something illegal."

"It came as a shock to all of us," she said. "We're doing everything we can to get this straightened out."

"If you need any paperwork about the land, just let me know." Justin paused. "I'm more than happy to testify that Ryan didn't even know that land was ours."

"I'll make sure his lawyer knows," she said before thanking him one more time. "Would you mind texting me your mother's number? I'd like to give it to Ryan."

He agreed before they ended the call.

"I think I have a pretty good handle on the conversation," Dylan said. "I need to call Ryan's lawyer and give him the update. I don't think he's going to like the fact that Justin knew they owned the land."

"Hold on a sec," she said. "Didn't the feud between Alcorn and Ryan's dad happen because Alcorn couldn't get that land? Makes you wonder why he was so set on getting it in the first place, doesn't it?"

"I'll dig around and see if I can find anything there." Dylan poured himself another cup of coffee to take out to his office with him. "Stay inside and let's keep the doors locked. Call if you need anything."

"Okay." She didn't want to say that she knew why he'd make such a request. Because with Ryan temporarily out of the picture, Beckett could plan an attack.

"Mrs. Anderson took Maribel to the playground. Said she'd bring her back in time for lunch."

He nodded as he left, locking the door behind him.

"It'll all work out," Samantha reassured her. "Look at us. I never would've thought in a million years that I'd be planning a wedding with Dylan and becoming someone's mom all at the same time. Especially after what happened. These guys are tough. If it wasn't for Ryan's help, we never would've gotten to Alcorn in the first place."

Lisa thought about another reason Alcorn might target Ryan.

"Maybe he wants revenge."

Chapter Seventeen

Ryan had answered the same half dozen questions until he thought his brains might fall out. "I've already told you everything I know."

"Then, where were you with your friends out in the middle of the night?" Deputy Adams asked.

"We were scouting places to set up camp for hog hunting," Ryan said. Again.

With the deputy's sour look, Ryan was about to lose it.

"Are you planning to arrest me?" he finally asked.

"I didn't say that exactly."

"Then, if you don't start asking different questions I'm going home." Ryan made a move to get up.

The deputy's hand came up to stop him.

"Home to your property?" Adams asked.

"I already told you that I don't own any property other than the land my house sits on."

"I've got a deed here that says otherwise." He waved the piece of paper in front of Ryan's face. Again.

Wave it one more time and see what happens, Ryan thought bitterly. He was tired, worried about Lisa, and being separated from her was making him cranky.

The deputy had better get on with it if he knew what was good for him.

"I'm Mr. Hunt's attorney. I'd like a moment alone with my client." Higby Stern's face popped into the room.

Now this really was getting interesting. Dylan must've hired him.

The deputy looked none too thrilled to see Stern. And that made Ryan like the man even more.

Stern was five foot eleven, middle-aged and with a body that looked as though he stayed on top of his game at the gym. He was the best lawyer in town, heck, in the whole county. Ryan didn't think about calling, because he didn't think he needed an attorney.

He guessed Dylan felt otherwise.

He was probably right.

The system didn't always work. Innocent people went to jail. Ryan had read about several cases.

"Fine," Adams relented. He stood, gave a stern look toward Ryan and closed the door behind him.

"I already know you're not a terrorist, so let's get you out of here so we can talk about your case." Stern wasted no time. "They don't have any real evidence against you, so my guess is that they're hoping you'll confess. What have you told them so far?"

"I had no idea I owned the land. I still think they're sipping some crazy tea on that one for starters," Ryan said.

"Is there another party involved or are you the sole owner?" Stern already had a notebook out and he was scribbling notes.

"According to the deed, I'm co-owner with my brother." Ryan didn't like the way Stern's eyebrow went up. "Don't get too excited. He doesn't even live in town. He got out of here a long time ago. He's a family man and sure as hell isn't a terrorist."

"The sheriff's office is asserting that the materials found in the warehouse on your land are consistent with the bomb at the funeral home," Stern said.

"I'm not surprised." Ryan was about to punch a wall.

Stern's eyebrow went up.

"Not because I know what the bomb was made out of, but because I was at the funeral. Beckett Alcorn dropped by with a few of his henchmen. Not twenty minutes later a bomb exploded. Almost killing me, by the way. You really think I'd be stupid enough to kill myself or my friends?"

"I didn't say you were," Stern said quickly. "I have to know the answers to these questions so I can speak on your behalf. I don't trust any one of the Alcorns and not just because of this latest round of accusations against them. I know how they operate." The look of disdain on his dark features said more than enough. "I also know they hire the best. Alcorn has already managed to find a way to get out on bail. Word on the street is that he wasn't even in town during the kidnappings fifteen years ago and can prove it."

"Why didn't he come forward before?"

"Says he was having an affair and didn't want to ruin his marriage. He's provided an ironclad alibi. His wife is standing by him, of course."

"I would expect nothing less from a woman like her," Ryan interjected. "Her son is a scumbag who deserves to be locked away forever."

"You won't get an argument out of me on that," Stern said. "My job is to get you out of here and keep you out. It's clear to me that you've gotten on the bad side of a family with the power to squash just about anything or anyone they want. How did you get yourself in such a position?"

"Good question." Ryan didn't think it was his place to say what Beckett had done to Lisa. "Suffice it to say I'm taking care of someone Beckett is trying to erase."

"I take it this someone is a woman."

"Yes."

"Has she filed charges against him?"

"Afraid not." Ryan shook his head. "He's after her because of something that he did to her a long time ago."

Stern seemed to catch the undertone of what Ryan was saying. He nodded with a sympathetic look and made a couple more notes, mumbling something that sounded a lot like the word *bastard* under his breath.

Ryan liked Stern even more.

"Are they planning on arresting me?" Ryan asked.

"They haven't yet. And that's good. My guess is they were trying to sweat you. Get you to tell them something they could use. Doesn't sound like you fell for it."

Ryan shook his head. "Can't say what you don't know. When it comes to that property, I honestly had no idea what they were talking about."

He had every intention of calling his brother to find out as soon as he got the heck out of there and made sure Lisa was safe.

"I'll want to launch my own investigation into your case," Stern said.

"Be my guest. You let me know if you need anything from me to get started."

"Let me see about getting you home." Stern stood and extended his hand.

Ryan shook it, sizing Stern up one last time. He had that honest but tough look about him. He'd have a jury eating out of his hands with his sharp wit and good-old-fashioned looks.

"I'll be back in a few minutes. Hang tight, okay?" Stern winked before walking out the door. His dark jeans and button-down shirt gave him a surprisingly professional look. He carried himself well and that would come in handy should a trial become necessary.

Damn. Ryan still hadn't figured out when and how he'd gotten himself pinned with a possible terrorist charge.

The door opened and Stern filed in, flashing a quick smile at Ryan, with the deputy close behind him.

"You're free to go," Adams said. "Contact this office if you plan to leave town any time soon."

Ryan agreed.

The sun hit him in the face full force as he followed Stern to the parking lot.

"You need a ride?" Stern asked. "We can talk a little more about our next move on the way."

"Sure." Stern seemed to have personal feelings toward the Alcorns. Ryan wanted to know more about that.

"Dylan asked me to tell you that Lisa is fine. He and Brody have been at the house the whole time," Stern said as they secured their seat belts.

That Ryan felt relief was an understatement. He needed to talk to Lisa to tell her how he really felt about her. He had no idea if she would be game for giving a relationship with him a go, but he had no plans to go to his grave without finding out. The only thing he knew for certain was that he loved her. And maybe that was all he needed to know for now.

But there was something else on his mind that he needed to address with Stern.

"Can I ask you a personal question?"

"Yes."

"During our earlier discussion, I picked up on the fact that you have strong feelings toward the Alcorns in general but Beckett more specifically. Why?"

"Other than the fact that early in my career his father's lawyers used to eat me for breakfast?" Stern said, and Ryan appreciated the honesty.

"Yeah. This feels deeper than that."

"You don't know many good lawyers, then, do you?" Stern said. "We build our business on our reputation. We build our reputation off winning cases. Alcorn's attorneys never played fair. I'm honest. I believe in justice, in the law, in the system. You should know that about me up front."

"Good. Then it sounds like we'll get along just fine," Ryan said, and meant it.

"But you're a good judge of body language. I have personal reasons for not liking that family."

Ryan waited for Stern to decide if he was going to share more than that.

"There was an incident with my niece about five years ago." Stern stopped long enough to navigate his sedan onto the highway. "She never would discuss the details with her family or with me."

"Do you mind if I ask her age?" This sounded all too familiar. Ryan fisted his hands at the thought of any little girl being hurt by Beckett.

"She's eighteen now, getting ready to start her first

semester at Duke, but she was thirteen at the time. The only thing we know for certain is that she went to a birthday sleepover at her girlfriend's house. She came back the next morning traumatized. All we could get out of her was that her friend's much older stepbrother had a few friends over that night. She was terrified to talk about it. She'd called her mother to pick her up at six o'clock the next morning. At first, it didn't register with my sister that anything sexual could've happened. My niece was shy and she'd tried a few sleepovers in the past only to call her mom to have her pick her up early."

"And you know for sure Beckett was there?" Ryan asked.

"I can't prove it and she won't talk. My sister didn't think we should press the issue. I disagreed then and I still do. But I do understand that she was trying to do what she thought was best for her daughter by giving her time and space to speak up about it. Carolina never did. She just retreated from her friends and didn't want to leave the house for weeks."

"So how do you know he was involved?" Ryan asked.

"Every time my niece was within earshot of his voice, she tensed up. It took me two years to finally fit the pieces together. I went to my sister with what I believed to be true. Carolina was doing better and my sister didn't want to dredge up the past by forcing her to talk about it," he said. "I didn't agree with the decision. I'm convinced Katy was in denial that something horrible could've happened to her daughter on her watch. We had terrific parents and Katy always had a hard time feeling like she measured up."

His voice had a wistful quality to it.

"You think your sister would let me talk to Carolina now?" Ryan asked.

"I doubt it. However, I might be able to arrange something if you give me more to go on."

"Your niece isn't alone. He's done this before. I suspect there are many others, too," Ryan said, trying to keep his voice steady through the anger. "One of my friends was a victim of his when she was twelve. That bastard can't be allowed to prey on girls."

"My niece most likely won't talk to you about what happened," Stern said. "I wish she'd speak to someone. It isn't healthy for her to hold this inside."

Ryan wondered if he could ask Lisa to speak to her. The young woman might be more comfortable speaking to another woman. "There might be another way to come at this."

"I appreciate your concern and I would like to see all of the Alcorns behind bars. Right now, though, I've got to focus on keeping you out of jail. You can't help anyone there."

True.

"How bad does it look for me?"

"Right now? It's not that horrible. But they're trying to put together a case against you and I don't like that one bit. This tells me that they're listening to someone else and I believe that someone is Charles Alcorn."

"With enough money, I guess you can get away with just about anything." Ryan didn't mask his contempt. "We're almost there. You're going to want to take a right onto that gravel road."

"It's my job to prove you had no prior knowledge of owning the property. Have you been there?" Stern cut the wheel and turned.

Ryan didn't immediately answer.

"Let me ask that question another way, then. Will investigators find any traces of your DNA on the scene?"

"No," Ryan said emphatically. Although he couldn't guarantee someone wouldn't place his DNA there or lie about it.

"Good. It'll be tempting to go there. Don't."

"Not a problem."

"They'll mark the place off as a crime scene, anyway. Then they're going to try to link you to the scene while they're proving that the bomb at the funeral home came from the materials there." Stern parked the sedan.

Lisa bolted out the door as the two men exited the vehicle.

Dylan was already on his way to greet them from his office out back.

"Thank heavens you're okay," she said to Ryan.

He introduced her to Stern.

Then, not really caring who was watching, Ryan hauled her against his chest and pulled her in close. "I'm here. I promise that I'm not going anywhere. We have a lot to talk about when this is over."

He kissed her, a quick peck on the lips. He couldn't help himself. She felt like home and he had every intention of telling her. They could decide what to do from there.

Now was not the time. Besides, his situation didn't look promising. After talking to Stern, Ryan realized how easy it would be for a tainted deputy or the sheriff to plant evidence linking him to the scene. If Alcorn could see to it that Ryan spent some time behind bars, it would be easier to get to Lisa. All he'd have to do would be to create another "accident."

It looked as though Charles Alcorn was going to walk. That family was about to get away with another crime.

"I'll be in the house in a minute. Think you can rest?" Clearly, she hadn't slept all night.

She nodded. She had to be dead on her feet by now.

"Good. I'll be in shortly." He hugged her one more time before heading to Dylan's office, where he waited with Stern.

It didn't take long to update Dylan. Stern excused himself and left to work on the details of the investigation.

"I'm not taking any chances. I called in a few favors, brought in extra security. We've dealt with these jerks before and we know how dangerous they are," Dylan said. "This place is fortified as long as we need it to be."

"We're going to have another helluva fight on our hands," Ryan said. "I can't guarantee that they won't find DNA at the warehouse."

"It's a good thing the deputy didn't ask to search Brody's vehicle. We would've had a hard time explaining the contents of those backpacks." Dylan leaned back in his chair.

"Damn right."

"What's next?" Dylan asked.

"That's a good question. They have us on the defensive and that was a smart move," Ryan said. "I might be able to dig up some dirt on Beckett that could create a stir. We keep backing him into a wall and he's going to make a mistake."

"With you under investigation and everyone at the sheriff's office aware of our friendship, I won't get any insider information on this case," Dylan said.

"Might be best to limit our interactions with that department for now, anyway." Ryan thought about taking Lisa, Lori and Grayson to the fishing cabin to hide out. Dylan's place was really the best spot to lie low while they figured out their next move.

"I'm going to try to get some sleep." Ryan bit back a yawn. "I can hardly think straight anymore."

"I was going to tell you that you looked like a sailor who'd been at sea for a month caught in a storm," Dylan teased.

It was good to keep a sense of humor.

Ryan slipped in the back door and down the hallway. All he wanted to do was make a beeline for the bed and he hoped like hell that Lisa was there waiting. Thoughts of pulling her body against his, holding her until he fell asleep, stirred more than a sexual reaction. Being with Lisa was like going home—and that was a foreign feeling at best.

Talking to her was easy, and so much of the crazy world seemed right when they were together.

Ryan figured they could build on that feeling and create something truly special. If she'd allow it.

As he neared the door, he heard her voice. She was on a phone call.

He should've just gone straight in and alerted her to the fact that he was there, but he stopped at the door instead.

And that was a big mistake.

Because the sense of betrayal stabbing him in the gut when he realized she was talking to his mother nearly knocked him over. He backed down the hall, mind reeling. Lisa might feel like home, but since when had he ever trusted anything or anyone at home?

Chapter Eighteen

What could be taking Ryan so long? Lisa threw off the covers and went out to search for him. She was surprised to find him sleeping on the oversize chair in the living room. He looked uncomfortable with his neck held awkwardly to one side. He was too big for the space and she thought about waking him and sending him to bed.

But why had he chosen the chair over her?

She decided to let him sleep and moved into the kitchen to find caffeine and food.

The refrigerator door had barely opened when the back door flew open and Dylan burst inside.

"We gotta get you guys out of here. Where's Ryan?"

"What's going on?" Lisa asked, but Ryan was already next to her.

"Who all needs to go?" he asked.

"Lori and the baby will stay here with Samantha and Brody. I have to get you two out of here. My contact called to say that the deputy is on his way."

It didn't take two minutes for the three of them to grab their cell phones and jump into Dylan's vehicle.

Dylan fired up the engine and gravel spewed underneath his tires as he hightailed it out of there.

He called Stern and put him on speaker.

"They'd need a warrant to track you using your phones, but as soon as this call is over, turn them off just in case," Stern said. "Is there any reason we wouldn't want them to get a hold of your cell?"

Lisa's heart pounded painfully against her ribs and she desperately wanted to ask Ryan why he'd done a one-eighty on her.

"There might be," Ryan said.

"Then get rid of them completely. Make sure no one can get to them again. Are we clear?" Stern asked.

"We are," Ryan said. He was already pulling the battery out of his. He located pliers in the backseat of the vehicle and shredded the SIM card in his phone.

"Do you save any of your data to a cloud or a source that can be subpoenaed?"

Ryan cracked a smile and she immediately knew why. This was one time his being a non-techy would pay off.

"Nope."

Dylan swerved. The crack of a bullet split the air.

"Dammit. We've been set up," Dylan said, muttering another stronger curse. "There's a vehicle coming up from behind and he's about to hit us."

Dylan delivered a few evasive maneuvers, but the other vehicle kept pace, hitting the bumper and knocking them forward several times.

"Can you give me the license plate of the vehicle charging you?" Stern asked.

Ryan spun around and read off the tags.

"I'll report this to the deputy. Keep me on the line. I'll use my landline to make the call."

Ryan's arm was around Lisa, but she knew that it

was only to offer another layer of protection to guard her from a bullet or keep her head from snapping back when Dylan hit the brakes.

"I finally figured it all out. The pieces didn't make sense before, especially when Alcorn provided an alibi. All evidence keeps leading back to Alcorn, and that's on purpose. He's protecting Beckett," Ryan said, venom in his tone. "His father has been covering for him all along and that's why they'll never be able to nail Alcorn. He isn't involved. He's there to cover up for his son. His alibi will hold. Linking Beckett to the case is going to be next to impossible. Turn this thing around. Take me to Beckett."

Dylan shot a look at Ryan as if he were crazy. Lisa had the same thought.

"It's not going to end," Ryan said. "Don't you see? He'll keep coming at her. This will never be over."

"Hold on. Not if I can help it," Stern said. "Don't do anything rash. It'll only make matters worse."

"That man hurt your niece, right?" Ryan asked.

Lisa was horrified. It had never occurred to Lisa that Beckett had been hurting other girls. It was time to end this once and for all. "Is it too late to tell my story? To bring charges?"

Ryan looked at her with shock.

"Hold on, people," Dylan said as he spun the wheel.

He was too late. The Escalade slammed into the side of him, sending them spiraling into the ditch. There was a small dip that the tire must've caught on, because the next thing Lisa knew they were spinning.

They landed upright; however, the airbags had deployed and it took Lisa a few seconds to shake off the shock of being alive. Was anyone hurt?

A cut on Dylan's forehead was gushing blood. Ryan was already maneuvering out of his seat belt, looking dazed, as well.

"We're okay," she said to everyone.

Stern didn't respond. They'd lost their phone connection with him. How would he know where to send the police? Now she understood why he'd had Dylan call out street names.

Maybe the law would get to them in time.

The passenger-side door opened and Lisa felt herself being yanked out.

Beckett.

She let out a yelp that could be heard two counties away. All the anger that had been building for fifteen years exploded inside her. She was no longer an innocent twelve-year-old girl. Lisa was a grown woman who could fight back. And she had every intention of doing so.

His grip on her arm sent pain shooting down her limbs.

She twisted and dropped to the ground, breaking his grasp. She slammed her fist into his groin on the way down and then he was the one on his knees, gasping for a breath.

"See how that feels?" She threw another punch, scrambling to her knees, but it was intercepted this time.

"You just won't die." Beckett knocked her the rest of the way to the ground. She had to give it to him, he was strong. But she was just as strong. She'd survived him twice and this time he was the one going down.

Before she could regroup, he had a handful of her hair and was dragging her toward his vehicle.

Dylan and Ryan had enough to deal with. They were

being double-teamed by men who were the size of line-backers.

No way did this bastard get to win. Lisa struggled for purchase on the ground and couldn't get any. She broke free from his grasp and he spun around to face her. She curled up, twisting and thrusting her feet at him. Her foot connected with his knee. He stumbled, but it wasn't enough to take him down. She kicked a second time, harder.

With curled firsts, she jabbed at his arms and kicked with every bit of strength she possessed. She pounded him for everything he'd done to the little girl inside her.

Well, that girl had grown and could no longer be hurt by him. She realized he only had the power over her that she was willing to give him.

And he didn't get to hurt her anymore.

He managed to pull her to her feet.

Lisa fought against him as he tried to stuff her into his vehicle. He cursed and dropped her when she delivered another blow to his manhood.

Her head smacked against the vehicle, an explosion of pain in her brain followed, but she no longer cared what happened to her physically. She fought, anyway.

Just as Beckett was about to deliver a blow to her head with the butt of a gun, Ryan came out of nowhere and dove on top of him, knocking him away from her.

Sirens split the air.

Ryan fought Beckett as Lisa struggled to stay conscious.

The deputies surrounded them, ordering everyone to drop their weapons.

Ryan, hands up, backed away from Beckett.

The last thing Lisa saw before everything went black

was Beckett's arms being thrust behind his back and his wrists being cuffed as he spewed swear words at the deputy.

LISA WOKE IN the hospital and immediately asked for Ryan.

"He never leaves," Lori said. "He just sits in the hallway close to your room. But he knows that you reached out to his mother."

"Is Beckett in jail?" Lisa asked.

"Whole town says the judge is going to throw away the key to his cell. He'll spend the rest of his life behind bars just like he deserves."

Lisa took a minute to contemplate that thought. It was over. It was finally over. She looked at her sister. "Will you ask Ryan to come in, please?"

Lori, tentative, did as told.

She didn't come back inside the room with Ryan. He didn't come all the way in, either. He just stood at the door, his frame blocking out the light from the other side.

"I'm sorry I went behind your back, Ryan. I'd change it if I could. I can't. This is me. I make a mess out of things sometimes, but you should know that I have never loved anyone the way that I love you," Lisa said.

"I can put up with not being perfect. Hell, I'm the poster child for messing up," he said, and a flicker of hope lit inside her chest. "There's only one thing I can't live with, and that's dishonesty. If you go behind my back, how will I ever be able to trust you?"

That spark of hope died as he turned away from her.

"You shouldn't have lied." With that, he walked away. Lisa rolled onto her side, pulled up the covers and cried. She'd blown it and she knew Ryan well enough to know he'd never be able to look at her in the same way again.

THE RIDE HOME was silent. Lisa was spent. Lori had taken the day off work and left Grayson with Brody and Rebecca.

"You look so much better," Lori said as she pulled onto the parking pad in front of Lisa's two-bedroom bungalow.

"It's good to be home." The words were empty, but Lisa didn't want anyone else to know just how much she was hurting inside.

"Hold on because I'm going to help you out." Lori parked, hopped out of the sedan and ran to Lisa's side.

If anything good came out of this, it was that Lisa could finally let others help her without feeling that she was doing something wrong.

It took twenty minutes to get Lisa settled, but being in her own bed again felt like heaven on earth. How long had it been? *Too long.*

Traveling home exhausted her. She asked for a pain pill and settled under the duvet.

Lori disappeared into the other room.

"Hope I'm not too late," Ryan said as he walked into her bedroom, chewing on a toothpick.

She blinked to make sure she wasn't dreaming.

"May I?" He motioned toward the bed. He had a tray in his hands with a glass of water and a couple of pills. He looked to be in pure agony.

She nodded, trying to ignore the rejoicing in her heart at seeing him again.

She took the pills, swallowed them and chased them with water.

"Do you believe in second chances?" He set down the tray and then threw away his toothpick.

"I do." Tears were already streaming down her cheeks.

"I messed this up once already. Can you forgive me?" He brushed a kiss on her lips.

She nodded.

"Will you let me stay and take care of you?"

"Yes."

"I don't mean for a few days. I mean forever." He caught her gaze and held it. "I love you, Lisa Moore. You're home to me. And I'm lost without you."

All Lisa could do in return was take his hand. He lifted hers to his lips and kissed her fingertips.

"You already know I love you, Ryan."

"Then once you're well, I have every intention of asking you to marry me."

"And I have every intention of saying yes."

Epilogue

The heel of Ryan's boots clacked against the narrow wood porch. He opened the screen door that looked as though it had seen one too many rainstorms. It was rusty and banged up, most likely from a hailstorm.

A moment of panic had him turning to look at Lisa for reinforcements.

He'd waited until she was well enough to travel to make the trip.

Her reassuring smile gave him the strength to do what he'd been wanting to do for a long time. It was time to see his mother.

They'd talked on the phone a few times and he finally understood how much she loved her sons.

That first call was the hardest to make. Forgiving her for leaving had turned out to be the easy part.

And now he wanted his whole family together.

* * * * *

*Don't miss TEXAN'S BABY,
the final book in Barb Han's
MASON RIDGE miniseries,
when it goes on sale next month
wherever Harlequin Intrigue books
and ebooks are sold!*

WHAT HAPPENS ON THE RANCH

USA TODAY Bestselling Author

DELORES FOSSEN

Chapter One

Anna McCord figured she had committed a couple of sins, maybe even broken a few laws, just by looking at the guy in the bed. He was naked, so it was hard not to have dirty thoughts about him.

Drool, too.

Mercy, he was hot.

Thick blond hair all tousled and bedroomy. Lean and muscled. At least what she could see of him was muscled anyway. He was sprawled out on his stomach, his face cocooned in the fluffy feather pillows of the guest bed. He reminded her of a Viking just back from a good pillaging, minus the bed and feather pillows, of course.

But who was he?

Even though she should have bolted out of there the moment she opened the guest room door and saw a partially exposed butt cheek, Anna stayed put. Someone had obviously glued her feet to the floor. Glued her eyeballs to the hot guy, too.

She glanced around the room and spotted a clue as to who he was. There was a military uniform draped over the back of a chair and a duffel bag on the floor near the bed.

Anna didn't actually need more clues to know he

was an Air Force officer and likely a friend that her brother Riley had brought home. But she also saw the dog tags. The ball chain holding them was still around the hot guy's neck, but the tags themselves were lying askew on the bed like smashed nickels.

Maybe he sensed she was there, because he opened an eye, and the seconds trickled by before it must have registered in his mind that he had a woman ogling him.

He made a grunting sound mixed with some profanity and rolled over, no doubt because that was the fastest way he could reach the sheet to cover himself. However, the rolling over gave her a view of his front side.

Definitely more dirty thoughts.

"Sorry, I didn't know anyone was in here," Anna said, as if that explained the gawking. The drool. The long, heated look that she was giving him.

But both the heated stuff and the drool came to a quick halt when Anna got a better look at his face. "Heath?"

He blinked. "Anna?"

Good gravy. It was Heath Moore, all right. Well, a grown-up Heath anyway. The last time she'd seen him had been nine and a half years ago when he was barely eighteen, but he had filled out a lot since then.

Oh, the memories she had of him came flooding back.

He'd been naked then, too—for part of those memories anyway, since she'd lost her virginity to him. Though she certainly hadn't seen as much of him during that encounter in the hayloft as she'd just witnessed. He had filled out *everywhere*.

He sat up, dragging the sheet over his filled-out parts, and still blinking, he yawned and scrubbed his hand over his face. More memories came. Of his memorable mouth. The equally memorable way he'd kissed her.

She fanned herself like a menopausal woman with hot flashes.

"Why are you here?" she asked at the same moment that Heath asked, "Why are you here?"

Anna figured he was going to have a lot better explanation than she did. "I thought I might have left a book in here," she told him.

A total lie. She had been in search of a book that the housekeeper, Della, had said she'd left in her room on the nightstand. But when Anna had seen the guest room door slightly ajar, she'd opened it and had a look.

She made a show of glancing around for a book that had zero chance of being there since it was all the way at the end of the hall.

"This is your room now?" Heath asked.

"No. But I come in here sometimes. For the view." Anna motioned to the massive bay window. She wouldn't mention that every bedroom on the second floor had similar windows, similar views. As did her own room on the first floor.

Heath glanced in the direction of the bay window as if he might get up to sample that view, but his next glance was at his body. Considering he was naked under the sheet, he probably didn't want to get up until she'd left, and that was her cue to leave. First though, she wanted an answer to her question.

"Why are you here?" she repeated.

"Riley. He saw me at the base in San Antonio and said I needed some…R & R before I left on assignment.

He was headed back here to the ranch to finish out his leave, and he asked me to come."

All of that made sense because Riley, too, was an Air Force officer and had indeed been at the base the day before. Yes, it made sense except for Heath's hesitation before R & R.

"You weren't here last night when I went to bed." She would have noticed Heath, that's for sure.

"We stopped for a bite to eat, then to visit some mutual friends, and we didn't get in until late. We didn't want to wake anyone up so Riley just sent me here to the guest room." Heath paused. "Riley's my boss."

Uh-oh. That wouldn't play well with Riley if he found out about her lustful thoughts over his subordinate. It wouldn't play well with Heath, either, since he probably didn't want to do or think anything—or have *her* do or think anything—that would cause his boss to hit him upside the head with a shovel.

A threat that Riley had first rattled off nine and a half years ago when he thought a romance was brewing between Heath and her.

If Riley had known what had gone on in the hayloft, he might not have actually carried through on the shovel threat, but Anna would have never heard the end of it.

And there was that whole underage-sex thing.

When Heath had first started working at the ranch, he'd been eighteen. But she'd been only seventeen. Riley and her other brothers had made a big deal about the attraction they'd sensed going on between Heath and her.

The term *jail bait* had been thrown around.

Since Heath had been making a big deal of his own about going into the military, it was an issue. Heath wanted to go into special ops, which would have required a lengthy background check for a top-secret clearance, and Riley had brought up her age for the sole purpose of scaring Heath into keeping his jeans zipped.

It had worked. Until the day Anna turned eighteen, that is. After that, she'd made the trip to the hayloft with Heath, and she had the memories of the orgasm to prove it.

Heath smiled at her, but it felt as if he'd had to rummage it up just to be polite. Again, the nudity was probably driving that. But the nudity didn't stop him from looking at her with those sizzling blue eyes. Also bedroomy like his hair. He slid his gaze from her head to her toes, lingering in the middle. Lingering especially on her breasts. Perhaps because she was wearing a T-shirt and no bra.

"Riley didn't mention you'd be here at the ranch," Heath said.

"Oh? Well, usually I leave the day after Thanksgiving, but I decided to stay a little longer." Since it was already two days after Thanksgiving, she probably hadn't needed to add that last part. "I'm in law school at University of Texas, but I finished my courses early this semester. I'm also planning a transfer. I need a change of scenery...or something."

And a life.

And perhaps sex, but she'd only gotten that idea when she'd seen Heath naked.

"Yeah, a change of scenery," he repeated, as if he were aware of what she meant by the *or something*.

"So, how long will you be here?" Anna tried to keep her eyes directed just at his face, but her gaze kept drifting a bit to that incredibly toned chest. Either he'd gotten very good with contouring body paints or the man had a six-pack.

"Until the cows come home," he said.

That's when she realized both her eyes and her mind had seriously drifted off, and she didn't have a clue what he'd been talking about before that.

The corner of his mouth lifted. A dreamy smile, and he hadn't had to rummage up this one. It was the real deal.

"I'll be here about two weeks," he said. Probably repeated information. "How about you?"

"Two weeks. More or less. I was going to stay until the final exams were over and the campus was less busy. Then, the plan was to talk to my advisor about the transfer."

"For that change of scenery or something?" Heath made it sound like a question.

Anna pretended not to hear it. No need to get into all that. Instead, she glanced at his left hand, the one part of his body she'd failed to look at during her gawking. No ring.

"I'm not married," Heath volunteered. "Never have been." He looked at her left hand, too, where she was still wearing the opal ring her Granny Ethel had left her.

Anna shook her head. "No I-do's for me, either." Close, though, but best not to get into that after her change-of-scenery slip. "So, catch me up on what you've been doing."

"Maybe I can do that after I've put on some clothes? Or we can talk like this?" Another smile.

He was flirting with her, a ploy she knew all too well since she'd been on the receiving end of his flirting that summer. Well, she could flirt, too.

"I guess I can restrain myself for a quick catch-up," she joked. "A *quick catch-up*," she emphasized. "What are you doing these days? I mean, other than sleeping naked, that is. How's the job going?"

The smile faded, and she was sorry she'd taken the conversation in that direction. Of course, it was something a normal nondrooling woman would have asked the man who had been her first.

Even though it was a dumb-as-dirt thing to do, she went closer. Much closer. And she sat down on the bed. Not right next to him, though, because she didn't want to move into the dumber-than-dirt category, but it was still too near him. Six miles would have been too near.

"Sorry," she added. "Didn't mean to hit a nerve. And I should have known better because Riley doesn't like to talk about his assignments, either. I think he believes it'll worry me, but whether he talks about it or not, I still worry."

"You shouldn't. Riley's been on plenty of deployments and hasn't gotten a scratch. Some guys are just bulletproof, and Riley's one of them."

Maybe. But Anna had a bad feeling about this deployment coming up. A bad feeling she definitely didn't want to discuss with Heath. Or Riley. If she didn't mention it aloud, maybe the feeling would go away. Maybe the danger would as well, and her brother would come back with his bulletproof label intact.

"You okay?" Heath asked.

That was a reminder to push aside her fears and get on with this catch-up conversation. "Riley always says if he tells me about his job, he'll have to hit me with a shovel afterwards. Riley really likes that shovel threat."

"I remember." Heath took a deep breath, causing the

muscles in his chest and that six-pack to respond. "Well, shovels aside, I can tell you that I just finished up a deployment in a classified location where there was a lot of sand, followed by eight months in Germany where there was a lot of paperwork. That's where Riley became my boss. Small world, huh?"

Yes. Too small, maybe. "Riley and you are in the same career field?"

"For now." The short answer came out so fast. As did his hand. He brushed his fingers over the ends of her hair. Even though he didn't actually touch skin or anything, it was enough of a distraction. "Your hair is longer," he said.

"Yours is shorter." And yes, she achieved dumber-than-dirt status by touching his hair, as well. Since it was on the short side, she also touched some skin.

She felt everything go still, and even though Anna was pulling back her hand, it seemed to be in slow motion. The only thing that was in the revving-up mode was this flamethrower attraction that had always been between Heath and her.

"Yeah," he drawled. No other words were necessary. They were on the same proverbial page along with being on the same actual bed. The flamethrower had had a go at him, too.

"I, uh…" Anna stuttered around with a few more words and syllables before she managed to say something coherent. "This could be trouble."

"Already is." He drawled that, too. Hitched up another smile.

The past nine and a half years just vanished. Suddenly, Anna was eighteen again and was thinking about kissing him. Of course, she hadn't needed vanishing years for that to happen, but it was as if they were back in that hayloft. On all that warm, soft hay. Heath had taken things so slow. Long kisses. His hand skimming over various parts of her body.

Then, into her jeans.

That had been the best part, and it'd all started with a heated look like the one he was giving her now.

Even though they didn't move, the foreplay was in full swing. His gaze lingered on her mouth. She picked up the rhythm of his breathing—which was too fast. Ditto for her heartbeat. Everything was moving in sync.

"Anna, we're playing with fire," he whispered. It was a drawl, too.

She was near enough to him now that his breath hit against her mouth like a kiss. "Yes," she admitted, but she was in the "fire pretty" mindset right now, and she inched closer, her drifting gaze sliding from his mouth to his abs.

"Is it real?" she asked, but was in the wrong mindset to wait for an answer. She touched that six-pack.

Oh, yes. Definitely real.

It probably would have been a good time to snatch back her hand and be outraged that she'd done something so bold, but she kept it there a moment and saw and heard Heath's reaction. He cursed under his breath, and beneath the sheet his filled-out part reacted, as well.

He cursed some more, but it was all aimed at himself. "I really do need you to leave now so I can get dressed. Once I can walk, that is. Maybe you can shut the door behind you, too."

That caused the past nine and a half years to un-vanish. Heath was putting a stop to this. As he should.

Anna was about to help with that stopping by getting to her feet and doing something that Heath clearly would have trouble doing right now—walking. But before she could budge an inch, she saw the movement in the doorway.

And saw the source of that movement.

Riley.

His eyes were so narrowed that it looked as if his eyelashes were stuck together.

"What the hell's going on here?" Riley growled. He opened his eyes enough to look at her. Then at Heath. Then at the other *thing* that was going on. "And what are you doing with my sister?"

No way was Heath going to be able to explain with the bulge of his filled-out part beneath the sheet. And neither could Anna.

Chapter Two

Well, hell in a big-assed handbasket. This visit was off to a good start.

Heath had known it wasn't a smart idea to come to the McCord Ranch, and he was getting a full reminder of why it'd been bad, what with Riley glaring at him.

"Get dressed," Riley ordered, and yeah, it was an order all right. "And we'll talk." Then he turned that ordering glare on his sister.

But Anna obviously wasn't as affected by it as Heath was, even though Riley was in uniform and looked thirty steps past the intimidation stage. Still, Anna matched Riley's glare with a scowl and waltzed out.

Thankfully, Riley did some waltzing as well and left, shutting the door behind him. Though it was more of a slam than a shut. Still, he was gone, and that gave Heath some time to take a very uncomfortable walk to the adjoining bathroom for a shower. Cold. Just the way he hated his showers. And if he stayed on the ranch, there'd be more of them in his near future.

It was time for a change of plans.

Not that he actually had plans other than passing time and moping. Yeah, moping was a definite possibility. At least it had been until Anna had shown up in the doorway. Difficult to mope in his current state.

Regardless, Anna was off-limits, of course.

He repeated that while the cold shower cooled down his body. Repeated it some more while he dressed. Kept repeating it when he went down the stairs to apologize to Riley and tell him that he'd remembered some place he needed to be. Riley would see right through the lie, but after what he had witnessed in the guest room, he'd be glad to get Heath off the ranch.

Heath made his way downstairs, meandering through the sprawling house. Since he was hoping for some coffee to go along with the butt-chewing he would get from Riley, he headed toward the kitchen.

He heard women's voices but not Anna's. He was pretty sure they belonged to Della and Stella, sisters and the McCords' longtime housekeeper and cook. Yep. And Heath got a glimpse of them and the coffeepot, too, before Riley stepped into the archway, blocking his path.

"I know," Heath volunteered. "You want to hit me on the head with a shovel."

"Hit who with a shovel?" Della asked, and when she spotted Heath, she flung the dish towel she was holding. Actually, she popped Riley on the butt with it and went to Heath to gather him into her arms for a hug. "It's good to see you, boy."

Heath hadn't even been sure the woman would remember him after all this time, but clearly she did. Or else she thought he was someone else.

"Nobody's gonna get hit with a shovel in this house," Della warned Riley, and then she added to Heath, "Have you seen Anna yet?"

"Earlier," Heath settled for saying.

"Well, I hope you'll be seeing a lot more of her while you're here. Never could understand why you two didn't just sneak up to the hayloft or somewhere."

Heath choked on his own breath. Not a very manly reaction, but neither was the way Riley screwed up his face. Della didn't seem to notice or she might have used the dish towel on him again.

"Have a seat at the table, and I'll fix you some breakfast," Della offered.

"Heath and I have to talk first," Riley insisted.

"Pshaw. A man's gotta have at least some coffee before he carries on a conversation. Where are your manners, Riley?"

"I think I left them upstairs."

Della laughed as if it were a joke and, God bless her, she poured Heath a cup of coffee. He had a couple of long sips, figuring he was going to need them.

"Thanks. I'll be right back," Heath said to Della, and he followed Riley out of the kitchen and into the sunroom.

No shovels in sight, but Riley had gone back to glaring again, and he got right in Heath's face. "Keep your hands off Anna, or I'll make your life a living hell."

Heath had no doubts about that. He didn't mind the living hell for himself so much, but he didn't want any more of Riley's anger aimed at Anna. "I'll get my things together and head out."

Riley's glare turned to a snarl. "And then Anna, Della and Stella will think I've run you off."

Heath had some more coffee, cocked his head to the side in an "if the shoe fits" kind of way. Because in a manner of speaking, Riley was indeed running him off. Except that Heath had already decided it was a good idea, too. Still, he didn't acknowledge that. He was getting some perverse pleasure out of watching Riley squirm a little.

"I'm guessing Anna, Della and Stella will make your life a living hell if they think you've run me off?" Heath asked. And he said it with a straight face.

Riley opened his mouth. Closed it. Then he did a wash, rinse, repeat of that a couple more times before he finally cursed. "Stay. For now. And we'll discuss it later. I've got to do some more paperwork at the base. Just keep your hands off Anna while I'm gone. Afterwards, too."

His hands were the least of Riley's worries, but Heath kept that to himself. Besides, Riley didn't give him a chance to say anything else. He lit out of there while growling out another "Stay" order.

Heath would stay. For the morning anyway. But it was best if he put some distance between Anna and all those parts of him that could get him in trouble.

He went back into the kitchen, got a hug and warm greeting from Stella this time, and the woman practically put him in one of the chairs at the table.

"How do you like your eggs?" Della asked.

"Any way you fix them." Heath added a wink because he figured it would make her smile. It did.

"Tell us what you've been doing with yourself for the past nine years or so," Della said as she got to work at the stove. "I seem to recall when you left here that summer you were headed to boot camp."

Heath nodded, took a bite of the toast that Stella set in front of him. "I enlisted in the Air Force, became a pararescuer and took college classes online. When I finished my degree, I got my commission and became a combat rescue officer."

"Like Riley," Stella said.

"Yeah, but he outranks me."

"How is that? Didn't you go in the Air Force before Riley did?"

Heath nodded again. "Only a couple months earlier, though. We've been in the service about the same amount of time, but for most of that I was enlisted. I've only been an officer for three and a half years now. And Riley's my boss. Well, until the rest of my paperwork has cleared. That should be about the time Riley leaves for his assignment in two weeks."

Della stopped scrambling the eggs to look at him. "You won't be going with him?"

There it was. That twist to the gut. Heath tried to ease it with some more toast and coffee, but that was asking a lot of mere food products. And Della and Stella noticed all right. He'd gotten their full attention.

"No, I won't be going with Riley this time," Heath said.

He still had their attention, and judging from their stares, the women wanted more. Heath gave them the sanitized version. "The Air Force feels it's time for me to have a stateside assignment. It's standard procedure. A way of making sure I don't burn out."

His mouth was still moving and words were coming out, but Heath could no longer hear what he was saying. That's because Anna walked in. Or maybe it was just a Mack Truck that looked like Anna because he suddenly felt as if someone had knocked him senseless.

She'd changed out of her sweats and T-shirt. Had put on a bra, too. And was now wearing jeans and a red sweater. Heath tried not to notice the way the clothes hugged her body. Tried not to notice her curves. Her face.

Hell, he gave up and noticed.

Not that he could have done otherwise. Especially when Anna poured herself a cup of coffee, sat down next to him and glanced at his crotch.

"Back to normal?" she whispered. Then she gave him a smile that could have dissolved multiple layers of rust on old patio furniture. Dissolved a few of his brain cells, too. "So, did Riley try to give you your marching orders?"

Since Della and Stella got very, very quiet, Heath figured they were hanging on every word, so he chose his own words carefully and spoke loud enough for the women to hear. "Something came up—"

Anna glanced at his crotch again and laughed. Obviously, a reaction she hadn't planned because she clamped her teeth onto her bottom lip after adding "I'm sorry." Too late, though. Because Della and Stella weren't just hanging on every word but every ill-timed giggle, too.

"Well, I'm sure whatever came up—" Della paused "—you can work it out so you can stay here for at least a couple of days. That way, Anna and you have time to visit."

"Especially since Anna needs some cheering up," Stella added.

Anna certainly didn't laugh that time. She got a deer-about-to-be-smashed-by-a-car look. "I'm fine, really," Anna mumbled.

Which only confirmed to Heath that she did indeed need some cheering up. Maybe this had to do with the "change of scenery or something" she'd mentioned up-stairs.

Well, hell.

There went his fast exit, and no, that wasn't the wrong part of his body talking, either. If Anna was down, he wanted to help lift her up.

Stella dished up two plates of eggs for Anna and him, and she smiled at them when she set them on the table. "You two were as thick as thieves back in the day." She snapped her fingers as if recalling something. "Anna, Heath even gave you that heart necklace you used to wear all the time. It had your and his pictures in it."

Hard to forget that. Heath referred to it as the great engraved debacle. He'd spent all his money buying Anna that silver heart locket as a going-away gift. Something to remember him by after he left Spring Hill and the McCord Ranch. It was supposed to be engraved with the words *Be Mine*.

The engraver had screwed up and had put *Be My* instead.

Since Heath hadn't had the time to get it fixed, he'd given it to Anna anyway, but he hadn't figured she would actually wear it. Not with that confusing, incomplete *sentiment*.

"Where is that necklace?" Della asked.

"I'm not sure," Anna answered, and she got serious about eating her breakfast. Fast. Like someone who'd just entered a breakfast-eating contest with a reprieve from a death sentence waiting for the winner.

Della made a sound that could have meant anything, but it had a sneaky edge to it. "I think Heath needs some cheering up, too," Della went on. "And not because Riley was going on about that shovel. That boy needs to get a new threat, by the way," she added to her sister before looking at Anna again. "I get the feeling Heath could use somebody to talk to."

Heath suddenly got very serious about eating his breakfast, as well. Either Della had ESP, or Heath sucked at covering up what was going on in his head.

Anna finished gulping down her breakfast just a bite ahead of him, gulped down some coffee, too, and she probably would have headed out if Stella hadn't taken her empty breakfast plate and given her a plate of cookies instead.

"I need you to take these cookies over to Claire Davidson at her grandmother's house."

"Claire's back in town?" Anna asked, sounding concerned.

Heath knew Claire. She'd been around a lot that summer he'd worked at the McCord Ranch, and if he wasn't mistaken Claire had a thing for Riley. And vice versa.

"Her grandmother's sickly again. Thought they could use some cheering up, too." Della shifted her attention to Heath. "And you can go with Anna. Then maybe she could show you around town."

"Spring Hill hasn't changed in nine and a half years," Anna quickly pointed out.

"Pshaw. That's not true. The bakery closed for one thing. And Logan bought that building and turned it into a fancy-schmancy office. It has a fancy-schmancy sign that says McCord Cattle Brokers. You can't miss it."

Logan—one of Anna's other brothers who ran the family business and probably also owned a shovel. Ditto for Logan's twin, Lucky. At least the two of them didn't stay at the ranch very often, so Heath might not even run into them. Well, he wouldn't as long as he avoided the fancy-schmancy office and any of the local rodeos since Lucky was a bull rider.

"I thought I'd go out and see if the ranch hands needed any help," Heath suggested.

That earned him a blank stare from the women. "You don't have to work for your keep while you're here," Stella said. "You're a guest."

"I know, but I like working with my hands. I miss it." He did. Not as much as he'd miss other things— like having the job he really wanted—but grading on a curve here, ranch work was missable.

"All right, then," Della finally conceded. "At least walk Anna to the truck. There might be some ice on the steps. We had a cold spell move in."

"Now, go," Stella said, shooing them out. "Della and I need to clean up, and we can't do that with y'all in here."

This wasn't about cleaning. This was about matchmaking. Still, Heath grabbed his coat so he could make sure Anna didn't slip on any ice. He only hoped Anna didn't ask why he needed cheering up, and he would return the favor and not ask her the same thing.

"So, why do you need cheering up?" Anna asked the moment they were outside.

He groaned, not just at the question but also because it was at least fifty degrees with zero chance of ice.

"Is it personal or business?" she added.

"Is yours personal or business?" he countered.

She stayed quiet a moment and instead of heading toward one of the trucks parked on the side of the house, she sat down in the porch swing. "Both. You?"

"Both," he repeated. But then he stopped and thought

about her answer. "Yours is personal, as in guy troubles?"

For some reason that made him feel as if he'd been hit by the Anna-truck again. Which was stupid. Because of course she had men in her life. Heath just wasn't sure he wanted to hear about them.

She nodded to verify that it was indeed guy trouble.

No, he didn't want to hear this, so he blurted out the first thing that popped into his head. He probably should have waited for the second or third thing, though.

"I had a girl break up with me once because I kept calling her your name," he said.

"*My* name?" She didn't seem to know how to react to that.

"Uh, no. I kept saying *your name* because I couldn't remember her name." And he added a wink that usually charmed women.

But, of course, it'd been Anna's name. The way stuff about her often popped into his head, her name had a way of just popping out of his mouth.

"Any other confessions you want to get off your chest and/or six-pack?" she asked. And she winked at him.

Man, that's what he'd always liked about Anna. She gave as good as she got. "Let me see. I don't wear boxers or briefs. I like mayo and pepper on my French fries. And my mother's in jail again."

All right, so that last one just sort of fell from his brain into his mouth.

Anna didn't question the *again* part. Maybe because she remembered the reason he'd ended up at the McCord Ranch all those years ago was that his mother had been in jail then, as well.

In jail only after she'd stolen and spent every penny

of the money that Heath had scrimped and saved for college. She'd also burned down their rental house with all his clothes and stuff still in it.

Heath had snapped up Riley's offer of a job and a place to stay—since at the time Heath had had neither. His father hadn't been in his life since he was in kindergarten, and what with him being broke and homeless, he'd had few places to turn.

If it hadn't been for his jailbird mom, he would have never met Anna. So, in a way he owed her.

In a very roundabout way.

"Want to talk about why your mom's in jail?" Anna asked.

Well, since he'd opened this box, Heath emptied the contents for her. "Shoplifting Victoria's Secret panties. She'd stuffed about fifty pairs in her purse—guess they don't take up much room—and when the security guard tried to stop her, she kicked him where it hurts. Then she did the same to the manager of the store next door. Then to the off-duty cop who tried to stop her. My mom can be a real butt-kicker when it comes to high-end underwear."

Anna smiled, a quiet kind of smile. "I do that, too, sometimes."

"What?" And Heath hoped this wasn't about butt-kicking or stealing panties.

"Diffuse the pain with humor. I'm not very good at it, either. Pain sucks."

Yeah, it did, and he thought he knew exactly what she was talking about. "You lost your parents when you were a teenager."

"Yes, they were killed in a car accident before you and I met. I was fourteen, and I thought my world was

over. That was still the worst of the *world's over* moments, but I've had others since."

"Is that why you need cheering up?" he asked.

She didn't answer. Anna stood. "I should deliver
these cookies before the ice gets to them."

Heath put his hands in his pockets so he wouldn't
touch her as she walked away. Not that he would have
had a chance to do any touching. Because someone
pulled up in a truck. Not a work truck, either. This
was a silver one that Della would have labeled as fancy
schmancy. It went well with the cowboy who stepped
from it.

Logan McCord.

The top dog at the McCord Ranch and the CEO
of McCord Cattle Brokers. He made a beeline for the
porch, passing Anna along the way. She said something
to him, something Heath couldn't hear, but it put a deep
scowl on Logan's face.

"Smart-ass," he grumbled. "She threatened to hit me
with Riley's shovel if I didn't make you feel welcome.
So—welcome."

Warm and fuzzy it wasn't, but at least it wasn't a
threat. Not yet anyway.

"Riley called," Logan continued. "He said I was to
come over here and convince you to stay."

"Because of Anna, Della and Stella."

Logan certainly didn't deny that, and his gaze drifted
to Anna as she drove away before his attention turned
back to Heath. "You're only going to be here two weeks
at most, and then you'll leave, right?"

Since that pretty much summed it up, Heath nodded.

"Well, the last time you did that, it took Anna a long

time to get over you. *Months*," Logan emphasized. "We all had to watch her cry her eyes out."

Hell. Crying? Months? This was the first Heath was hearing about this, but then he hadn't been around to see those tears. He'd been off at basic training at Lackland Air Force Base. He'd written her, of course. In the beginning at least. She'd written back to him, too, but she damn sure hadn't mentioned tears.

Logan took a step closer, got in his face. So close that Heath was able to determine that he used mint mouthwash and flossed regularly. "You won't hurt my kid sister like that again."

"The shovel threat?" Heath asked, aiming to make this sound as light as a confrontation with Logan could be. Heath wasn't sure friendly bones in a person's body actually existed, but if they did, Logan didn't have any.

"Worse. I'll tell Della and Stella what you've done and let them have a go at you. If you piss them off, the shovel will be the least of your worries."

Heath didn't doubt that. In fact, the whole McCord clan would come after him if he left Anna crying again. And that meant Anna was way off-limits.

He'd survived months in hostile territory. But Heath thought that might be a picnic compared to the next two weeks with Anna and the McCord brothers.

Chapter Three

Heath had been avoiding her for the past three days. Anna was certain of it. And she was fed up with it, partly because if Heath avoided her, it was like letting her knot-headed brothers win.

The other *partly* was that she couldn't get him off her mind, and she didn't know what riled her more—her brothers' winning or her own body whining and begging for something it shouldn't get.

Shouldn't.

Because another fling with Heath would only complicate her life and possibly get her heart stomped on again. That was the logical, big-girl panties argument, but the illogical, no-underwear girl wanted Heath in the hayloft again.

And the hayloft was exactly where she spotted him.

He was standing in the loft, tossing down bales of hay onto a flatbed truck that was parked just beneath. He was all cowboy today: jeans, a blue work shirt, Stetson, boots. Oh, and he was sweaty despite the chillier temps.

She wasn't sure why the sweat appealed to her, but then she didn't see a single thing about him that didn't fall into the appeal category.

Anna stood there ogling him, as she'd done in the bedroom, and she kept on doing it until his attention landed on her. Since she should at least make an attempt at not throwing herself at him, she went to the nearby corral and looked at the horses that'd been delivered earlier. It wasn't exactly the right day for horse ogling, though, because the wind had a bite to it.

An eternity later, which was possibly only a couple of minutes, the ranch hands drove off with the hay, and Heath made his way down the loft ladder. Then he made his way toward her.

"You've been avoiding me," she said. All right, she should have rehearsed this or something. For a soon-to-be lawyer, she was seriously lacking in verbal finesse when it came to Heath.

"Yeah," he admitted in that hot drawl of his. And he admitted the reason, too. "Your brothers are right. I'm not here for long, and they said you cried a lot the last time I left."

Her mouth dropped open, and the outrage didn't allow her to snap out a comeback. But her brothers were dead meat. Dead. Meat.

"They told you that?" She didn't wait for an answer. "I didn't cry. That much," Anna added.

Heath lifted his eyebrow, went to her side and put his forearms on the corral fence. "The fact that you cried at all tells me that I should keep avoiding you."

"Should?" she challenged.

He cursed, looked away from her. "You know I'm attracted to you. You saw proof of that in the bedroom."

She had, indeed. "And you know I'm attracted to you."

There, she'd thrown down the sexual gauntlet. But it caused him to curse again.

"I don't want to hurt you," he said.

"And I don't want to get hurt—"

A commotion in the corral nipped off the rest of what she was about to say. And it wasn't a very timely commotion.

Sex.

Specifically horse sex.

It went on a lot at the ranch. So often in fact that Anna rarely noticed, but because Heath was right next to her, she noticed it now. And he noticed that she noticed.

With all that noticing going on, it was amazing that she remembered how to turn around, but she finally managed it. She took hold of Heath's arm and got him moving away from the corral and toward the pasture.

Where she immediately saw cow-and-bull sex.

Dang it. Was everything going at it today?

Heath chuckled. "The Angus bull was getting restless, trying to break fence, so the hands brought in some company for him."

The ranch's version of Match.com. And the icy wind definitely didn't put a damper on things. Not for the bull anyway, but it did for Anna. She shivered and wished she'd opted for a warmer coat instead of the one that she thought looked better on her. It was hard to look your best with chattering teeth and a red nose.

"In here," Heath said. He put his hand on her back and maneuvered her into the barn.

"The scene of the crime," Anna mumbled. She'd fantasized about getting Heath back in here, but not like this. Not when she needed a tissue.

He glanced up at the hayloft, his attention lingering there a moment before coming back to her. The lingering lasted more than a moment though, and he took out a handkerchief and handed it to her.

"I should probably take you back to the house so you can warm up," he offered.

She considered it just so she could blow her nose. It was tempting, but Riley was inside. Della and Stella, too. So Anna touched the handkerchief to her nose and hoped that did the trick. In case it didn't, she went for what Riley would have called a tactical diversion.

"I'm surprised you're not off somewhere enjoying some *company* like that bull before you leave for your deployment," she said.

Anna figured that would get Heath to smile. It didn't. And she saw it again—the look on his face to remind her that he needed to be cheered up about something. Apparently, it had something to do with his assignment.

"Unless a miracle happens, I won't be deploying," he finally answered. The strewn hay on the floor was suddenly riveting because he stared at it. "The Air Force wants me to take an instructor job in Florida."

With the hay-staring and the gloomy look, Anna had braced herself for something a lot worse. "You make it sound as if you're being banished to Pluto."

"In a way, it is like that for me. I trained to be a combat rescue officer, like Riley. I didn't go through all of that to work behind a desk."

Anna wasn't sure how far she should push this so she just waited him out. Waited out the profanity he muttered under his breath. Waited out more hay-staring.

"I feel washed up," he added.

Ah, she got it then. "But the instructor job is temporary, right? You'll go back to being a combat rescue officer?"

"In three years."

She got that, too. It was an eternity for someone like Heath or Riley.

Anna touched his arm, rubbed gently. "The three years will fly by. Look how fast the past nine and a half years went."

The hay finally lost its allure for him, and he looked at her. "Yeah." Not so much of a sexy drawl this time. The hurt was still there. Time to pull out the big guns and do a little soul-baring.

"Remember when I told you I needed a change of scenery? Well, what I really need is to get away from my ex-boyfriend," Anna confessed. "We had a bad breakup."

Evidently, Heath didn't like this soul-baring so much because he frowned. "Are you telling me this is rebound flirting you've been doing with me?"

"No. The breakup happened two years ago, but he's getting married to one of my classmates. And they're having a baby. Twins, actually. The classmate is a former Miss Texas beauty pageant winner."

He nodded, made an "I got it" sound. "You're still in love with him."

"No!" And she couldn't say that fast or loud enough. "He's a lying, cheating weasel. My need for a change of scenery isn't because I still care for him but because I'm sick and tired of everybody walking on eggshells around me."

Her voice had gotten louder with each word, and she couldn't stop the confessions now that the floodgates were open.

"Poor pitiful Anna McCord got dumped for the beauty queen," she blathered on. "It reminds me of the stuff my brothers pull on me, and I'm tired of it. Tired of being treated like someone who needs to be handled with kid gloves."

She probably would have just kept on blathering, too, if Heath hadn't slid his hand around the back of her neck, hauled her to him and kissed her.

All in all, it was the perfect way to shut her up, and Anna didn't object one bit. In fact, she would have cheered, but her mouth was otherwise occupied, and besides, cheering would have put an end to this kiss.

She didn't want it to end.

Apparently, neither did Heath, because he put that clever mouth to good use and made the kiss French. And deep. And long.

All the makings of a good kiss even if Anna's lungs started to ache for air.

Heath broke the kiss just long enough for them to take in some much needed oxygen, and he went in for another assault. Anna was no longer shivering, could no longer feel her nose, but the rest of her was hyper-aware of what was happening. The heat zoomed from her mouth to her toes, but it especially fired up in her orgasm-zone.

Soon, very soon, the kiss just wasn't enough, and they started to grapple for position. Trying to get closer and closer to each other. Heath was a lot better at grappling than she was because he dropped his hands to her butt and gave her a push against the front of his jeans.

Anna saw stars. Maybe the moon, too. And she darn near had an orgasm right then, right there while they were fully clothed.

Her heart was pounding now. Her breath, thin. She was melting. And there was a roaring sound in her head. That roaring sound was probably the reason she hadn't heard the other sounds until it was too late. Not horse or bull sex this time.

Footsteps.

"Interrupting anything?" someone asked.

Not Riley or Logan. Her brother Lucky.

And he was standing in the barn doorway with a shovel gripped in his hand.

ONCE AGAIN HEATH was facing a McCord brother when he was aroused. Hardly the right bargaining tool for dealing with Anna's older siblings who were hell-bent on protecting their sister.

Anna stepped in front of him as if she were his protector, but Heath remedied that. He stepped in front of her. But that only prompted her to attempt another stepping in front of him, and Heath put a stop to it. He dropped a kiss on her mouth, a chaste one this time hoping it would get her to cooperate.

"I need to talk to your brother alone," Heath told her.

"No way. He's here to browbeat you, and he's got a shovel."

Lucky shrugged. Propped the shovel against the wall. "Riley said I should bring it and do my part to remind Heath that he should keep his jeans zipped around you." He shrugged again when he glanced at the front of Heath's jeans. "The zipper's still up, so my work here is done."

Lucky turned to walk away.

"That's really all you've got to say?" Anna asked.

Her brother stopped, smiled in that lazy way that

Lucky had about him. Heath knew Lucky loved his sister, but he'd never been as Attila the Hun as Riley and Logan. Heath suspected that's because Lucky got out all his restless energy by riding rodeo bulls. And having lots of sex.

"Should I ask you two to stay away from each other?" Lucky didn't wait for an answer though. "Wouldn't work. You two have the hots for each other, and there's only one way to cool that down." His gaze drifted to the hayloft before he turned again to leave.

Was Lucky really giving them his approval?

No.

This had to be some kind of trick.

Heath went after Lucky. Anna, too, and they caught up with him by the porch steps. However, before Heath could say anything else, the door opened, and Della stuck her head out.

"Anna, you got a call on the house phone. It's Claire."

Anna volleyed glances between Heath and her brother and then huffed. "Don't you dare say anything important before I get back."

She hurried inside. So did Lucky and Heath, but they stopped in the sunroom.

"Zippers and haylofts aside," Lucky said. "I don't want Anna hurt again. She sort of fell apart the last time you left."

"Yes. I heard about the crying from Logan." Heath paused. "Define *fell apart*."

"It wasn't just the crying." Lucky paused, too. "It was the pregnancy scare."

Heath felt as if all the air had just been sucked out of his lungs. Out of the entire planet. And if there was air on Pluto, it was also gone.

"Anna doesn't know that I know," Lucky went on. "No one does, and I'd like to keep it from my brothers. If Riley and Logan find out, they'd want to kick your ass. And mine since I didn't tell them. Then I'd have to kick theirs. If you don't mind, I'd rather not have to go through an ass-kicking free-for-all."

"Pregnancy?" Heath managed to ask. Considering there was still no air, he was doing good to get out that one word.

Lucky nodded. "A couple of weeks after you left, I went into Anna's bathroom to get some eye drops, and I saw the box for the pregnancy test in her trash can. She'd torn up the box, but I was able to piece it together to figure out what it was."

Heath managed another word. "Damn."

"Yeah. Two words for you—safe sex."

"I used a condom."

Lucky shrugged again. "Then, it must have worked because when I found the pee stick—it was in the way bottom of the trash can, by the way—it had a negative sign on it."

Heath heard the words. Felt the relief at that negative sign. Then managed another word.

"Hell."

Anna had gone through a scare like that, and she hadn't even told him.

"The only reason I dragged this up now was so that you'd understand why I'm protective of her," Lucky went on. "Now, go find her. Confront her about all of this. Then use a condom when you have makeup sex."

There'd be no makeup sex. Because Heath wasn't touching her again. Hell. She could have had his kid.

Heath went looking for Anna, and when he didn't

find her in the kitchen or any of the living areas, he went to her bedroom. Of course she was there. The one room in the house where he shouldn't be alone with her. The door was open, and she was still on the phone, but she motioned for him to come in. He did, but only because he wanted answers and didn't want to wait for them.

But he had to wait anyway.

He listened to Anna talk niceties with Claire. Several "you're welcomes" later, she finally ended the call and looked at him. The smile that was forming froze on her mouth though when she saw his expression.

Heath shut the door just as he blurted out, "You had a pee stick in the bottom of your trash can."

Anna gave him a blank look.

"The pregnancy test from nine and a half years ago," he clarified. "Lucky found it and just told me about it. I'm wondering why I had to hear it from him."

She laughed. Hardly the reaction he'd expected. "It wasn't my pee on that stick. It belonged to Kristy Welker. I bought it for her so her folks wouldn't find out, and she did the test here."

Heath had vague memories of this Kristy. Anna and she had been friends, and Kristy had come over a couple of times that summer.

Anna's laughter quickly stopped. "What the heck was Lucky doing in my bathroom?"

She was using her sister voice now, and it wouldn't have surprised Heath if she'd gone running out of there to confront her brother about it. She might have done that if Heath hadn't done something so unmanly as having to catch on to the wall to steady himself.

"Whoa. Are you all right?" She slipped her arm around his waist, led him to the bed.

Heath didn't even try to say he didn't need to sit down. He did. "I thought… Well, I thought…"

"Trust me, if you had knocked me up, I would have told you about it."

Of course she would have. But it might take a year or two for his heart rate to settle down.

She gave his arm another rub like the one she had in the barn. "Relax. You were my first, but I wasn't totally clueless." She stopped, paused. "I wasn't your first though, and that's why you knew to bring a condom to the hayloft."

Even though Heath was still coming down from the shock-relief whammy, he heard her loud and clear. She'd given him something that a girl could only give once. Her virginity. That upped the encounter a significant notch, and maybe she was looking for some kind of assurance that she'd given it to the right guy.

"You were the first one that mattered," he said. "I risked being hit by a shovel to be with you. That should have told you something."

No smile. No more arm rub, either. "And yet you left."

He nodded, tried to ignore the sting of that reminder. "I was leaving for basic training, and you were barely eighteen."

Anna waved that off. "I know where this is going. We were too young for it to have been real love."

"No, we weren't too young."

Okay, he hadn't meant to say that, and it was another opened box with contents that Anna was clearly waiting to be spilled.

"What I felt for you was real," Heath said. And strong.

He hadn't cried as Anna had done, but leaving her had left a hole in his heart. Best not to mention that, especially since he would be leaving again soon.

"I knew I couldn't give you a good life," he added. "Not when I was still trying to figure out my own life."

She stayed quiet a couple of seconds. "Fair enough. And if you'd stayed, you would have resented me because you gave up your dream of being in the military. Your wanderlust and need for an adrenaline fix would have come into play. We would have fought, broken up, and all these years later we would have cursed the mere mention of each other's names."

Heath frowned. He didn't like that version of what could have been, but she was probably right. Probably. Now he was cursing her name for a different reason. Because it reminded him of how much he wanted her.

"I still have the need for that adrenaline fix," he admitted. "The need to be…something. Somewhere. It's easier if I stay on the move."

"I get it." She motioned around the room. "That's why it's hard for me to be at the ranch sometimes."

He was pretty sure they were talking about her parents now, about the hole in her heart that their deaths had no doubt left. "Are the memories of your folks harder to deal with while you're here?"

"Every now and then. But sometimes it's hard no matter where I am. Sometimes, I wake up, and I can't remember what they looked like. That sends me into a panic. So I run to grab one of the photo albums just to remember their faces."

"It's your way of keeping them in your life," Heath said around the lump in his throat.

"Yes. The past has a way of staying with you like

that." Anna took a deep breath, then sighed. "And you can't run away from your past. I know, I've tried. It's like that little mole I have on my right butt cheek. It just goes with me everywhere." She looked at him. "I know what you're thinking."

Because he thought they could use some levity, Heath asked, "You have a little mole on your butt cheek?"

"All right, I didn't know what you were thinking after all. I thought you might be wondering if I was trying to outrun my past by transferring colleges."

That hadn't even crossed his mind, mainly because he wondered why he hadn't noticed that mole on her butt cheek. He was also wanting to see that mole. Clearly, he had a one-track mind here.

He shook his head. "I didn't think the transfer was about running, more like ulcer prevention. No need for you to have to face a daily dose of Mr. Wrong and his new family."

"Exactly." She smiled in a triumphant *I didn't think you'd get that* kind of way.

Heath got it all right. He got a lot of things when it came to Anna. A lot of things because of her, too. Like that tug below his belly that nudged him to kiss her again. That was his red-flag warning to get moving, and he would have done just that if he hadn't spotted the silver heart locket on her nightstand.

When she saw that he'd spotted it, she tried to put it in the drawer, but Heath took hold of her hand to stop her.

Yes, it was the locket he'd given her all right.

"After Della asked about it, I found it in my old jewelry box," she said. Then, she frowned. "All right, I wear it sometimes. Okay?"

She didn't sound especially happy about that, but it pleased Heath that she still had it. Pleased him even more than she occasionally wore it. What didn't please him was the reminder of the two words engraved on it.

"Be my." Anna ran her fingertips over it. "I wasn't sure what you were saying—be my heart, be my locket. Be my lay in the hay." She chuckled, poked him with her elbow.

"It was a fill-in-the-blank kind of thing," he joked, poking her back with his elbow.

"It sounds to me as if you didn't know what you wanted to say." No elbow poke that time.

"I was eighteen. I didn't know."

"And now?" she asked.

For two little words, it was a mighty big question. One that he didn't have to answer because there was a knock at the door, and the knocker didn't wait for an invitation to come in. The door opened.

Riley.

Well, at least Anna and he weren't in a butt-grabbing lip-lock as they'd been in the barn when Lucky had found them.

"I need to talk to you," Riley said, looking at Heath. Then his gaze swung to his sister. "And no, this isn't about you. It's business."

Damn it. That didn't sound good.

Anna must have thought so, too, because she gave Heath a sympathetic look as Riley and he headed out. They didn't go far, just into the foyer.

"I just found out that you're still trying to get out of your instructor assignment, that you put in a request to go on another deployment," Riley threw out there.

Heath cursed. He wasn't exactly keeping it from

Riley. Okay, he was, but he didn't want to justify what he was trying to do.

"You've already had two back-to-back deployments as an officer," Riley reminded him. "Before that, you had back-to-back-to-backs as a pararescuer."

"You're going on another one," Heath reminded him just as fast.

"I've had breaks in between. In the past ten years, the only time you've been stateside is for leave and training." He put his hand on Heath's shoulder. "You don't have anything to prove."

"No disrespect, *sir*, but I have everything to prove. To myself anyway."

Riley huffed. "You can prove it by being the best Air Force instructor you can be."

"That sounds like a recruitment pitch."

"It is." Riley took his hand from Heath's shoulder, and his index finger landed against Heath's chest. "And here's some more advice—sometimes life gives you crap, and you just have to make crappy lemonade out of it."

Heath frowned, thinking he might never again want another glass of lemonade. Or another lecture from Riley. Of course, there wouldn't be any more Riley lectures if Heath got stuck with that instructor job he didn't want. Then Riley would no longer be his boss.

Frowning, too, possibly over that bad lemonade analogy, Riley walked away. Heath would have, as well. He would have headed back to the pasture to do something, anything, to burn off some of this restless energy inside him.

Yeah, he needed an adrenaline fix *bad*.

He figured in that moment that his thought must have

tempted fate, because his phone dinged with a text message. There was that old saying about when the gods wanted to punish you, they gave you what you wanted. Well, it wasn't from the gods.

It was from Anna.

And the text flashed like neon on his phone screen. A sort of warning from the gods out to punish him.

Meet me in the hayloft in one hour.

Chapter Four

Anna figured she wasn't just going to be able to sneak out of the house without anyone seeing her.

And she was right.

As she was cutting through the sunroom, Della spotted her. Anna smiled, tried to look as if she weren't up to something, but that was sort of hard to do considering she had a six-pack of beer in a plastic grocery bag. A six-pack Anna had just scrounged from the fridge.

Della glanced at the bag and its distinctive shape. Then gave Anna no more than a mere glance.

"What are you up to?" Della asked.

Anna shrugged. "I'm considering playing with some fire. Running with scissors. Taking candy from some guy I don't know."

Falling hard for an old flame she shouldn't fall hard for was something Anna could add to that list of no-no's.

"So, you're going to the barn again with Heath," Della said. It wasn't a question.

"No. Yes," she admitted when Della gave her that liar-liar-pants-on-fire look. Anna huffed. "Don't give me a hard time about this. I'm tired of everyone babying me."

"They do that because you're the baby."

"Was the baby," Anna corrected. "I'm a grown woman now, but none of them can seem to accept it."

"They love you," Della pointed out.

"And I love them, but I want the key to my own chastity belt."

Della smiled that sly little smile of hers which meant she could be up to something. But she only kissed Anna on the cheek. "Honey, you've had that key for a long time now. Might be time to see if it works the way you want it to work."

Anna opened her mouth to respond, but she had nothing to say. Not a word. Instead, she returned the cheek kiss, tucked the beer under her arm so the bottles wouldn't jiggle and clang, and headed out the back.

No brothers in sight. No ranch hands, either.

But she also didn't see Heath.

Since it was—Anna checked the time on her phone—three minutes to rendezvous, she'd hoped she would see him waiting for her. He better not have blown her off. Except Heath wouldn't do that. Well, he might have done it with a text, call or chat, but he wouldn't do an unannounced blowing-off.

And he hadn't.

The moment she stepped in the barn, she saw him. Not in the hayloft, but standing by the steps that led up to the loft.

"You came," she said.

"Of course I came. I'm a guy and I'm not stupid. All right, maybe I am stupid, but the guy part's still true, and I've got the junk to prove it."

She smiled, chuckled. All nerves, and she hated the nerves because they didn't go well with this blistering attraction. "Yes, I got a glimpse of your junk. You're definitely a guy."

He smiled, too. "Beer?" he asked, tipping his head to the bag.

"I thought you might be thirsty. It was either this, milk or a questionable green smoothie."

"You made the right choice. I've already had my quota of milk and questionable green smoothies for a while."

He reached out, took her by the fingertips. That was it. The only part of her he touched. It was like being hit by a really big dose of pure, undiluted lust.

"You may have made the right choice with the beer," he added a heartbeat later. "But asking me to meet you here might fall into the stupid category."

"Might?" she repeated. Well, it was better than an out-and-out "this ain't gonna happen."

"Is this going to happen?" Anna came out and asked.

With only that teeny grip on her fingertips, he inched her closer. So close that when she breathed, she drew in his scent. Mixed with the hay and the crisp November air, it gave her another dose of lust.

"It shouldn't happen," Heath said. "I've tried to talk myself out of it."

"And?" She was still breathing, through her mouth now. Still taking in that scent. Still feeling him play with her fingers. "I hope you're really lousy at talking yourself out of things."

He closed his eyes a moment. Groaned. And, as if he were fighting—and losing—a fierce battle, he brought her another inch closer. She figured if the lust doses kept coming that she was going to launch herself into his arms.

"I'm leaving soon," he reminded her. "And I'm trying to do the right thing here."

She wanted to point out that unless he was leaving within the hour, then this could indeed happen, but that would just make her sound needy. Which she was. So very, very needy.

He let go of her fingertips, and she figured this was it. Heath would send her on her way. But he took the beer from her, and as if he had all the time in the world, he set the bag next to a hay bale.

"So, what now?" she asked.

Heath didn't answer her. Not with words. He reached out, and just when she thought she was going to get more fingertip foreplay, he took hold of her, snapped her to him and kissed the living daylights out of her.

Anna forgot all about the stupid argument that he was leaving soon. She forgot how to breathe. But other feelings took over, too. Probably because Heath didn't just kiss.

He touched.

He slipped his hand between them and ran his fingers over her right breast. Nice, but he double-whammied it with a neck kiss, and Anna felt herself moving. At first she thought it was just her body melting, but nope, she and Heath were walking.

"What are we doing?" she asked.

"Complicating the hell out of things."

"Good. I like complications." At the moment she would have agreed to a lobotomy.

Heath kept kissing her, kept moving. Not up the steps of the hayloft but rather toward the tack room. Maybe because it had a door. Maybe because it didn't require the coordination of step climbing with an erection. Maybe because it was just closer.

It was the erection thing, she decided, and since she could feel it against her stomach, Anna added some touching of her own. She worked her hand over his zipper and would have gotten that zipper down if Heath hadn't stopped her.

She heard herself make a whiny sound of protest, but then he put her against the back of the door that he'd just shut, and he lifted her. Until his hard junk was against her soft junk. Everything lined up just right to create a mind-blowing sensation.

"Let's play a game," he said. And yeah, he drawled.

Anna nodded. She would have agreed to a second lobotomy.

"On a scale of one to ten, rate the kisses, and then I'll know which parts to concentrate on."

She wasn't sure she could count to ten, much less rate kisses, but Heath jumped right into the game. He kissed her mouth.

"A ten," she said after he left her gasping for air and reaching for his zipper again.

He put his hand over hers to stop her, but Anna just used the pressure of his hand to add pressure to his erection.

"We'll play that particular game later," he promised.

Heath moved on to the next kiss. He placed one in the little area just below her ear, and he must have remembered that was a hot spot for her because it didn't seem like a lucky guess.

"Fifty," she blurted out. If Heath hadn't held her in place with his body, she would have dropped like a rock. There were no muscles in her legs, and her feet had perhaps disappeared.

"I'll definitely put that on my playlist," he said and added a flick of his tongue in that very hot spot that needed no such licking to further arouse it.

She went after his zipper for a third time, and the only reason she failed, again, was because he pushed up her sweater, pushed down her bra and did that tongue-flicking thing over her nipples.

"A seventy," she managed to say.

"Scale of one to ten," he corrected.

"Ten plus sixty."

He chuckled, which made for some very interesting sensations since he still had his mouth on her nipple.

"And this one?" he asked. He went lower, kissed her stomach.

"Ten," she admitted, and she was about to pull him back to her to breast and neck.

Then he went down a few more inches.

Heath clearly had some experience in zipper lowering. *Fast* zipper lowering. He slid down, unzipping her and dragging her jeans just low enough so that he could plant the next kiss on her panties.

Anna threw back her head, hitting it against the door and perhaps giving herself a concussion. She didn't care if she did. That's because the only thing that mattered now was the pleasure. Such a puny word for the incredible things Heath was doing with his mouth.

"Your rating?" he asked, and mercy, he added some breath with that question.

"Six million," she managed to say.

He laughed.

"One more kiss," he said. "Then it'll be your turn."

Oh, she wanted a turn all right. Wanted it badly. Until he shimmied down her panties, put her knee on his shoulder and kissed her again. A special kiss.

Tongue flicks included.

After a couple of those flicks, Anna went into forget mode again. The thought of taking her turn went right out of her head. Everything vanished. Except for the feeling that she was about to shatter. And fall. And shatter some more.

Heath made sure he gave her the *more* she needed for shattering. One last well-placed kiss. An equally well-placed tongue flick. And all she could do was fist her hand in his hair and let him shatter her.

She had to take a moment to gather her breath. Another moment to keep gathering it. But even with the ripples of the climax tingling through her, she wanted to get started on her turn. And she was going to torture the hell out of Heath and his junk.

"Damn," Heath growled.

It took her a moment to realize that he was reacting to something he heard.

A knock at the tack room door.

"Heath?" Riley called out.

Hell.

"Uh, Heath, I need to talk to you," Riley added. "It's important."

Unless the world was about to end and Heath could stop it, then it wasn't that important, but Anna conceded that was the lust talking.

"How important?" Heath asked.

"Very."

Heath and she both cursed.

"Anna's in here with me," Heath volunteered.

It took Riley several snail-crawling seconds to respond to that. "Yes, I figured that out. Didn't think you'd go into the tack room alone and close the door. But this isn't about Anna. It's about your assignment."

Heath groaned, stood back up, helping her fix her jeans and panties. "You can wait in here if you want," he offered.

"Not a chance," Anna argued. "Riley knows what we've been doing. Or rather what we started doing, and the assignment thing could be a ruse to draw us out so he can ambush you with a shovel."

He brushed a kiss on her mouth. "You've got a very active imagination." Though she knew there might be a grain of truth in her theory.

Heath went out ahead of her, and Riley was indeed right there. He was sitting on a hay bale, drinking one of the beers. She braced herself for him to say something snarky like had she been trying to get Heath drunk or why did she have this thing for barn sex?

He didn't.

Riley did give her a look that only a big brother could have managed, but it had some, well, sympathy mixed in with the brotherly snark. A strange combination.

"I just came from the base," Riley said to Heath. "They want to see you about your deployment request."

"Deployment request?" Anna repeated. "I thought Heath was going to Florida."

Riley remained quiet, clearly waiting for Heath to explain.

"I asked to be diverted from the instructor job to another deployment," Heath said.

Riley's arrival had been a killjoy in the sexual-pleasure department, but hearing about Heath's request was a different kind of killjoy. Although obviously not for Heath since this was something he wanted.

Very much.

After all, he'd told her that the instructor job made him feel washed up, and maybe now he wouldn't have to feel that way because he could go back to one of those classified sandy locations. Where people shot at him and where he could be hurt or killed.

Mercy.

That felt as if she'd been slammed with a truckload of bricks. And there was no reason for it, because this was Heath's job. No logical reason anyway. But Anna wasn't feeling very logical at the moment.

"They want to see you out at the base right away," Riley added.

Heath nodded, looked at her as if he needed to say something, but Anna let him off the hook. She smiled, brushed a kiss on his cheek.

"Go," she insisted, trying to keep that smile in place. "We can talk when you get back."

Heath hesitated, gave another nod and then walked toward the house. Anna managed to keep her smile in place until he was out of sight. Riley opened a bottle of beer and handed it to her.

"Will he get to come back here to the ranch if the deployment is approved?" Anna asked, though she was afraid to hear the answer. "Or will they send him out right away?"

"Hard to say."

Or maybe not. The next thing Anna saw was Heath leaving the house, carrying his gear. He put it in his rental car and drove off. Obviously, he was prepared to go.

Anna took a long swig of that beer and wished it was something a whole lot stronger.

"Best to forget him," Riley said as they watched Heath drive away. "Heath isn't the settling-down type."

If only that weren't true.

"It's just a fling," Riley added. "That's what it was nine and a half years ago, and that's what it is now."

If only that were true.

Chapter Five

The McCord brothers were waiting for Heath when he got back from the base, and they didn't even try to make it look like a friendly, casual meeting. They were in the living room just off the foyer, and the moment Heath stepped inside, they stood.

No shovels. Not physical ones anyway.

"Where's Anna?" Heath asked. "You didn't lock her in her room, did you?"

The joke didn't go over so well, but Heath didn't care. He was tired, frustrated and wanted to talk to Anna, not the kid-sister police.

"Anna's Christmas shopping in San Antonio," Logan answered. "She'll be back any minute now."

Good. Well, sort of good. Heath definitely wanted to see her even if she probably hadn't liked his news. Hell, he hadn't liked it much, either.

"My request for deployment was denied," Heath explained. "The Air Force wants me to report to the base in Florida day after tomorrow so I'll have to cut my visit here short."

He expected them to jump for joy. Or at least smile. They didn't.

Riley immediately shook his head. "I didn't have anything to do with that."

Heath nearly snapped out "Right," but he knew in his gut that Riley was telling the truth. He wouldn't do anything like that even if it meant saving his sister from having sex with a guy Riley didn't think was right for her.

And Riley was spot-on.

Heath wasn't right for her. End of subject.

"I'll leave tomorrow," Heath added. "I just want a chance to say goodbye to Anna first."

None of the brothers objected, and Heath wouldn't have cared if they did. Yeah, it was the pissed-off mood again, but he had to get something off his chest.

"I know you think I'm a jerk, that I'm here only to try to seduce Anna, but I do care about her. Always have. If I hadn't cared, I would have never had sex in the hayloft with her nine and a half years ago."

There. He'd said it. But they weren't saying anything back to him. Maybe because Riley and Logan hadn't known about the sex. Lucky had, of course, because of the pee stick discovery, but even Lucky might have been stunned to silence to hear the de-virgining had taken place in the barn.

"Anna cares about you, too," Lucky finally said.

"She'll cry a lot again when you leave," Logan added.

"She'll be hurt," Riley piped in.

Maybe. Probably, Heath silently amended. Yeah, he was a jerk all right, but he was a jerk on orders, and that meant leaving whether he wanted to or not.

And he did want to leave, Heath assured himself.

He did.

Silently repeating that, Heath went to the guest room so he could finish packing.

HER BROTHERS WERE waiting for Anna when she got home. Hard to miss them since they were on the sofa in the living room.

She so didn't have the energy to deal with them now.

"You're all grounded," Anna said, going on the offensive. "Now, go to your rooms."

Of course, they didn't budge. Well, except to stand, and judging from the somber looks on their faces they had something serious to tell her. But she had something to say, too.

"I already know about Heath's deployment being denied. He texted me right after he got the news. He was at the base and couldn't talk, but he wanted to let me know that he's leaving tomorrow."

They stared at her as if expecting her to sprout an extra nose or something. Then Riley's hawkeyed gaze moved to the Victoria's Secret bag she was holding.

"Yes, I bought it for Heath," Anna admitted. "For me to wear for Heath," she amended when their stares turned blank. "It's red and slutty, and if you don't quit staring at me like that, I'll give you lots of details about what I want Heath to do to me while I'm wearing it."

Logan's eyes narrowed. Riley's jaw tightened. Lucky shrugged and went to her. He pulled her into his arms despite the fact she was as stiff as a statue from the mini hissy fit she'd just thrown.

"I've got two words for you," Lucky whispered to her. "Condom."

She pulled back, looked at him. "That's one word."

"If you wear what's in that bag, you'll need two condoms. Three if you skip what's in the bag all together and just show up in your birthday suit. Either way, condoms."

In that moment he was her favorite brother. Lucky had always been her champion and not judgmental. Most of the time anyway. Plus, he was the only brother who talked safe sex with her. Or any kind of sex for that matter. He wasn't just her brother, he was her friend.

Anna kissed his cheek. "Thanks."

He shrugged in that lazy but cool way that only Lucky or a Greek god could manage. It was as if he drawled his shrugs. And his life.

Lucky returned the cheek kiss and apparently considered his brotherly/friendly duties done because he strolled toward the door and headed out. Logan went to her next.

"I love you," Logan said. "And no matter what happens, I'll be here for you. You can cry on my shoulder all you need. Or if you prefer, I can kick Heath's ass for you. Your choice."

She had to fight a smile, but she didn't have to fight it too hard because the nonsmiling emotions were just below the surface. "I don't want his ass kicked, but I might need the shoulder."

Logan tapped first one shoulder, then the other. "Any time. They're reserved just for you, and I swear *I told you so* will never cross my lips or my mind. You're a grown woman, and if you want to wear what's in that bag, then you have my blessing."

In that moment she loved Logan best. Logan had been her father more than her brother, mainly because he'd been the one to step up after their folks died. He'd been the one to bust her chops when she needed it and had been a whiz helping with her math homework.

Logan would walk through fire for her and not once complain. Well, maybe he would complain, but he'd still do it.

He kissed her forehead and headed off, not out the door but to his old room. Since he lived in town and no longer spent many nights at the ranch, Logan must have wanted his shoulders to be nearby in the event of an impending crying spell.

Uh-oh.

It was Riley's turn.

"If Heath makes you cry again, I'm hitting him with the shovel," Riley growled. "And wear a robe with whatever's in that bag."

Anna sighed. The support of two out of three wasn't bad.

Riley sighed as well, and he pulled her into his arms. "FYI, Heath did some crying, too, after he left here that summer."

Anna wiggled out of his grip so she could see if he was serious or not. He was.

"I don't mean he actually shed tears," Riley went on, "but he cried in his own man kind of way."

"How do you know that?" she asked.

"Because I'm the one who drove him to his basic training." A muscle flickered in his jaw. A sign that he was remembering that day as unfondly as she was. Some of the anger returned. "Heath asked me to make sure you were okay. Can you believe it?"

"The bastard," Anna joked.

"He said it as if I needed to be reminded of it. I didn't. Not then, not now. If you need someone to make sure you're okay, I'll do it. As long as I don't have to hear any sex details. Or see what's in that bag. And I'll do that—minus the exceptions—because you're my sister."

Anna blinked back tears. In that moment, she loved Riley best. Yes, he was hardheaded, and they had a history of sibling squabbles. Plus, there was the time when he'd ruined all her dolls with camo paint and duct-tape combat boots, but still she loved every stubborn, camo-painting ounce of him.

Riley wasn't her father or her friend. He was her brother.

And sometimes, like now, that was exactly what a sister needed.

Chapter Six

Heath paced. Cursed. He figured this much debate hadn't gone into some battle plans, but a battle plan would have been easier than trying to figure out what to do about Anna.

Or better yet what to do *with* Anna.

If he went to her room, sex would happen. Then tomorrow he would leave—just as he'd done nine and a half years ago. That hadn't turned out so well, what with all the crying and her brothers wanting to shovel him.

If he didn't go to her room, sex wouldn't happen. But then he would have to leave things unsettled between them—again—as he'd apparently done before.

He was screwed either way, so Heath decided he might as well go for it. He threw open the door and nearly smacked right into some idiot wearing a hoodie and an army-green vinyl poncho.

Except this was no idiot. It was Anna, and in addition to the garb, she was also carrying a blue sock.

She practically pushed him back into his room and shut the door. "Shhh," she said. "Della and Stella's book club is meeting tonight."

He was still wrapping his mind around the fact that Anna was there, that she had come to him, and maybe that's why Heath couldn't quite wrap his mind around the book club or the poncho.

"There are six of them in the living room, and I had to sneak past them," Anna added when he gave her a blank look.

When Heath kept that blank look, Anna pulled off the poncho, and he saw the hoodie. No pants. No shoes.

Just a pair of really tiny devil-red panties.

He was sure his blank look disappeared because his mouth dropped open. This was the best kind of surprise.

"I didn't have a robe here at the ranch, and the plastic poncho felt sticky against my skin so I put on the hoodie," she explained. Then she unzipped it.

No top. No bra. Just the Be My heart locket dangling between her breasts. Heath thought maybe his tongue was doing some dangling, too.

"And the sock?" he asked.

She smiled and emptied the contents onto the bed. Condoms. At least a dozen of them.

"I took them from Lucky's bathroom," Anna explained. She was still whispering, but it had a giddiness to it. "The poncho and hoodie didn't have pockets so I put them in the sock. I only brought the normal-looking ones. Some had pictures on them and some were glow in the dark." Anna looked at him. "Why would a man need that?"

Heath didn't have a clue. He didn't need any illumination to find anything on Anna's body. His most vital organ agreed. In fact, it wanted to go on that particular search mission right now.

But there was a problem.

"You got my text saying I was leaving, right?" he asked.

She nodded. "Tomorrow. That's why I didn't want to wait until after the book club left. Sometimes they hang around until midnight if Della breaks out the tequila, and we don't have much time."

Not if they were planning on using all those condoms, they didn't, but Heath had to make sure that Anna was sure. She stripped off the hoodie, and he was sure she was sure.

At least he wanted her to be.

He wanted that even more when she slipped into his arms and kissed him. Heath was stupid and weak so it took him a moment to break the kiss.

"Anna, I don't want you hurt," he said.

She frowned. "I think that ship's sailed. I'll be hurt, but I'll get over it. And tonight you'll give me some really good memories to help me get over it, right?"

Yeah.

Whether they had sex or not, Anna would be hurt. Or at least she would be sad to see him go. Ditto for him being sad to leave her. But at least this way they'd have new memories, and they didn't need glow-in-the-dark condoms to do it.

Now that he had a clearly defined mission, Heath pulled her back to him to kiss her. One of those kisses that reached scorch level pretty darn fast. But Anna was aiming for fast, too, and not with just the kisses. She was already going after his zipper.

"We're going to play that scale-of-one-to-ten game," she insisted.

Maybe. But the way she was tugging at his zipper, it was possible she was also trying to finish this all way too fast. Tonight, he didn't want the kissing game, and he didn't want fast.

Heath stopped what she was doing by catching on to her wrists and putting her against the wall. He liked walls because it gave him some control...

Damn.

He had no control. Anna ground herself against him, sliding her leg up the outside of his so that the millimeter of red lace was right against his crotch. Apparently, the orgasm she'd had earlier in the barn hadn't done anything to take the edge off because she was going for another one very quickly.

Again, Heath tried to slow things down. With her leg still cradling his, he turned her, intending to put her against the dresser, but he tripped over the poncho and fell onto the bed.

With Anna on top of him.

"Let's play a game," she said. Definitely not a virginal tone or look. "I'll use just my tongue to find all your special spots. You don't have to give it a number rating. Just a grunt for pleasure. A groan for find another special spot that's more special."

"Men only have one special spot," he told her. Heath took her hand and put it over his sex.

She laughed. Not a humor kind of laugh but the sound of a woman who'd come to play. Or maybe give a little payback for the things he'd done to her in the tack room. Well, Heath wanted to play, too. After all, he had a nearly naked Anna straddling him, and her breasts were making his mouth water.

He managed a quick sample of her left nipple before she moved away. Anna didn't waste any time. With her hand still on his special spot, she went in search of others. His earlobe.

He grunted, but Heath didn't know if that was because, at the same time, she started lowering his zipper.

"That wasn't a loud enough grunt," she said and went
after his neck.

Heath grunted. Again, mainly because she lowered
the zipper, and when she did that, her breasts got closer
to his mouth again. She didn't grunt when he kissed her
there, but she did make that silky sound of pleasure that
Heath would never tire of hearing.

He would have kept on kissing her breasts, but apparently it was special-spot search time again because
she scooted lower and ran her tongue over his own left
nipple.

Oh, yeah. He grunted.

Grunted some more when she circled his navel with
her tongue. All that tonguing and circling though didn't
stop her from getting his zipper all the way down, and
as he had done to her earlier, she shimmied his jeans
lower.

"You really do go commando," she said.

"Yep—"

He might have added more. Something clever or at
least coherent, but her hands were on him. The condom, too. Heath wasn't sure when she'd opened one
of the packets. Nor did he care. The woman had clever
hands after all—

Hell.

He grunted loud enough to trigger an earthquake
when she dropped down onto him. That's when he figured out really, really fast that the panties were crotch-
less and that he was in her warm and tight special place
all the way to the hilt.

"That's not your tongue," he said through the grunts.

"So, I cheated."

The woman was evil. And damn good. Heath usually liked to be the alpha when it came to sex, but even more than that, he liked taking turns with Anna. Apparently, she was going to make the most of her turn, too. She had the whole *ride 'em, cowgirl* motion going on. So fast that Heath knew this would all end too soon.

Of course, sixteen hours was going to be too soon.

As if she'd read his mind, she slowed. Anna put her palm on his chest and, still moving against his erection, leaned down and kissed him.

"After this," she said, "I want you all the way naked."

Heath thought that was a stellar idea. He wanted those panties off her, too, even though they fell into the *why bother* category of women's undergarments.

The locket whacked him in the face, but even that didn't put a damper on the moment. Heath just pushed the locket aside, gathered her close and let his cowgirl screw his brains out.

Chapter Seven

Anna wished there were some kind of anticry shot she
could take. Even one that worked for just an hour or so
would do. She figured she'd do plenty of crying after
Heath had left, but she didn't want any tears shed in
front of him.

Or in front of her brothers.

She wanted Heath to remember her smiling. Or
maybe naked, since that's how he'd seen her for a good
portion of the night. It was certainly how she wanted
to remember him.

With that reminder/pep talk still fresh in her mind,
Anna left her bedroom and went in search of Heath so
she could give him that smiling goodbye she'd prac-
ticed in the mirror. But he wasn't in his bedroom. Or
the living room. Or the kitchen. In fact no one was, and
she figured they'd all cleared out to give her a chance
to have a private goodbye with Heath.

Or maybe they'd cleared out because Heath was already gone. She had several moments of panic when
she sprinted to the back porch to make sure his rental
car was still there.

It was.

And so was Heath.

He was at the fence pasture, looking at some cows that'd been delivered that morning. He made a picture standing there with his foot on the bottom rung of the fence, his cream-colored cowboy hat slung low on his face.

He must have heard her approaching because he turned, smiling. It looked about as genuine as the one she was trying to keep on her face. Until he reached out, pulled her to him and kissed her.

Then the smiles were real.

"How soon before you leave?" she asked.

"Soon."

That reminder made her smile waver. Anna wasn't sure how far to push this part of the conversation, but there was something she had to know. "Are you feeling any better about the instructor job?"

"I've accepted it. Sometimes, that's the best you can do with crappy lemonade. Sorry," Heath added when she frowned. "It was just something Riley said. An analogy of sorts."

Riley not only needed a new threat, he needed new analogies, as well.

Since their time together was about to end, Anna reached into her pocket and took out the "gift" she'd gotten him on her shopping trip the day before. She hadn't wanted it to be a big gift because that would have made this goodbye seem, well, big.

Which it was.

But she didn't want it to feel big to him.

She took his hand and dropped the smashed penny in it. "It reminded me of your dog tags, and it's supposed to be good luck."

He stared at it, gave a slight smile. "Thanks."

"I was going to give you the red panties," she added, "but I thought it would look strange if the TSA went through your luggage."

Now she got the reaction she wanted. A bigger smile. A bigger kiss, too.

"I have something for you," he said. He took out a silver heart locket. It was similar to the other one he'd given her nine and a half years ago. Very similar.

Right down to the Be My engraving.

Anna checked to make sure she had on the original one. She did. And she was shaking her head until Heath opened it, and she saw what was inside. Not pictures of him and her.

But of her parents. Her dad on one side of the heart. Her mother on the other.

"Della got the pictures for me," he explained. "You said sometimes you forget their faces, and this way you won't forget."

Oh, God.

She was going to cry.

No matter how hard she blinked, the tears came, and they just kept coming.

"I'm sorry." Heath pulled her back in his arms. "I didn't know it would upset you."

"It doesn't," she said, sobbing. "It's a good kind of upset." Still sobbing. "Thank you, Heath, thank you."

He held her while she sobbed, and it took Anna several long moments to stop.

"I got you something else," he added.

Anna couldn't imagine getting anything better than the second locket. It was even more precious to her than the first one. But Heath must have thought "the more the better" because he took out a wad of lockets from his coat pocket.

"I went to the jewelry store this morning and bought every locket they had."

She had no doubts about that—none. There was another silver one, one gold and another in the shape of a cat's head.

"They're, uh, beautiful." Though she couldn't imagine needing that many lockets. Or the ugly one with the cat's head.

"I had them engraved," he added, "and this time I watched to make sure they did it right. You can choose which one you want."

It took her a second to realize he'd finished his sentence. Not "which one you want *to wear.*" Not "which one you want *to keep.*" Not "which one you want *to remember me by.*"

Heath turned over one of the silver ones, and she saw the engraving there. One word.

Lover.

He put the Be My locket next to it, and she got the message then. Be my lover.

She laughed. "Does this mean you want to see more of me?"

"Well, I've already seen more, but I'd like to see more of you more often."

That dried any remnants of her tears, and she blurted out an idea she'd been toying with for days. "I could look into transferring to a law school in Florida." And she held her breath.

No smile from him. "I don't want you to sacrifice going to a school that maybe doesn't have as good of a reputation as the one you're in now."

"No sacrifice. There are a couple of really good ones. And besides, I was transferring anyway. Might as well transfer so you can—" she held up the two lockets to finish that thought "—Be My Lover."

Anna tested his neck again with a kiss. And her tongue.

"Keep that up, and you'll be my lover again right now," he grumbled.

"If that's supposed to make me behave, then it won't work. Not with the hayloft so close. How much time do you have before you need to leave for your flight?"

"Not enough time for the hayloft."

She kissed him again, and he seemed to change his mind about that. He started leading her in that direction.

"Not enough time for the hayloft unless we hurry," Heath amended.

Good. The kisses were working.

Since she'd already put her heart on the line, Anna put the rest of herself out there, too. "I don't want a fling."

"Good. Flings are overrated." He kissed her again. "And temporary."

She released the breath she didn't even know she'd been holding. Heath didn't want temporary. Nor a fling. He wanted sex.

That was a solid start since she wanted that, too.

"I'm not done," he said. "Remember, you pick the locket you want." He held up the next one, the gold one, and it also had a single word engraved on it.

Woman.

As in Be My Woman.

Yes, they were so going to that hayloft, and then

she was going to the university to start that transfer to Florida.

"Can I wear both the *Lover* and *Woman*?" she asked. Because she wanted both.

"You haven't seen the third one yet."

And she probably couldn't see it before the next kiss crossed her eyes. Along with singeing her eyelashes.

Still, he put the locket in her hand just as her butt landed against the ladder. Anna backed up one step at a time, which wasn't easy to do with Heath kissing her like that. And he kept on kissing her until they made it all the way to the top of the hayloft.

But Anna froze when she saw what was engraved on the tacky cat's head locket.

Love.

"Be My Love," she said, putting the words together.

Putting *everything* together.

"The *L* word?" she asked.

Heath nodded. "Sometimes it's the only word that works. What about you? Does the *L* word work for you?"

Anna had to catch her breath just so she could speak. "It works perfectly for me." She kissed him. "Does this mean we're going steady?"

"Oh, yeah," Heath confirmed. "That, and a whole lot more."

* * * * *

COMING NEXT MONTH FROM

◆ HARLEQUIN®

I N T R I G U E

Available March 22, 2016

#1629 TROUBLE WITH A BADGE
Appaloosa Pass Ranch • by Delores Fossen
Lawman Levi Crockett would never turn his back on PI Alexa Dearborn and the baby girl in her care. But as a serial killer stalks them, Levi must fight a powerful enemy—the desire between them.

#1630 DECEPTIONS
The Battling McGuire Boys • by Cynthia Eden
Secrets from their pasts threaten Elizabeth Snow and Mac McGuire—as much as the killer who seems to know their every move. Can they trust each other again? Or will a shocking truth prove fatal?

#1631 NAVY SEAL CAPTIVE
SEAL of My Own • by Elle James
Being abducted wasn't part of Sawyer Houston's R & R mission. Jenna Broyles claims she's rescuing the navy SEAL from unknown assailants. Only, it's her life on the line when the jilted bride becomes a target.

#1632 HEAVY ARTILLERY HUSBAND
Colby Agency: Family Secrets • by Debra Webb & Regan Black
When someone tries to kill security expert Sophia Leone, she's rescued by her husband, Frank—an army general she *thought* died a year ago. Now Sophia must trust her life to the man she married...the man she never stopped loving.

#1633 TEXAN'S BABY
Mason Ridge • by Barb Han
Bodyguard Dawson Hill is committed to protecting the woman who left him two years ago. Melanie Dixon has returned to Mason Ridge...with his son. Now a madman is threatening the family Dawson never dreamed he could have.

#1634 FULL FORCE FATHERHOOD
Orion Security • by Tyler Anne Snell
Fatherhood was never in the cards for Mark Tranton, until widow Kelli Crane and her daughter wrapped themselves around his heart. But digging into their past riles someone who won't rest until Kelli pays the ultimate price...

YOU CAN FIND MORE INFORMATION ON UPCOMING HARLEQUIN® TITLES, FREE EXCERPTS AND MORE AT WWW.HARLEQUIN.COM.

HICNM0316

REQUEST YOUR FREE BOOKS!
2 FREE NOVELS PLUS 2 FREE GIFTS!

(H) HARLEQUIN®

INTRIGUE

BREATHTAKING ROMANTIC SUSPENSE

YES! Please send me 2 FREE Harlequin® Intrigue novels and my 2 FREE gifts (gifts are worth about $10). After receiving them, if I don't wish to receive any more books, I can return the shipping statement marked "cancel." If I don't cancel, I will receive 6 brand-new novels every month and be billed just $4.74 per book in the U.S. or $5.49 per book in Canada. That's a savings of at least 12% off the cover price! It's quite a bargain! Shipping and handling is just 50¢ per book in the U.S. and 75¢ per book in Canada.* I understand that accepting the 2 free books and gifts places me under no obligation to buy anything. I can always return a shipment and cancel at any time. Even if I never buy another book, the two free books and gifts are mine to keep forever.

182/382 HDN GH3D

Name _____ (PLEASE PRINT) _____

Address _____ Apt. # _____

City _____ State/Prov. _____ Zip/Postal Code _____

Signature (if under 18, a parent or guardian must sign)

Mail to the **Reader Service:**
IN U.S.A.: P.O. Box 1867, Buffalo, NY 14240-1867
IN CANADA: P.O. Box 609, Fort Erie, Ontario L2A 5X3
**Are you a subscriber to Harlequin® Intrigue books
and want to receive the larger-print edition?
Call 1-800-873-8635 or visit www.ReaderService.com.**

* Terms and prices subject to change without notice. Prices do not include applicable taxes. Sales tax applicable in N.Y. Canadian residents will be charged applicable taxes. Offer not valid in Quebec. This offer is limited to one order per household. Not valid for current subscribers to Harlequin Intrigue books. All orders subject to credit approval. Credit or debit balances in a customer's account(s) may be offset by any other outstanding balance owed by or to the customer. Please allow 4 to 6 weeks for delivery. Offer available while quantities last.

Your Privacy—The Reader Service is committed to protecting your privacy. Our Privacy Policy is available online at www.ReaderService.com or upon request from the Reader Service.

We make a portion of our mailing list available to reputable third parties that offer products we believe may interest you. If you prefer that we not exchange your name with third parties, or if you wish to clarify or modify your communication preferences, please visit us at www.ReaderService.com/consumerchoice or write to us at Reader Service Preference Service, P.O. Box 9062, Buffalo, NY 14240-9062. Include your complete name and address.

HI15

SPECIAL EXCERPT FROM

⊞ **HARLEQUIN**®

I N T R I G U E

*When a Texas lawman discovers a woman from
his past and an innocent baby in danger, he has every
intention of keeping them safe…even though it could
cost him everything.*

*Read on for a sneak preview of
TROUBLE WITH A BADGE,
the next book in USA TODAY bestselling author
Delores Fossen's gripping new miniseries,
APPALOOSA PASS RANCH.*

Levi eased into the shadows away from the pulsing neon
bar lights, and he listened. Waiting. It was hard, though,
to pick through the sounds of the crackling lights, the
wind and his own heartbeat drumming in his ears.

But somewhere there was the sound of an engine
running.

Because the driver had the headlights off, it took Levi
a moment to realize the car wasn't approaching from
the street but rather from the back of the bar. No road
there, just a parklike area that the local teenagers used for
making out. It could also be the very route a killer would
likely take.

Before the car eased to a stop, Levi whipped out his
gun and took aim. He froze. And not because of the
weather.

The person stepped out from the car, the watery lights
just enough for him to see her face. Not the Moonlight

HIEXP0316R

Strangler but someone he did recognize. The pale blond hair. The willowy build.

Alexa.

Of all the people that Levi thought he might run into tonight, Alexa Dearborn wasn't anywhere on his radar. Heck, she shouldn't be anywhere near him, this bar or the town of Appaloosa Pass.

Because she had a bounty on her head.

Word on the street was that the hired guns who were after her had orders to shoot to kill.

It'd been five months since Levi had seen her, as the marshals had whisked her away into WITSEC to an unnamed place. A change of name, too. But five months wasn't nearly long enough for the memories to fade.

Don't miss
TROUBLE WITH A BADGE
by USA TODAY *bestselling author Delores Fossen,*
available in April 2016 wherever
Harlequin® Intrigue books and ebooks are sold.

www.Harlequin.com

EXCLUSIVE
Limited Time Offer

$1.⁰⁰ OFF

USA TODAY Bestselling Author

DELORES FOSSEN

The McCord Brothers are the most
eligible bachelors in Spring Hill, Texas.
But these cowboys are about to get
wrangled by the love of some very special
women—the kind who can melt hearts
and lay it all on the line.

TEXAS ON MY MIND

Available February 23, 2016.
Pick up your copy today!

H
HQN™

$7.99 U.S./$9.99 CAN.

$1.⁰⁰ OFF the purchase price of
TEXAS ON MY MIND by Delores Fossen.

Offer valid from February 23, 2016, to March 31, 2016.
Redeemable at participating retail outlets. Not redeemable at Barnes & Noble.
Limit one coupon per purchase. Valid in the U.S.A. and Canada only.

52613249

5 65373 00076 2   (8100)0 12116

PHDF0316COUP